Girl, Unstrung

Also by
CLAIRE HANDSCOMBE

NON-FICTION

Conquering Babel:
A Practical Guide to Learning a Language

Walk With Us: How The West Wing *Changed Our Lives*

FICTION

Unscripted

First published in the USA in 2021

© Claire Handscombe, 2021

ISBN: 978-0-9975523-4-8 for paperback
ISBN: 978-0-9975523-6-2 for e-book

Girl, Unstrung

CLAIRE HANDSCOMBE

In memory of my mum, who taught me Scrabble.

One

You might think it's cool to have a famous actor for a dad. But you'd be wrong, and let me tell you why.

Maybe you're sitting at the Cheesecake Factory after orchestra rehearsal one Saturday, and you've just taken a bite of Dulce de Leche Caramel cheesecake. You're telling your dad about the solo you've been assigned for the next concert. A girl from school comes up to say hi, and you think maybe she wants to ask you what high school you've enrolled at because she could use someone to sit with in homeroom. Or maybe she wants to invite you to the escape room she's doing for her birthday. But then it becomes very obvious that, in fact, she just wanted a selfie. With your dad.

And you should have known, because this kind of thing happens all the time. Each time, like Lucy and the football, you are hoping it will turn out differently. But you've learned your lesson now.

So when you start at your new school, you are wary.

Take me, for example. It's the first week of freshman year and I'm leaning against my locker, peering at the campus map, frustrated with myself for not being able to figure out where orchestra rehearsal is.

It should not be this hard.

I know how to read a map.

The cool metal of the locker digs into my back. Small doors clang around me. Sneakers squeak along the shiny floor. Laughter rings out and mingles with snatches of conversation.

How long? I don't think she meant it.

He broke up with her?

Vacation.

How old is it?

I hate freshmen.

Groups of friends swerve out of each other's way. And I'm still trying to make sense of this map.

I look up and make eye contact with a boy, and I see it in his face right away. The flicker of recognition. Of triumph. Like he's unearthed some great secret treasure. The same flicker that makes it seem like someone's interested in me until I realize that they're looking past me, through me, at my dad, deciding whether to ask for that selfie. I can almost see the thought bubble above this guy's head now. *I heard Thomas Cassidy's daughter was going to be at this school, and here she is!*

I'm unmistakable, after all, with the way my light brown hair looks red under this harsh hallway lighting and with the smattering of freckles across my nose and cheekbones. Thanks for those, Dad. But I'm kidding myself: it's not a smattering. That sounds more elegant than they actually are. It's a *clump*. A clump of freckles.

I can see this guy thinking, *hmmm, she could be useful to me in the future. Think of the Instagram likes! She could make me Internet famous.* He knows that offering to help me with whatever I'm confused about is a good plan. An investment in his future, or at least in his social status. He can forever be the guy who helped Clara Cassidy find orchestra practice. He can tell those stories forever at those basic Hollywood parties where everyone tries to outdo each other with tales of their brushes with celebrity.

"Hey," he says. Smooth opener. Can't fault it so far. And I have to say, it's nice not to be invisible all of a sudden. To hear kindness in someone's voice. "Looking for something?"

I look down at the red viola case resting on the floor between my feet.

"The orchestra rehearsal room," I say. I want to add, *genius*, but I don't know who this guy is yet. I have my own social status to work on. There is, after all, always a chance that some kids here won't know whose daughter I am, and I don't want those people to hate me. To think of me as the girl who was unaccountably mean to Greg or Darren or Paul or whatever his name is. Especially if it turns out that this Greg or Darren or Paul is actually as nice as he seems. And if he is, then I definitely want him on my side.

My dad isn't even that famous. I can't imagine what it's like for the Brangelina kids, or what it was like for Miley Cyrus growing up. Still, she's done pretty well out of it, I guess. It probably doesn't hurt to have the doors to the world of show business already open so that all you have to do is sing a note vaguely in tune and they hand you a TV show and a recording contract. Me, I'm going to have to work my way to success. Nobody in the symphony world is going to care that my dad was on some TV show about teachers that ended forever ago, even if he did go to Juilliard and that's where I want to go too. And that's the way it should be, right? Those of us who work the hardest and have the most talent should be the ones to make it. It's only fair.

"The orchestra rehearsal room?" the boy says, shaking his head once to get the bangs out of his eyes, à la Dean from *Gilmore Girls*. "I think I know where that is. C'mon, I'll show you."

I'm unconvinced by the *I think*. But annoyingly, he's kind of cute with his swoopy brown hair and his chin dimple. So I tell myself that wanting to be close to something like fame is only natural. And I really do need to find orchestra practice, so I let him lead me to the Performing Arts Center, down the winding hallways and across the sunny courtyards. Secretly, I can't imagine ever knowing my way around this school.

"You're Clara, right?" he says.

I was hoping he wouldn't try to make conversation. Four days into high school and I'm already sick of the small talk. *Which part of town do you live in? Do you have brothers and sisters? What school were you at before?* Like we're all foreign exchange students having some English conversation lesson. I nod at his question and leave some silence between us. In the distance, there's a whistle, the sounds of diving into a pool. I don't correct him on the pronunciation of my name. I like people to say Clah-ra, the way my British friend Libby does. "And that's your viola?" He points at the case over my shoulder—a rectangular case, which could have anything inside it for all anyone knows. Yet somehow he's picked exactly the right thing. And he's even said it right: vee-ola.

"How d'you know?" I can't resist asking him.

He shrugs. I'm guessing it's *People* magazine.

Or just living in Pasadena, where everyone's always up in everyone else's business.

"Viola," he says again. "That's kind of like a violin, right?"

"Kind of," I tell him. "But a little bigger. And a lot better."

"What makes it better?"

I think about this as we carry on walking. I consider telling him about when my first teacher put a viola in my hands, when I was ten, and the way it felt. She had the instrument in an open case, just lying on the table when I went to her house for a violin lesson. She didn't say anything, just let me wonder about it all the way through warmups until I couldn't take the curiosity anymore. Then when I finally asked, she explained the viola is similar to the violin, with the same fingerings and the same skills but a deeper tone, like a man's voice compared to a woman's.

She told me hardly anyone plays it, and so when you're the one who does, it's easier to get noticed, to get assigned the good parts. She told me about the extra challenge of reading music for it because it's written using the alto clef, so that each staff—each line of music—starts with a shape that almost looks like the outline of a viola, rather than the more usual treble clef, which is the swirly one you've probably seen on Pinterest and in Etsy shops.

She picked up the viola and played the beginning of a piece by Glazunov, a piece that's not obviously elaborate but really showcases how the viola can sing, and I sort of forgot to breathe as I listened to her. Then she put the viola in my hands, and it felt exactly right, like an extension of me. Like the violin had been something I'd held and used, but the viola was part of who I was.

But no way am I going to explain all of this to someone I've barely met, someone who probably only cares about me because of my D-list dad, even if his voice is warm and mellow and he sounds like he's genuinely interested. These are things I don't tell just anyone. I keep them close to me. The way I feel about playing the viola transcends logic, and so it can scare me a little, because I'm not sure what to do with that feeling. I keep it hidden away, like the light might tarnish it.

"Anyone can play the violin," I tell Greg or Darren or Paul instead, as we push open the doors to the Performing Arts Center. "The viola is special. You read the music differently, and the tone is deeper. And you get to stand out, because there's only a few of you in an orchestra, not a whole load like with the violin."

I turn my head and make eye contact with him when I say *special*. I don't know why it matters in this moment, but I want him to get it. For some reason, I want him to get *me*.

In the meantime, we've arrived at the orange music room door.

"Well, anyway," the swoopy-haired boy says, outside Practice Room A. "I'm Tim."

"Hi, Tim," I say, remembering my manners. "It's nice to meet you. Thank you for delivering me here safely."

"No problem," he says. "We have a pretty great orchestra. It's not LACHSA, but you know. Maybe you'll still like it." And then he's gone and I didn't get the chance to say, *wait, what, LACHSA? You know about LASCHA?* I was hoping no-one else knew about that.

Thanks, *People* magazine.

Two

My dad's house is in one of the curvy, zigzaggy Pasadena streets that's almost in San Marino but technically not quite. It's still close enough for me to walk from there to the Huntington Gardens, though. You might know the Huntington from *La La Land*. It's a blink-and-you-miss it moment, but if you're paying attention, there's a split second in the summer montage where Emma Stone and Ryan Gossling (sigh) are walking through this green jungle-like place, all shade and dark, giant leaves. That's the Huntington, the part of it unsurprisingly called the Jungle. There's also a Japanese Tea Garden and a Rose Garden and all kinds of things like that. I like going there sometimes, between orchestra rehearsals on the weeks I'm at Dad's, to sit on a wooden bench and watch families go by, kids chasing butterflies, babies snoozing in carriers as their parents stop to smell the flowers or read the little signs with the Latin names of them.

It's my favorite place to think or to make adjustments to my life plan, like I had to when I didn't get into LACHSA. On the first page of my red leather bullet journal it says three things.

LACHSA

JUILLIARD

SYMPHONY

I could be flexible as to which symphony I'd end up playing in. Obviously, the LA Philharmonic is the dream, with its exciting repertoire and shiny new concert hall, and especially if Gustavo Dudamel is still conducting there, with his unruly hair and his dimples and all his energy and passion. It's like he draws every detail and emotion out of the score and sends it directly to my brain and heart. It would be amazing to be conducted by him someday, but it might be fun to try different things first, see different things and go to different places. Maybe the London Symphony Orchestra in England. (I love their red swirly logo, which stops looking like letters at all if you look at it hard enough. And I know I'm going to love London. I've got a trip planned there next spring, to see my friend Libby, and I can't wait.) I know I'd need to work my way up through city orchestras and then regional ones first.

In the end, though, I realized I didn't have to make any adjustments to my life plan. It was still:

LACHSA

JUILLIARD

SYMPHONY

It's just that I was hoping and expecting that by now the front of my bullet journal would say

LACHSA ✔

JUILLIARD

SYMPHONY

In case you've been living under a rock or something, or maybe just not in California, I should probably explain what LACHSA is. It's the Los Angeles County High School for the Arts. It's Fame Academy, in other words. Not that I care about fame, because as you'll have picked up by now, as far as I'm concerned fame actually kind of sucks. But I do care about the viola, and being great at the viola, and it would be kind of cool to have people applauding me for how great I am at the viola. At LACHSA, you have to do the normal school subjects, which makes sense, because I hear Pythagoras' Theorem is super-helpful in everyday life when you're an adult. In fact, just the other day my dad and Ebba, my new stepmom, were discussing it over dinner. (Or they could have been talking about politics, since that's all anyone is talking about this fall. I can't wait for 2016 to be over and everyone to be done ranting about this.)

But anyway, at LACHSA, you learn all that stuff in the morning, and then you get to spend the afternoon doing the things you actually care about—dance or drama or music or whatever. How cool is that?

So I've been dreaming about walking between the red pillars on my first day there ever since I was ten and started to be able to play real music on my viola, not just, like, when you do *Three Blind Mice* and *Twinkle Twinkle Little Star* on the violin. I would close my eyes when I was holding a long note and listen to the sound, sweet like honey, feel it travel through my body, and picture myself on the stage at the Kennedy Center in Washington, DC. I'd be the first chair—the leader of my section, looking out onto rows and rows of red velvet seats filled with people who know how to appreciate good music.

Of course, now I know I was pretty terrible back then, and long notes were just long notes without the wave-like beauty of vibrato. If the note's pitch jiggled as I passed my bow across the string, it was because the fingers on my left hand weren't holding it down firmly enough. It wasn't deliberate, but I loved wobbly notes then because I could imagine it *was* vibrato, imagine I'd just nailed the slow movement of the Walton concerto, and I knew I could do it, the LACHSA-JUILLIARD-SYMPHONY thing, knew I wanted to. But then, I don't know what happened last year. I sent in my audition tape to LACHSA and I never got called in for the next part, the in-person audition. Maybe they had more violists than usual applying that year. Maybe everyone's finally figured out that the viola is not just the violin's more sophisticated cousin, deeper and more mellow and unsqueaky, cello-like without the hassle of lugging an enormous instrument around, but also that, if you're good, you get to rise through the orchestra ranks faster than with a violin because fewer people play the viola. Maybe now it's going to be all about the viola and I won't be special anymore.

It doesn't matter, though, because I'll work doubly hard this year and get into LACHSA for my sophomore year. Let's call this a minor setback. I know how to persevere.

So back in February I sat at the Huntington on a wooden bench in the shade of the giant leaves at the Jungle Garden and I got out my pink highlighter and underlined it.

<u>LACHSA</u>
JUILLIARD
SYMPHONY
There. No problem.

Three

I love having the house to myself to practice the viola. Somehow, I can play better when no-one's listening. Without the sound of people padding up the stairs and the ever-present threat of a sibling coming into my room to ask me something, I can really just get lost in the music, open my door and let it fill the whole house. I can close my eyes and play by heart. There's something about just letting the music become part of you. Your fingers remember, your body remembers, and so your mind is freed up to engage, to be fully present.

You have to work at this, though. It's easy, when your hands are just doing what they do automatically, to let your brain roam elsewhere: to wonder what's for dinner or to start thinking about what you're most excited to do in London during your spring break. You mustn't let your mind go there. You're wasting a golden opportunity to lose yourself in the music. To let it make you feel things. And you especially mustn't let your brain make the leap from imagining yourself on a stage in a floor-length, electric-blue dress, playing the solo from the second movement of Brahms' Symphony Number Four, to standing on the stage at your LACHSA audition and failing it again, and then what?

You especially mustn't think about all that because then you'll have lost all the benefits of playing for yourself, of relaxing into the music. Instead, your heart rate will increase and your sweaty fingers will slip a little on the strings and the tuning of the notes will waver and you'll be snapped out of the moment, out of the beauty of it, out of why you are even doing this in the first place.

Today, Harry is at a playdate and dad's driving Juliette to her ballet class. No idea where Rosie is. The library, if I had to guess. Ebba's working, probably, or something. Who knows what that looks like today? She might be in a coffee shop writing a novel, or teaching a ballet class, or rehearsing a play. As far as I can tell, it's always one of those things—at least, that's what I've picked up over dinner when Dad asks her about her day, looking at her like she is his whole world, acting like she's the most interesting person he's ever met. And maybe she is. I don't know her well enough to have an opinion.

I go into my bedroom but don't bother shutting the door. That's another nice thing about being alone in the house. My rooms are basically the same at both Mom's and Dad's houses. Pride of place in both of them goes to a framed poster of the famous Juilliard red stairs. I have a red bedspread and red-accented drapes, and there's a decal of an alto clef above my bed. Rosie thinks I'm crazy: her rooms are different in our two houses, or at least different-ish, both with zillions of shelves of books, but one is *Harry Potter*-themed and the other is *Anne of Green Gables*. Her bed is against the wall at Mom's and in the middle of the room at Dad's. I'm not sure I could cope with that. I think I'd wake up in a cold sweat, not knowing where I was.

So I'm in my Juilliard-themed bedroom at Dad's house, playing the Glazunov *Elégie*, the piece my teacher played me to convince me to ditch the violin and take up the viola instead. This piece gives me goosebumps. I want to give people goosebumps when I play it, too. I'm playing by heart, and no-one is around to judge me, so when I lose my place or forget what comes next I improvise and play around, play my way back to something I remember.

The other thing I do when everyone's out of the house is a lot of repetition. It winds my family up when I go over the same few bars over and over until I get the fingering just right, or when I'm learning a piece in C sharp major and I keep forgetting the B sharps. Today I worked on the Telemann Concerto in G major for a long time, for my LACHSA audition, and now as a reward I'm playing the Glazunov. I love the way this piece is seemingly so simple but requires perfect bow control and really shows off the tone of a viola. I like the acrobatics of more technically challenging pieces, too, for different reasons—the double stopping which is where you play two notes at once, the quick changes between positions of the left hand that sometimes make my wrist ache a little afterward—but sometimes it's just nice to lean into a piece like the Glazunov, to let the music carry you.

I'm there, in that place, the place some people call *flow*, the place where the good kind of butterflies slowly flutter in my stomach, the place where it seems like the viola is an extension of me, where it's part of my body, when I notice something shift in the air. I'm not alone. I can feel it. I open one eye during the next long note and am jerked right out of the moment. My stepmom, Ebba, is standing in the hallway outside my bedroom, watching me, her blue eyes all excited and this goofy smile on her face. My mood splutters and dies. The bow in my right hand slows to a stop.

"Keep going," Ebba says. "I love watching you play."

"I don't like to be watched when I'm practicing," I say.

"I love the creative abandon on your face."

"I don't like to be watched," I say again.

I can see her mulling over what to say to me. I hope I don't have to explain to her the difference between being watched at a concert, when you've worked your ass off for months and you're as damn near perfection as you're ever going to get, when your hair has been coaxed into a vaguely elegant updo and you're wearing your best concert dress, the simple black of it making you feel somehow grownup and poised, and being watched at home, in your yoga pants and your dad's old Juilliard t-shirt, as you play only for yourself and allow imperfection.

"You're beautiful when you play," she says.

"Thank you," I spit out automatically, like a vending machine. Really, I'm thinking, *oh, and I'm not beautiful the rest of the time?* (I know I'm not. Not like her, with her bouncy brown hair and her perfect posture.) Really I'm thinking, *leave me the hell alone.* This is more or less what I'm always thinking when she tries to be nice to me. Why does she have to be so nice? Dad already married her. She doesn't have to prove anything.

"I should get back to it," I say, though I know that I won't. That she's ruined the mood and the moment. I stand and wait for her to leave. Our eyes lock in some kind of unspoken battle. She wants me to keep playing with her there, I'm pretty sure, so she can keep watching. Ummm, no.

She gets it eventually. She turns to leave, her shoulders stooping a little. I've won this round. But it somehow doesn't feel like I have.

Four

Ebba and my dad first dated way back when dinosaurs roamed the earth, in the 1990s I think, when he was at Juilliard and she was at NYU. But she broke his heart when she left him for this superstar screenwriter, which is very sad except when you consider that if she hadn't done that he wouldn't have met Mom and I wouldn't exist, or maybe I would exist and I'd be Ebba's daughter instead, I don't know, that kind of thing blows my mind.

The story goes that Mom and Dad, who obviously weren't Mom and Dad yet, were both in the audience of the same play, and the play had this dark humor that nobody else seemed to get except the two of them, so they were the only two laughing. And at one point they both turned to see who the other person laughing was, and at intermission Dad bought Mom a drink, and fast forward a little and you have a wedding, four kids, divorce. A true love story for our times.

Two years after the divorce, when we'd just about gotten used to our new lives as "one family under two roofs" (okay, Mom and Dad, whatever you need to tell yourselves), Ebba's book got published. It's a memoir mostly about her love affair with this screenwriter dude she'd left Dad for, and Dad went all starry-eyed over it because she mentioned him in it, too, and I guess wrote some nice things about him. Apparently, he was quite the charmer back then. (If Twitter is to be believed, a lot of women still think he is, and that totally weirds me out.) I didn't know any of this at the time, but I've pieced it together through savvy eavesdropping and the creative use of my more-than-adequate brain.

You might think that if Dad and Ebba were going to start dating again, it would have been then. But in fact, things got even more complicated the summer I was twelve, because that was when this British woman Libby came to live with us in the apartment above the garage. I'm fuzzy on the detail and how it all came about, but basically Libby was writing a screenplay with my dad. (Or so he claimed. There's been no evidence of an actual movie yet.) And then one day, I walked in on them kissing, which, let me tell you, is not what you ever want to see. Parents kissing each other is bad enough. But parents kissing other people—especially people who are way too young for them: ugh.

I watched the whole thing happen and I could've stopped it just by clearing my throat or dropping something loudly on the floor, but I guess part of me was morbidly curious, like when you're driving past the scene of an accident or watching a murder on TV and you can't stop staring. I saw Dad and Libby get tied up in knots trying to fix some scene, then high five when they figured it out. So far, so okay, I guess. But then out of nowhere they were hugging and then kissing while I just stood there, glued to the spot, willing myself to yell *stop*.

Long story short, Libby left eventually, and Dad and Ebba started dating again. I'd been so worried about whether Libby would be my new stepmom that I completely missed the Ebba signs until it was too late. Libby would actually have made a great stepmom, so I don't know what I was worrying about, except that it would have been weird because she was really more of a big-sister kind of age than a mom kind of age. I bet she wouldn't have stood in the doorway watching me play without asking first, though. She would have realized how weird that was.

Five

It turns out that swoopy-haired Tim was right about the orchestra at this school. It is pretty great. We play real music, not simplified film music like back at middle school, and on days like today, even with the windows closed, the smell of freshly cut grass comes in from the football field. The room is oval-shaped, with wide steps so that the different families of instruments are on different levels: snare drums and other percussion at the back, clarinets and flutes and trumpets and the other wind instruments a little lower, and then us strings at the front, with the violas next to the second violins.

I'm second chair, so I'm not the leader of the viola section. It's apparently completely random. There were no auditions and the freshmen sit wherever there are spaces from the seniors graduating and everyone moving up to take their place, like we're the British royal family and it's an unquestioned and unquestionable line of succession. It's a stupid system, if you ask me, because clearly what needs to happen is everyone should audition every year, since for all anyone knows the incoming freshmen are every bit as good as and maybe even better than the newly appointed seniors. As, for example, is the case this year.

I share a music stand with Esther, a sophomore, and she's okay, but she doesn't like it when I turn the pages too quickly, so we keep missing notes. It won't matter after a few weeks, when we know our part of *Scheherazade* off by heart, but at the moment it's kind of annoying, plus it makes me look bad. You're supposed to glance at the last few bars on the page, imprint that on your brain, and then turn the page as soon as a rest will allow, even if it's before you really need to. But she's too busy tapping out the rests with her foot and counting under her breath—*one two three four two two three four three two three four*—to memorize the notes.

Still, we're making progress.

The orchestra teacher is kind of funny looking. He's tall and wiry and bald, and says things like *flutes, imagine those top notes need to reach up to the clouds!* If it was me, I'd just say, *watch your tuning, you're way flat, it's hurting my ears,* but weirdly this stuff does seem to work.

He told us the story of *Scheherazade* to "get us in the mood". It's about an Arabian king who kept having his wives executed, until he met Scheherazade. She was super-smart. She kept him interested because of the way she told stories, always stopping on a cliffhanger so that he couldn't kill her till he found out the ending. The teacher says that's how we should play—as if we're telling a story that we want the audience to be desperate to know the ending of. I think about that a lot whenever I play now, not just in orchestra practice.

Tuesday of the fourth week, swoopy-haired Tim is waiting outside the music room when I come out, chewing gum and kicking his right foot with his left foot, his left foot with his right, over and over. I'm almost not surprised to see him there. I've been expecting something like this, I'm not sure why. He seemed the type to want something from me—something to do with my really-not-all-that-famous-let's-all-calm-down dad, probably, and the type not to rest until he gets it.

"Hi," I say, because being polite and moving on seems like a good strategy for getting him off my back. My dad taught me that: be as nice as you can be, then leave as soon as you can. As soon as I can is now. And I have a worthy excuse: I'm being picked up by my mom, and I don't want everyone's dinner to go cold because I'm late for her.

"Hold up," he says, when I'm a step or two past him already.

I turn and look at him, size him up. "Were you waiting for me?"

"I was," he says. He looks down, like he's suddenly shy. I'm not buying it, but my stomach does a weird somersaulty thing that is probably related to the length of his beautiful eyelashes. Then he looks back up at me through them with those ocean-colored eyes.

Ugh. Listen to me. I can't help it if he's hot, okay? It would be rude and stupid not to notice. I don't have time for boys. Instead of teardrops on my guitar I have stickers on my viola case. Stickers from music camp and from countries I've toured around with different orchestras.

But I'm just stating objective fact when I say that Tim is hot. It might be useful for some scientist's doctoral project someday: the effect of long eyelashes on the guts of teenage girls.

"I wanted to be sure you knew about the school ski trip," he says.

Of course I do. It's all anyone's been talking about this week.

"I don't ski," I say. I'm not the outdoorsy type, unless you're counting lying on the beach flipping through *Teen Vogue* or *Strings Magazine*.

"You should," he says. Other kids are pushing past me. We are completely in the way. And I'm wishing I could raise one eyebrow the way Ebba can. An eyebrow that would say, *who do you think you are, exactly, to tell me what I should and shouldn't do?*

"Should I?" I say instead, hoping all of that is somehow obvious from my tone.

"Yes. Skiing is really fun. And the trip was a blast last year."

"Uh huh," I say.

He presses a flyer into my hand. He barely touches me but I feel like I'm the body in that Operation! game I sometimes play with Harry. Like every part of me is buzzing and lighting up. Then Tim leans in and whispers, "It'd be a chance to get to know each other." The word *chance* tickles my ear with its *ch* and its *ssss* sounds. My stomach does that thing with the somersault again. And I think, who speaks like this, in this weirdly formal way? It's like he's swallowed a Jane Austen novel. Although that's what some people say about me sometimes, too. I've liked long words since I competed in spelling bees when I was in elementary school.

"Okay," I say. Really I'm just saying, *okay, I'll think about it. Okay, I'll take the flyer.* Also: *okay, stomach: let's calm down. He's just a boy. You don't have time for boys. Or for ski trips.* But swoopy-haired Tim grins and walks away, and my stomach doesn't say *okay* back.

Six

Mom likes to have heart to hearts with me when she picks me up from orchestra. It's one of the few times we're alone, uninterrupted, and because we're both looking in front of us and not at each other, it's easier sometimes to say what we really think. Plus, I'm trapped there, no getting away, with my viola in its bright red oblong case between my knees, and I'm usually in a good mood after orchestra. The chosen topic today is Friends At High School. Mom tries to make conversations like this seem spontaneous and light-hearted, but I know she thinks about them in advance. I'm not, after all, my mother's daughter for nothing. I believe in planning, too.

When I mention Esther, my stand partner, she spots a plausible segue and pounces.

"I don't hear you talking about your new friends much," she says.

"My new friends?"

"From school."

It's only September 20. I've not even been at this school a month, though it feels like an eternity. I just want to be out of here and at LACHSA. "Oh. Well. If I'm only going to be there for a year, it seems pointless to get attached to anyone."

This, it seems to me, is flawless logic, but my mother sighs. "It's always worth getting attached," she says.

I turn my head to look at her, like—*really? You're kidding me with this, right?* But her eyes are behind sunglasses and on the road. Pretty sure she can feel mine boring into the side of her head, though.

"And what about Katie?"

Katie's been my best friend since the third grade. We always planned to go to LACHSA together—her for acting, me for music. Guess which one of us got in. Well, obviously, you already know which one of us got in because you know which one of us didn't. Of course, we made all these pacts our entire childhoods about how unless both of us got accepted, neither of us would go, our pinkies entwined or our names solemnly signed in purple ink in our journals, but you know how those pacts go. And let's be honest, I'd have done the same. You can't put your dreams on hold while you wait for someone else to catch up. I don't blame her, not really. That doesn't mean I particularly want to talk to her, though.

"What *about* Katie?" I ask.

"You should invite her over sometime. I miss her."

Katie is the perfect friend to bring home. She's unfailingly polite, vocally grateful for every meal and snack and glass of lemonade, and she loves being around my crazy family for reasons that I have never completely been able to fathom. But I'm pretty sure my mom doesn't mean she misses her. She's worried about me and my Lack Of Friends.

"I don't really want to hear about LACHSA," I say. I didn't mean to be so careless, to open my mouth and have the truth just fall out that way.

"You might be surprised," Mom says. She doesn't elaborate, and I have no idea what she means by it. "Besides, a friendship like that is a precious thing. You can't just throw it away over jealousy. It's such a waste."

Then we're home, which means Mom's had the last word, and she gets to underline her point with a thud of the car door.

But instead of calling Katie, I go to my happy place: research for my London trip. I can't wait to visit over spring break, to get on the plane by myself like I'm already a star, a flight attendant looking out for me, no Juliette yabbering on about ballet, no Rosie ignoring me with her nose in a book, no Harry wriggling next to me or watching Paw Patrol with the volume up so high I can hear it through the viola music playing in my own earphones. No teacher walking up and down the rows telling us to keep our voices down, or worrying what the kid across the aisle is saying about me, or having to sit next to a sophomore making out with her boyfriend all the way to Italy for the orchestra tour.

Just me, winging my way across the ocean to see castles and palaces, actual history, the Royal Albert Hall where I'll play one day with the London Symphony Orchestra.

I can't wait to see Libby again, either. You're probably wondering why I'm visiting someone I didn't even like when she stayed with us, someone who made me cringe so hard. And that would be a fair question. The thing is, I warmed to her after a while. I was determined not to like her, and I was mad after Dad told me they were "just" working together and made it sound like I was paranoid for thinking that something was going on between them, and then I caught them kissing. But then, this one night when it was just her and me in the house, we put on a movie and painted our nails, and even though I knew she was *trying* to bond with me, it didn't stop me bonding with her back.

I wouldn't have hated having Libby as my stepmom. She's smart and funny and I could listen to her accent forever. At first, I hated the way she said my name, Clah-ra, but Dad kept trying to tell me that it was sophisticated and cool, and even though I didn't see it at first, I kind of agreed with him by the end. I was sad when she left, and a little mad too that things were changing on us again, first the divorce and the move and now this, and so I guess that's part of the reason I started getting everyone to say my name the British way, as a kind of protest and also so I could feel like, in a weird way, Libby was still with us, even though Dad was dating Ebba by then.

When I found out I didn't get into LACHSA for freshman year, Libby invited me to go to London to "cheer me up" and honestly, I'm not sure my parents would have said yes in any other circumstances. But I was pretty miserable and not much fun to be around, so I think they agreed as much for their sake as for mine. Since then, I've made Pinterest boards and followed a load of London-related hashtags on Instagram. I text Libby back and forth about our plans. She Snapchats with me sometimes too, sending me pictures of things we can do together when I'm there. And I'm excited about spending more time with her, talking about real life stuff with her and not just the memes and "this made me think of you" things we share now. I've decorated the inside of my locker with posters of red buses and Big Ben, and every time I open it to grab a textbook it makes me smile, no matter how much of a crappy day I'm having.

And Mom's right—the days at this school *are* pretty crappy. I miss having a friend like Katie. In my room, I toggle out of Instagram and onto my phone app and scroll down to her name in my contacts.

But no.

I'm not ready.

I don't know if I'll ever be ready.

Seven

I'm walking past Dad and Ebba's room the next week, my feet cool on the hardwood floor, when I catch a snippet of their conversation through a sliver of open door. Only a snippet. I don't even realize it's about me until my brain is done processing the sentences, and by then I'm too far down the hallway on the way to my room to double back. I'd risk being a little too obvious if I did. Eavesdropping requires stealth.

I hear Ebba's voice first. "How long do you think she's going to be mad at me for?"

"A couple more days," my dad says, but he doesn't sound sure. "That's about the right penalty for this type of minor offence."

"Minor?"

"She pretends not to like being watched, for her art or whatever, but Clara lives for admiration." It's harsh, and I'd argue with him if I wasn't hearing this from the hallway, but let's be honest: it's probably fair.

"No," Ebba says. "Not that. How long do you think she's going to be mad at me for being in your lives? It's been two years. I'm exhausted. I feel like I've tried everything."

It goes quiet and I hear the rustle of clothes, like they're hugging or getting ready to—

No. Do not go there, brain. I forbid it.

"Well," my dad says, in this ridiculous voice, the kind that usually comes with puppy dog eyes. All sweet and adoring. Ugh. "If it makes you feel better, I'm unspeakably glad you're in our lives. In my life."

It's clearly about to get gross at that point, so I tiptoe the rest of the hallway and into my room for viola practice. As I lift my viola out of its case, I think about Ebba's question. How long am I going to be mad at her? Another year? Maybe. She's right: it's exhausting being mad all the time. I twizzle the end of my bow to tighten the horsehair and think about it some more. It's not like I'm furious or punching walls or throwing plates at the floor or anything like that. It's just this constant, low-level anger, like the way the fridge hums and you don't notice it till it stops. Only this anger never does stop and that's why I hadn't really noticed it until I heard Ebba mention it. Kind of like the way I didn't really think about how weird it is that viola bows are strung with horsehair anymore until I told you just then.

I flick to the right page of the *études* book on my music stand and secure the pages with metal clips so it doesn't close in on itself. I run through my scales absent-mindedly, forgetting to alternate *staccato* and *legato* notes. I feel like my anger protects me, you know? Like a forcefield. It stops Ebba getting too close. I let Libby get close and she left and I miss her. I let Katie get close and now she's getting on with her life without me and leaving me behind. What's going to happen if I let myself get close to Ebba? Anyway, she likes Juliette more and loves going to the library with Rosie and talking to her about books and curling up on the couch with her, one on each end, their feet touching, sharing a fuzzy blanket, each of them silently turning pages. Who even needs a blanket, anyway? This is California. Like, turn the AC down if you're cold.

And yeah, sure, maybe I'm missing out. I have no reason to think she'd be anything but nice to me if I pulled down the barriers. I've heard Juliette laugh with Ebba till they're both wiping tears away. I've seen how Harry lights up when she claps his ridiculous dive-bombing in our pool, and her kindness the time Rosie fell off her bike and scraped her knees badly. And she's right: she's really tried, and I haven't always let her. But we have our mom, and I have Libby, even if she's far away, and I don't want to be disloyal to them. It's too complicated, and too uncomfortable, all these different emotions, and I don't have time for complicated emotions. So for now, I choose to keep my distance, and the easiest way to do that is to lean into the anger. The forcefield of protection.

Eight

Every October and February, my school puts on a talent show. Student Arts Showcase, they call it. You have to apply to be in it and get a teacher of the relevant subject to sign a slip guaranteeing you're not going to completely and forever embarrass yourself and the school by attempting to do something in public that you're so bad at you shouldn't even be attempting it in the privacy of your own bedroom. Those evenings double as fundraisers and photo opps. The school invites reporters and prospective donors and then the article in *Pasadena Now* gets framed and put in the Hall of Fame, the part of the hallway that houses the sport trophies and signed photos from illustrious alumni and all that kind of stuff. We all know we're basically being exploited for the financial good of the school but I've already picked up that, somehow, it's still a big deal to get to perform or display your artwork for the Showcases.

Mr. Giovanni, the wiry teacher from orchestra, smiles when I present him with the form after rehearsal. The room is bustling, still. People are disassembling their flutes, loosening their bows, clicking instrument cases shut. Then there are one or two show-offs running through some of the harder passages we've played, allegedly to seal it in their muscle memory but more to demonstrate to the rest of us that *they* weren't the ones slowing us down, thank you very much.

"Good job, Clara," he says. He pronounces my name right, the way Libby does. It's also the way Clara Schumann pronounced her name, since she was German. She was also pretty great. She was a child prodigy at the piano, and later some people called her the High Priestess of Art—kind of an awesome title. She even earned more than her famous composer husband at first, which in the nineteenth century was really rare. I love that about her, and I'm glad we share a name. "It's great to see freshmen get involved in these showcases," he adds. "What are you going to play?"

I've been practicing the Stravinsky *Elégie* with my viola teacher for a while, and it's almost up to scratch. (Dad would approve of that pun.) Although it's got the same name as Glazunov's, it couldn't be more different—it's just you up there, with no piano accompaniment, and there's not so much a distinct melody as a series of chords, almost as if it's designed for you to impress the audience with your viola tricks, like double stopping. I've got two weeks. If I practice for an extra hour every day, it should be plenty good enough. Major scales, minor scales, arpeggios, *étude* of the week, the Telemann, and then the Stravinsky.

"That's ambitious," Mr. Giovanni says when I tell him. Something in his voice or the slightest arch of his eyebrow makes me think that maybe *ambitious* is code for *crazy* or even *impossible*. He clearly doesn't know me very well yet, doesn't know that with my special sauce of talent and hard work and determination I can basically do anything. "It's a hard piece," he says. "With all that tricky double stopping."

"I'm almost there with it," I say, which is almost true. Playing two notes at the same time is one of the hardest things to do on a stringed instrument, but I'm determined to get skilled at it. You have to get the angle of the bow just right, and both the notes have to be exactly in tune, so your left hand has to know exactly what it's doing too, pressing down on the strings to get them to make the right pitch.

"Okay," he says. He's still holding the paper, still sucking on the end of his pen. He still hasn't signed his name. He's about to do it when he lifts the pen off the paper again and asks, "You don't think it would be better, you know, just this once, for your first one of these, to play a piece you know really well?"

"Where's the fun in that?" I ask. And by *fun*, I of course mean *challenge*.

"Okay," he says again, and this time pen meets paper and he actually signs.

"Thank you," I say, taking it from him before he changes his mind, but what I mean is *watch me*. Watch me dazzle you.

Nine

Right after dinner that night I head back to my room to start my new practice régime. We're at Mom's this week, and we're all marathoning *Malcolm in the Middle* on Netflix there, but I don't have time for that. It hurts a little. I don't like to be left out of family moments. But this is what it takes to be great: you have to make tough decisions.

"Yay! More space for me on the couch," Rosie says, and I think about staying just to get her back for that, but I need to be strong. Real artists don't compromise.

"Do what you gotta do, honey," my mom says. She's making real popcorn in the pan, the way I like it, with a clear lid so you can watch the kernels implode and jump into life, steam escaping through the vent in the lid and letting through a slightly salty scent. She says it lightly, not in that passive-aggressive way some mothers might. She's in the acting business, like Dad, so she understands sacrifices for the sake of art.

Upstairs, I pop my viola case open. I choose the bow, my favorite one, the one that's a tiny bit heavier and has a slight indent where my thumb has worn it down. I run it across the cube of amber rosin I keep in my case: the rosin is sticky and helps the bow grip the strings better and make a smoother sound. But it can be messy and that's why after each practice and each orchestra rehearsal I wipe my viola off with a cloth before I put it back in its velour-lined bed. We all have routines like this at orchestra. Woodwind players have to shove a cloth down their instruments to wipe away the spit. (Gross, if you ask me, unlike rosin, which is made of tree sap and smells like pine.) Sometimes the flautists use cigarette papers on the keys to blot them when they get sticky. They shine the body of their flutes with a cloth, too. I'm never jealous of the woodwind players—the spit thing alone, come on!—but there is something really cool about the shininess of the flutes, the way they catch the light on a stage, the way that light seems to travel from one end to the other in one smooth motion.

I play my scales, major and minor, but halfway through the arpeggios my left wrist starts to cramp. I've already done my two usual hours of practice today, plus two hours of orchestra, so I guess I shouldn't be surprised. Am I going to have to do some kind of weight lifting to get the strength in my arm up? Where am I supposed to find the time for that?

I lay my viola down on my red bedspread and stretch out my wrist, back and forth, back and forth. I draw circles with it, spread my fingers out, massage the inside of my wrist. On my nightstand, in front of a framed picture of Mom, Dad, and me in the pre-divorce era, my phone lights up with a notification. It's Katie. She must have sensed us talking about her the other day. A disturbance in the universe—we used to joke about that. Or maybe my mom contacted her and told her to text me.

The text, imaginatively, says *hey*. I wait for more. My left wrist is still cramping. I can't go downstairs and risk being mocked by Rosie for not even making it fifteen minutes into a practice session. I might as well text Katie back. *Hey yourself*, I write, which I admit is also a little basic.

How's it going? She writes. *How's your new school?*

Does she actually want to know, or does she just want to brag about how great LACHSA is? Hard to tell, so I don't really know what to write back. And then I realize I also don't know what to write back because I don't know what the answer to her questions is. How *are* things? How *is* my new school? Fine, I guess. Orchestra is good. Freshman algebra is good. Other classes are okay. I don't have a ton of exciting new friends, but who cares, right? School is just a thing to get through between orchestra rehearsals and viola lessons. Do I miss Katie? Do I miss sitting cross-legged on her purple bed making lists of the ten cutest boys in our class? (Purely hypothetical—she doesn't have any more time for that stuff than I do.) Do I miss eating rolls of raw cookie dough even though we promised our moms we wouldn't and then lying on our backs, clutching our stomachs and moaning about how sick we feel? Sure. That must be why my cheeks are wet and I'm sniffing. Well, either that or the pain in my wrist.

I miss you, I type. *Come over to my mom's on Saturday?*

I have rehearsal, she texts back. Too quickly, like she's mad, like she's been waiting to cut me off. But then the little dots in the app tell me that there's more. *But maybe after?*

Ten

At my mom's that Saturday afternoon, Katie and I paint our nails and catch up, just like old times. We're well into October now, so it's time to switch from the bright yellows and pinks of summer to the darker reds and purples of fall. (I've picked out a color called *Madam President* in the new range OPI brought out for the election.) On the surface, it's like nothing's changed with Katie and me. These have been our routines since forever. But of course plenty *has* changed. We don't see each other every day. I haven't met her new friends. We don't know every detail of each other's lives anymore. I miss that. And I miss that I can't ask her about it without a knot in my stomach. But I don't want things to be weird with us. I want her to be able to tell me about her life, even though it feels like tiny knives are stabbing me in the throat and I worry she'll be able to hear that in my voice.

I swallow hard.

"So how's LACHSA?" I ask her, focusing on painting my thumbnail first. We're each sprawled out on a squishy grey couch in the TV room, ready to watch a movie next. I'm using my mom's technique of not looking directly at Katie. I want to know the answer to my question, and also I don't, but mostly I don't want Katie to see any of that in my face and to feel like she has to hide things from me.

"It's," she says. And then she pauses for what feels like a long time. From the corner of my eye, I can see her curling the strand of her hair that's fallen out of her ponytail around and around her finger. Luckily, she hasn't opened the nail polish yet, or it could get messy. "It's intense. That's probably the best word for it."

"What are some other words?"

"Crazy. Hard. Fun. Competitive."

That sounds perfect. I love competition. There was a while in middle school when I was really into the spelling bee, but really that was for the fun and adrenaline of the competition, not for the words themselves, even though I've ended up with weirdly good vocabulary because of it. It was before I switched from violin to viola and got serious about music, so I had time to read through the dictionary and make index cards to test myself and write out a load of words in a load of different colors. I came second in the fourth grade and lost with *voyage*, which seems so obvious now, but I don't know, in the moment, there was all the pressure, not to mention that I was only nine years old. In the fifth grade I won (*triceratops*) and went through to regionals. I was thrown by *epistrophe*, though, and I missed out on nationals, which still gets to me.

"I know you love competition," Katie says, like she's read my mind, "but this is different. You can never be sure that anyone's really your friend. Because nobody really wishes the best for anyone. Everyone's always waiting for someone else to trip up so they can get ahead. Even me." I look up to see her expression when she says this, because I can't totally read her tone of voice. She looks ashamed, like she might cry.

"I find that hard to believe," I say. "You always want the best for everyone." We did this test called Myers Briggs one time, and she came out an ENFJ. Which apparently is the type of person always looking out for others. I wasn't surprised. Sometimes I think our friendship has only lasted as long as it has because she's way too forgiving and much kinder to me than I deserve, like the time I got pretty insufferably whiny after I lost in the regionals of the spelling bee in the sixth grade. (It mattered, okay? It still matters, if I'm completely honest. It bugs me that I didn't even get to compete in nationals.)

"It's true, though," she says. "It's the atmosphere there. It brings out the best in people's talents and hard work. But the worst in their character."

Katie's always been sensitive. I can imagine that's hard for her.

"I don't think it'd be a very good place for you," she says quietly, like she knows I'm going to be mad but she also knows she has to say it. "I'm sorry."

I *am* mad, so she was right to be worried. How could it *not* be the right place for me, with that amazing stage, a grand piano in a corner, waiting to accompany me as a spotlight shines on my nimble fingers? But I've also missed Katie, and I don't want to fight. I'll fight with her later in my head.

"Okay," I say. "Let's talk about something else."

We focus on picking out a movie—and my anger fades as the beginning credits of *High School Musical 3* roll. But long after she leaves I'm still thinking about it. Not a good place for me? LACHSA is the best place—the only place I've ever wanted to be. I'm going to need to practice my heart out so I can prove Katie wrong.

♫ ♫ ♫ ♫ ♫ ♫

When I finally fall asleep, I dream about Juilliard again. There are always some weird details in these dreams: a llama running through Lincoln Center Plaza, some random friend from kindergarten handing me a coffee, faceless teachers who turn into Libby or Dad. But for the most part, I've fed my brain enough of a blueprint that my subconscious knows which images to call up—like the huge library with its dark green desks and shelves filled with 77,000 musical scores or the shiny white stairs in the lobby. I love the picture Dad took of me sitting on those stairs the last time we were in New York City—it sits framed on my desk to remind me of the prize, of what it is I'm working so hard for.

In my dreams, sometimes I'm lost in the maze of practice rooms and rehearsal rooms and classrooms on the fourth and fifth floors where the music department is. Sometimes I'm looking out from my dorm room onto Broadway, people hurrying past with coffees or backpacks or instrument cases, fall leaves fluttering down the street. And sometimes I'm playing at Carnegie Hall, because getting to play there is one of the amazing things about studying at Juilliard, and two thousand people are clapping from their red velvet chairs. And Tim is standing up and wolf whistling. When I wake up from dreams like that, I let myself stay in a half-asleep state, let myself linger in a world where I walk through Central Park in the snow on the way to the ballet or the Met, or where I sit at lunch with other musicians as talented and dedicated as me, talking techniques and our favorite pieces of music, or where I wander down the same halls that Nobuko Imai and Nigel Kennedy once walked down. And then when I get up for morning practice, somehow my notes are brighter, like even my viola is smiling in anticipation. Even more than LACHSA, I can't wait for Juilliard to be my reality, and not just a dream. Me and my viola, on an adventure in New York City.

Eleven

It's October 12, the day of the recital—the Look How Great The Kids At This School Are, Your Kids Could Be This Great Too Showcase.

I'm ready.

Mom took me shopping for a dress, and it's jade green and a little shiny and it falls just above the knee and I love it. She's French-braided my hair for me, too, and I wonder if that makes me look too little-girly, but I love her hands in my hair, love the undivided attention she gives me as I sit on the floor in front of her and she threads strands of my hair together.

I pull out a couple strands toward the front to soften the hairstyle, and she frowns.

"Won't those get in the way for reading the music?"

I admit I didn't think of that, but I shrug.

"It'll be fine," I say.

I know the piece by heart, so the music will only be there for reassurance.

Mom takes a photo of me and I post it to Instagram. Across the ocean, even though it's the middle of the night in England, Libby comments almost immediately. "Wish I could be there to hear you!" She's always wishing she could be here for things. I miss her, too. It's hard to believe we only spent a summer together and I didn't even like her at first.

I'm fourth on the program at the recital, and that gives me tons of time to get nervous, and also to look around the audience on their plush blue chairs beneath the mahogany-framed pictures of famous alumni and notice swoopy-haired

Tim. I swear my stomach registers him before my eyes or my brain do. It immediately and predictably ties itself into a knot. *I'll show him*, I think, clenching my teeth. *I'm so much more than Thom Cassidy's daughter. I'm so much more than the girl who didn't get into LACHSA.*

Mom passes me a tissue when it's my turn. She knows from past experience that I need to wipe my nervous, sweaty hands. I wonder, not for the first time, if putting rosin on the tips of my fingers would help with their grip on the strings, too. Now is probably not the time to experiment, though.

The girl before me introduces me when she's done with her clarinet piece, using the words I wrote. It's weird, writing about yourself as if you're someone else.

"Clara Cassidy is a freshman. She's played the viola since she was ten and has toured extensively with Pasadena Junior Orchestra with her viola, and her violin before that."

It makes me sound so professional. Apart from the *Junior* part. I wish the PJO had a better-sounding name.

Then I'm on the stage and I'm playing. My fingers are doing what I've trained them to do over so many hours, the fingers on my left hand positioned exactly on the fingerboard so that exactly the right pitch oozes out with every steady bow stroke. I sound good. I can feel myself smiling. My viola teacher is always telling me to smile when I play, and I always want to say, *there's so much else to think about, my face is the least of my worries*, but I can tell that somehow the smiling relaxes me, eases the tension in my shoulders and makes my playing even better.

It's over too quickly. I bow and go back to my seat between my mom and dad. They always come to these things together, in some grand show of unity. It's unbearably awkward but today I don't mind. I'm glad they're both here, that they both got to see me do that.

"Great job," my dad whispers into my ear over the applause for the next player I've just introduced. "You looked like you were enjoying yourself up there."

"I was," I say. He puts his arm around my shoulder, gives it a squeeze. I wait for the inevitable pun.

"Another string to your bow," he says.

There it is.

♫ ♫ ♫ ♫ ♫ ♫

There's always a reception after these things, too, as if to underline the point: not only will this school nurture your children's talents and possibly make them into prodigies, we also have great cheese! And some grapes! We wander to the room where there's confetti on the tablecloths, Diet Coke and sparkling cider for the kids, much more interesting drinks for the parents, all prettily arranged on silver trays. Dad has even stopped rage-tweeting about the election and put his phone away. Mr. Giovanni meets my eye after getting his champagne and walks over to us—he's sorry, I imagine, that he ever doubted me.

"That was wonderful, Clara," he says. "Wonderful." He introduces himself to my parents and I hold my breath. I wait for the backtracking when they say their names and Mr. Giovanni realizes he is supposed to know who they are. But there's no backtracking. Not even a vague flicker of recognition.

"You have a very determined daughter," he says, and they laugh at the suggestion that this could possibly be news to them. *And talented*, I mentally add. I will my parents to say it. They don't, but that's okay. Anyone can be talented. But not everyone is as determined as I am to make the most of their talent.

That's when, out of the corner of my eye, I see swoopy-haired Tim, looking even hotter than normal in a blue shirt that brings out his eyes. He's not supposed to be back here in the reception area. This part is just for the performers and their families and donors and potential donors. Not for the riff raff. Who do we even think this school is *for*?

"Thom," he says, coming toward us. I hate the way people do this: call my parents by their first names as if they know them. Dude, he might be on your TV all the time, but he's not your buddy. Did he say you can call him Thom? How do you know he doesn't prefer Thomas?

But my dad, being my dad, chilled and polite and always just so *nice* to everyone, stretches out his hand.

"Hi," he says.

"Big fan," Tim says. Can't people, just for once, come up with something more creative than that?

"Thanks." How does my dad put up with this crap?

"Do you mind?" Tim says, and before my dad has a chance to ask *do I mind what*, Tim pulls out his phone, reaches his arm out for a selfie. "Big fan," he says again. Then he walks away.

It's like he hasn't even seen me.

Twelve

"Call Juliette for dinner," my dad says the next night after poking around at the roasted chicken to make sure it's cooked right through. The whole house smells like thyme and rosemary, and the skin looks so crispy I could die just thinking about eating it.

I open my mouth to yell for my sister, and he says, "Not like that. Go to the basement and speak like a civilized human being."

My dad is normally pretty chilled when he's not firing off a million political tweets, so who knows what's up with that, this sudden insistence on "civilization." Our weeks with him were always a little more relaxed, a little rougher around the edges, more takeout pizza and fuzzier bedtimes. Until Ebba, of course. Now there's a scented candle in the downstairs bathroom and we eat at the same time every day and there are always flowers on the dining room table. They look nice enough, but honestly, they're a little impractical sometimes and we could really do with the extra space for, you know, actual food and food-related items.

So I make my way to the basement, where Juliette has her own mini dance studio, complete with a barre and wall-length mirrors. I open the door and climb down the first couple of steps. The music from the *Nutcracker*'s party scene is playing on a tinny iPhone. I can see Juliette from this angle, the back of her, and the front of her reflected in the mirror. She's standing with her hands lightly on the barre, and she's sticking her tongue out a little, deep in concentration. Her left foot is pointing out, and her right leg is up in the air at an angle. And next to that leg is Ebba, giving her instructions.

"Okay, now point that right foot. Good. Much better. Now turn your heel inward a little. No, inward." Juliette is struggling—her tongue is poking out further. Ebba moves to stand behind her, and takes her right foot in her hand. She turns it slightly, so slightly it's almost imperceptible to the naked eye, certainly to the naked eye of a non-dancer. That's what Ebba and Juliette call us: non-dancers. Which is a bit offensive, actually. I don't go around calling people non-musicians or tone-deaf chumps. Not out loud, anyway. Not to their faces.

"See?" Ebba says, and Juliette nods. Then she smiles at Ebba widely and gap-toothed, and my heart pinches. They're two peas in a pod, there at the barre. Two brunettes with buns. Juliette has Mom's coloring, and Ebba … well, so does she. Let's just say that Dad has a type.

The way Ebba is holding my sister's foot, like a precious glass slipper, it's—tender, is the word that comes to mind. Which is weird, because that's a word we only ever use in the context of steak in this house. I back away, up the stairs, and close the door gently. For some reason, I don't want them to know that I've seen them.

"Well," Dad says. "Are they coming, or what?"

They? Did he know that Ebba was down there too? Did he send me down there just so I could witness their beautiful moment of stepmother-stepdaughter interaction?

"Did you send me down there on purpose?" I ask.

"With the purpose that you would call them for dinner," he says. "Yes."

"No, I mean—so that I would see them practicing together."

"I wish you'd give her a chance," he says, which sounds like he's not answering my question, but of course, he is.

"I'm always perfectly civil to her," I say.

"No," he says. "You're not." I know he's thinking of the other day when I pretended not to hear Ebba when I got back from orchestra. She asked me how it was but I decided it was the TV I was hearing and I went straight to my room. "You're not always perfectly civil." He's taking knives and forks from the silverware drawer, crashing them together like cymbals to underline his point. "And even if you were, she deserves a lot more than that, okay? A lot more."

Dad looks at me, waits for me to make eye contact. I don't want to, but the silence is so excruciatingly awkward that eventually I can't bear it anymore and I do, just to get out of the moment.

"What does Libby say about her?" he asks.

I'm about to ask if he's been snooping through my phone for her texts, because that's not okay, but something in his eyes tells me not to go there. Libby was always trying to convince me that Ebba's really great, not just talented and beautiful but also kind. It got so bad that I had to ask her to stop. She probably thought she was being subtle, slipping it in under the radar, sending me subliminal messages. *Say hi to everyone! Tell Ebba I miss her.* Or, *I'm reading this novel Ebba recommended. I love it, she has such great taste in books.* Or, *Ebba said this really wise thing to me once …* In the end, I was like, look, Libby, I know you love Ebba, but I just don't really want to talk about her. I saw the little dots on my phone start and stop, start and stop. Who knows what essay she was composing to guilt me. *You could do a lot worse for a stepmom, you know,* is what she eventually sent. *But okay. I won't mention her again unless you do.* Which means I can't complain to Libby about Ebba now either, because that puts the subject back in play.

"Libby loves her," I tell my dad.

"See," he says. He hands me the silverware. "Finish setting the table. I'll go get them."

Thirteen

I check my phone during the break at orchestra rehearsal one Thursday in November and I have a text from Katie. Though what I see first isn't who it's from, it's what it says. I KISSED A BOY AND I LIKED IT!!!!!

Immediately, as I stand right there with my back against the foam acoustic panels and my backpack between my feet, my brain splits into two halves like it always does when people tell me good things about their lives. Half my brain (don't ask me which half, my theory isn't fully developed yet) is all, like, *what, who, where, when.* In this case, I know the *how* at least technically, and the *why* I assume is obvious, but I want to know everything.

I'm wishing I hadn't seen the text while I was at orchestra. I'm going to be so distracted now. It's not like I haven't seen the movies, or heard other girls talk about it, but Katie is (was? is!) my best friend and there are certain details only your best friend will tell you. Like, what does his tongue taste like? How did you control the flurry of butterflies in the pit of your stomach? Where did you put your hands? And the eternal question, which I've googled but whose answer still seems unclear: where, oh where, did you put your nose?

And then the other half of my brain, at the same time, is all, *what? But what about me?* It's not that I have time for boyfriends and all that stuff or even that there's any particular boy I want to kiss. (Well, except maybe swoopy-haired Tim, but I'm not falling into that trap—I know he's only using me, though I can't figure out what for. Something to do with

Madison Harper, I guess. She played my dad's daughter on TV for a while, so that makes her, what, my screen half-sister? We hung out a bit around then, and whenever she posts something on Instagram and tags me in the picture I get a zillion new followers, mostly girls our age. I assume it's not because they like my glob of freckles or want to know more about why the viola is clearly the best instrument in the world or because they like my artsy pictures of sunlight streaming onto crisp new sheet music. I guess for some people it might be fun to bask in Madison's reflected glory but I've already been basking in my dad's and my mom's my whole life, and who knows, maybe one day I'll get to bask in my sister the ballerina's, and I'd quite like some of my own glory, you know?)

Anyway, back to the point, which is that the only guy I might consider kissing is swoopy-haired Tim, but I also wouldn't consider kissing him because I don't want to kiss someone who will be thinking about Madison Harper the whole time. Eww. So I guess my brain is actually splitting into halves of halves at this point and it's kind of no wonder I'm having trouble with *Scheherazade* when we come back to it after the break.

"Clara Cassidy, are you with us?" Mr. Giovanni says, pausing mid-bar, and I realize my bow is going in the opposite direction to everyone else's.

"Yes, yes, sorry," I mumble, and I can feel my cheeks getting pink. I've never been called out like this at orchestra—any orchestra—and it's mortifying. This is what I mean about boys and not having time for them. One text about one boy, who isn't even my boy, and I'm a total mess.

I try to focus. I tap my foot in time and I count out the bars of rests: *One two three four, two two three four, three two three four*. But half my brain is still on Katie's text. It's bad enough that she's left me behind and gone to LACHSA without me. But now she's leaving me behind on this too? Shouldn't the LACHSA code forbid this kind of thing, discourage anything that doesn't contribute to a laser-like focus on the arts? After all, I'm giving up the chance to go on a ski trip where I too could potentially be kissed as snow falls around me and lands prettily in thick flakes in my hair. I am giving it up so I can practice for my LACHSA in-person audition, because I'll definitely get past the video audition part this time. This is it. The beginning of the rest of my life. The first bullet point on my big life list. What is a kiss compared to that?

Unless … unless I make sure I can play the music perfectly even before the ski trip, and then I could go, and maybe take my viola with me to sneak in a few run-throughs while I'm in Colorado? Maybe that would be okay? Because if Katie is going to be kissing boys then I should be kissing boys too. It's only fair.

I'll make it work. I have to.

Fourteen

Ever since I can remember, we've always gone to see *The Nutcracker* the weekend of Thanksgiving. It used to always be Friday, till we (I) convinced Mom and Dad to let us actually use the best shopping day of the year, so now we go on Saturday. Well, except for Juliette, who goes every day because she's in it every day. She started when she was five, as a mouse. The mice don't actually do any real ballet, but they do get to wear pretty costumes and run around on stage and be around the ballerinas who think they're all oh-so-cute, probably feeling nostalgic for their own childhoods, and that's what made her want to take lessons, I think.

The performance we go to is at the Pasadena School of Dance—Dad always takes the opportunity to lecture us about the importance of supporting local art—and because they're smaller and less prestigious than some other places, they were auditioning even non-dancers for the mouse roles. Juliette was only just five, and super-small, and super-sweet. She was a mouse for four years and now that she's nine she gets to be a party girl, her long hair all ribbons and curls, a fuchsia bow around her waist.

She was, of course, stoked about it when she got the part and that was when she made Dad install a barre and mirrors downstairs and now she can practice obsessively. Mom's house doesn't have a basement or anywhere else where it could easily go, so Juliette's here a lot more than the rest of us, using her dance studio. These last few weeks, we've hardly seen her. She disappears down there constantly. It's unclear how much of that time is spent actually at the barre doing actual exercises, and how much is spent just prancing around in front of the mirror, imagining being *en pointe* and getting to dance the leading role of Clara one day. But she says she's serious. So we'll see.

The first year after the divorce we all went to the show together, except for Harry who was four and hyper and unlikely to sit still through even just one act of ballet. He stayed at home with the babysitter. It was super-awkward, actually, you could tell Mom and Dad had just had a fight (*just a little disagreement, honey*, my mom told me when I asked her about it afterward—ooookay then). They both just sat there with these smiles, the kind you can tell are forced because your lips are making the right shape but your eyes don't change from when you're frowning. The advantage of them having so many kids is that we can make up a significant physical barrier between them, though with Harry at home and Juliette on stage that only left me and Rosie, which wasn't quite enough to cut through the ice. So since then, even though things are much better between Mom and Dad now, we alternate parents for *The Nutcracker*. This year, it's Dad and Ebba's turn.

"I used to go every year with my parents too," she's told us at least three times, in an effort to bond with us or something. "I love *The Nutcracker*." Like that's any huge coincidence, like everybody doesn't love *The Nutcracker*. There are plenty of people who like ice cream or puppies or think the best Harry Potter movie is clearly *Prisoner of Azkaban*, but that doesn't mean I want them to come live in our house.

I'm sitting between Dad and Harry with Rosie and Ebba the other side of him. Harry, of course, is fidgeting, shifting his weight from one butt cheek to the other. He told us this year he was sick of being left out and he wanted to wear a tux and bow tie and come with us (he looks ridiculous and adorable at the same time, if that's possible), but a few minutes into act two he's probably thinking that popcorn and his annual viewing of *Home Alone* would have been a wiser choice. He was riveted for the first half, sitting the stillest I've ever seen him sit and with the straightest of backs, but the spell was broken at intermission. I think he thought that was the end and couldn't quite believe he had to go back in there and sit and not speak for as long all over again. I want to put him on my lap, but I don't know if it's okay to do that, if he'll be too high up and block the view of the people behind me, so I take his little warm hand in mine instead. Sometimes he just needs to know that we see him, that we know he's there.

My favorite part of *The Nutcracker* is in the first half, too: it's the snow scene. And this year, my mind goes right to the ski trip. I convinced my parents, handed in my form, and now I'm counting down the days till the beginning of winter break. I like to imagine I'll look as graceful as these ballerinas as I whizz down the slopes.

Ebba's super-focused on Juliette, watching every step, willing her to get them right. Not that she needs to. Juliette is graceful and elegant—at nine years old! So unfair!—and she's confident, too, every *jeté* and *échapé* and *pas de bourrée* in the right place, at least to my "non-dancer's" eye. I can actually hear Ebba exhale when she's done, like she's been holding her breath the whole time.

At the curtain call, Juliette is smiling wider than I've ever seen her smile, showing off the gap between her front teeth. She looks so pleased, and she should be. She did well, and she knows she did well, and if there's one feeling in the world that's better than that, it's the feeling of other people knowing you did well, too, and standing up and wolf-whistling and shouting *brava*! She's still smiling, still pink under her makeup when she comes out of stage door to find us.

"I'm so proud of you," Dad says, hugging her. "So proud, so proud." Ebba puts her arm around her and squeezes her tight. "You were wonderful, honey." Juliette beams up at her, her eyes full of worship. They walk back to the car like that, Ebba's arm around Juliette, laughing and comparing ballet memories and dreaming together of the day when Juliette will get to be Clara.

The thing is, though, I'm Clara. I'm supposed to be the one with the starring role.

No-one stops us to ask for dad's autograph. No-one spoils this moment for Juliette. Dad's holding Harry's hand, swinging his arm, and Rosie's talking about some author she thought she saw in the audience. And even though it's a warm night for November, I'm suddenly cold.

Fifteen

I've practiced and I've practiced and it's time to record my video for the LACHSA audition. The closing date isn't till January, and it's only the beginning of December now, but I want to be prepared, to get my tape sent in plenty of time. What if they watch them in the order they've received them? I know from sitting backstage at recitals that the more solos you listen to, the more they all blur into each other. By the fifth Telemann in G major they'll be bored of the syncopation and less easily impressed by the fast notes or the cadenzas, no matter how fun the off-beat or semi-improvised passages are. I don't want to risk that being me, boring them.

For some reason they specifically want the home-made kind of video. Mom says it's so as not to disadvantage the people who don't have the money for professional video sessions, which I guess makes sense.

It's not like I would hate being professionally recorded. It could be fun, could give me a taste of my future career. But I don't want any extra advantages. I don't need them, either. I've practiced and I've practiced—I had to take a lot of Advil— and I even had extra lessons, two a week instead of one for the last month. I made Dad and Ebba sit still on their blue couch and Mom on her brown leather one, and listen and tell me if there's anything wrong, not that they know a ton or have anything close to perfect pitch like me, but it can help to get feedback from the untrained ear, and it definitely helps my nerves to play in front of people, especially people I know. Having one of them hold an iPhone to record me won't be as big of a deal after they've already watched and heard me.

I still get self-conscious when I perform. I always have those clichéd dreams right before a recital, where I'm on stage naked, and that's totally how I feel when I play in front of others: look at me, here's a little piece of my heart, please don't crush it. I'm standing in front of you being the best I can possibly be, please tell me it's good enough. Tell me you love my playing. That it moves you or makes you want to play the viola too or convinces you once and for all that neither the violin nor the cello are any match for its beauty. The stakes for this taped audition are even higher than all of that, because as well as the LACHSA people seeing how good I am, I also need them to see how good I could be, how much potential I have. So it's a good thing I've exorcised some of my nerves on my parents already.

The other kids are with Dad and Ebba this week, so I've come to Mom's empty house, to the silence here, to practice a few final times and have her record me. The light falls differently in my room here, and at certain times of the evening there's a patch of sun almost like a spotlight, and I love playing in that. And when it's just the two of us, Mom and me, she likes to try to have more heart-to-hearts than we get to in short car rides, *Gilmore Girls* style, and honestly, it's kind of nice to have her all to myself. I like that she takes the time to do my hair differently every day as I sit on the floor in front of her, my back against the leather couch. That's usually when she asks me the more personal questions. It's another version of the car talk—she thinks I'll be more honest if I don't have to look at her. And it's true, I really am more honest in those moments, but I think it's because having someone's hands in my hair relaxes me. I told Mom that once and she laughed.

"Honey," she said. "You wouldn't know relaxed if it walked up to you and smacked you in the face."

But when she's brushing my hair it feels like relaxed *is* smacking me in the face, the sound of the bristles over and over like playing scales when I'm trying to calm my nerves before a concert. I feel safe, somehow. Like it's okay to be me. Like it almost—almost! —doesn't matter if I get the highest grade in the math test or get accepted into LACHSA.

"You excited about skiing?" she asks me today, French braiding the left side first.

I'm counting the days using an app on my phone, but I can't think about it properly yet. Not till this audition tape is done. Focus on the thing in front of you: my first viola teacher used to say that a lot. Don't worry so much about what's coming next. Get great at the first movement of this concerto, and then we'll talk about the second. But then my next teacher was the opposite. *Anticipate!* she would say, not letting me turn the page until I'd already started playing what was on the next one. *Anticipate! Always know what's coming next.* So I blame both of them for my confusion, but it was the advice of that second one that really stuck with me.

"I can't wait," I say to Mom, even though I've always thought that was a weird turn of phrase. Clearly I can wait, because I'm going to have to. And when you have to do something, you make yourself able to. Whatever it takes. You don't have a choice.

"Which of your friends are going?"

Friends is a strong word for the loose collection of people whose names I know and whose smiles I return as we jostle past each other in the hallways. But I rattle off the list anyway. "Olivia, Nguyet, Alicia, Abigail, Imani, Tim." I didn't mean to mention Tim. His name just slipped out, I guess because it's always there at the back (okay, the front) of my brain, on the tip of my tongue. Katie calls that *mentionitis*.

"Did I tell you Tim invited me skiing? Have I mentioned Tim? Did I tell you I met this guy called Tim?"

It's unnerving how much she sounds like me when she demonstrates what she means. I think she's trying to make me laugh when she does that, but I elbow her and tell her to shut up.

My mom's hands are halfway down my scalp on the right now, which means we have to wrap up this conversation soon, because otherwise I'll have to look at her, and while we're on this topic, I definitely don't want to do that. I can feel I'm blushing, and I don't want her to see it.

"Tim?" she says. "I don't think you've mentioned him before." In my head I can hear Katie do the snort-laugh she does, and her sarcastic voice. *No, never. Never ever.* I haven't actually mentioned Olivia, Nguyet, Alicia, Abigail or Imani to Mom before either, but she's only interested in Tim. Like there might be a reason I'm mentioning him now and a reason I never have before. Which is very heteronormative of her. Like, how does she know it's not Abigail or Nguyet or Olivia or Alicia I have a crush on?

I guess she's my mom, and that's how.

It's not a crush, anyway. More of an intrigue. An interest, purely out of curiosity. An appreciation of his swoopy hair and his long eyelashes and his chin dimple.

"Yeah," I say. And then, probably because of the magical powers of the hair braiding, I add, "It was him that invited me on the trip, actually."

"Oh," she says. So casually. I can feel her undoing some of the braid on the right side. "It's uneven," she says. But I know her game. She's buying us more time for this conversation. "And you like him, this Tim?"

"You're a poet and you don't know it," I say. I am good at this deflecting thing, but my mom will not be deterred. Her hand pauses in my hair, and she waits for me to really answer.

"Remember my school recital? When a guy came up to get a selfie with Dad? Big fan and all that unoriginal crap?"

She's still not braiding, but probably now it's because she is digging into her memory. There's a lot to keep track of, what with four kids and their four sets of friends (and, I am pretty sure, a boyfriend's children and their set of friends).

"Hair all in his eyes?" she tries.

"Yep. That's him."

"He was cute."

It's clear by the *hair all in his eyes* comment that this is not what she actually thinks. That what she actually thinks is he needs a haircut before she can even contemplate his blue eyes and his chin dimple and his long eyelashes. She's trying to get a reaction from me. Gauging if *I* think he's cute.

"I guess," I say. "I hadn't really thought about it."

"Uh huh," she says, in that way she does when it's clear she doesn't believe me. She brushes the part of my hair that isn't braided yet. Trying to relax me some more, coax more honesty out of me.

"Do you think he likes you too?"

"I don't know," I say. I've fallen right into the trap, by just letting the *too* sit there, unargued with. It's the hair brushing. Its actual magical powers. "I mean, he invited me on the trip, so, I guess so. But sometimes I think boys only like me because of Dad. Not just boys. Girls, too. Everyone."

The words rushed out in an honest whoosh before I had the chance to think about them. But they're an effective deflection, pointing to a Bigger Issue Into Which We Should Probably Delve.

"How do you know they don't like you because of me?" my mom says. Now she's deflecting, too. Making a joke to relax me further, to cause more words to tumble out of me as she finishes my braid.

"Ha," I say. "Good point."

She starts massaging my neck and shoulders. This is definitely not part of the usual hairstyling deal.

"That's good," I say. She's doing it pretty softly, on my neck then down each shoulder. I know that in order for it to be effective it needs to hurt at least a little, like so many things in life. You play till your wrist aches, and then way past that point. Till the skin on your neck is purplish. That's how you know you're pushing yourself anything close to hard enough.

"You've got a good head on your shoulders," my mom says, like it's some great achievement to have figured out that people in Hollywood's orbit are a little superficial. Still, I like the compliment. "But you have to let people love you. You have to let them like you for who you are."

I think about Ebba, for some reason. Which is not at all what we're discussing, so who knows where that came from.

"Maybe not sophomore boys on school ski trips," she adds. I never mentioned he was a sophomore. How does she know? Does she speak to Dad more than I thought? Is Dad not as distracted by politics as he always seems to be? Was all of this conversation some kind of elaborate bluff? I don't want to sound paranoid, though. I let it go. "Be careful," she says. "Okay?"

I've got a supply of condoms, if that's what she means. You know, just in case. Just in case things escalate quickly at the top of a mountain or after a hot apple cider.

Would he taste sweet when I kissed him? Would I taste it if I've been drinking it too? How does that even work? Always prepared. I suspect that isn't what my mom means, though. I suspect she's talking about my heart. She doesn't need to worry about that. I'm always careful with my heart.

Sixteen

Since Mom's an actor too, she understands the importance of multiple takes. Of keeping going till you get it just right. Till you get it perfect. Except, of course, there's no such thing as perfect in music. That's why we're supposed to say *Practice makes progress*, not *Practice makes perfect*. (I've told my dad this a million times. It's like he doesn't listen.) It's possible, I guess, to be technically perfect, with your fingers in all the right places on exactly the right beats, with your vibrato exactly even. And that's primarily what I'm going for in this video: technical perfection. The other stuff, it's so subjective. My expressiveness. My musicality. My potential, even. These things can't ever be perfect. Not objectively. So I'm focusing hard on the things that can, because secretly I agree with my dad on the fact that you can get there if you just put the effort in. The other stuff is icing on the cake. It's not the cherry, because strictly speaking you don't need a cherry. It's nice, but it's superfluous. Some people don't even like the cherry. But icing is different. Icing, like the musicality, needs to be there. It's not the main thing, but a cake without icing isn't going to impress anyone, no matter how perfect its execution.

My fourth take today is great, and not just because Mom got the angle exactly right so that my round face looks a bit thinner, and the lighting makes my freckles less prominent. No, it's great because of my technique. To continue this slightly overwrought metaphor, the cake has risen perfectly. The testing knife has come out clean. But where the metaphor fails is here: you make the cake perfectly, then you add the icing

CLAIRE HANDSCOMBE

and in theory at least if the icing isn't good enough you can scrape it off and start again until you get that part right, too. With playing the viola, you have to do both at the same time. Technical perfection *and* musicality. The cake *and* the icing.

I'm at my most musical when I'm not thinking too hard about the notes, when I'm able to just relax into the melody, to let intuition guide me. There are two ways to achieve that. Either you fudge the notes and the tempo, or you know the notes and the tempo so well that it's okay to relax because your muscles can be trusted to do their thing. Mom and Dad say it's the same thing with acting. That you've got to know your lines so well that you don't need to think about them, so that all of your energy can go into being the fictional character, which guides the other stuff—how you move, your facial expression, your tone of voice. In a way, it's muscle memory for them, too, and that's why they memorize out loud, to train their mouths to just make the right sounds while they focus on the other things.

So now that I've achieved technical perfection I need to keep doing takes until I get one that's also musical and moving. After four takes, though, I don't really feel capable of moving anyone—or moving anything, even my bow across the strings.

"What did you think of that one?" I ask Mom, hoping she felt something I didn't. Hoping there was musicality in it that I didn't hear because my brain is mush at this point. But, to be fair, maybe hers is, too. And in any case, here's the thing. I'd know. I can feel it down in my gut when I'm doing it right. This wasn't that.

"I think let's call it a day," Mom says. "We'll try again tomorrow."

I'm exhausted, suddenly. I have no energy left to fight my imperfections.

"Okay," I say.

Seventeen

The seventh take is the winner, but I'm not at Mom's when I do it. She got called for an audition the night after our first four takes, and it was for a show she's always wanted to be on. She got the call when we were together and I acted like it was no big deal, that I could totally just do the taping with Dad instead.

The truth is, though, it is kind of a big deal. Being with Mom is calming in a way that being with Dad isn't. He's fun, but he's not calming. And Ebba—well, Ebba just makes everything more complicated. But I didn't want to guilt Mom out of the opportunity. I'm back at Dad's now, and he's out working too, or what passes for working, some party somewhere, a première of some movie or other. Ebba usually goes with him to these things, but it can get complicated when it's our week with Dad. So, lucky her, she's stuck with trying to get Harry to eat a spoonful of peas at the kitchen island, her phone wedged between her head and her shoulder as she organizes a car pool for ballet class for Juliette, against the background thrum of Rosie talking and talking about the latest book she's reading.

Ebba looks a little frazzled, to tell you the truth, too frazzled to do a good job of recording me, let alone of helping me get my head in the game. Strands of hair have fallen out of her ponytail, and not in an artsy way. So I go upstairs to try to figure out if I can somehow position my iPad to video myself at a good angle. I play the first few bars of the Telemann and then I look, and it's awful, awful, the camera practically peering up my nose and somehow also giving me a double chin. In theory, it doesn't matter what I look like, but first impressions, and all that. I don't want the LACHSA people to think I'm some kind of weirdo with no friends to take the video for her. I've made my peace with not being allowed "unfair" advantages, but I'm not going to allow myself unfair disadvantages either.

LACHSA only takes rising ninth and tenth graders, so this is my last chance. Dad likes to sing me that line from *Hamilton* about not throwing away a shot from time to time, in what I think is supposed to be an encouraging way. "When are you going to get us tickets?" I ask him when he does, and he says, this is not about that. This is about *you*. You not throwing away your shot. But annoying as it is, it's kind of become my mantra. I'm going to make it this time if it kills me, and sometimes I think it just might. At night, sometimes, the throbbing of my wrist wakes me up. I have to swallow a couple Advil about an hour before each practice session so it kicks in in time. I've thought about asking my parents to take me to the doctor so I can get prescribed something stronger, but I think Mom and Dad would probably both decide I was unnecessarily obsessed or something, and make me cut down my hours of practice or whatever, not throwing away my shot be damned. But I'm so close now, so close, I just need to get this video done and then a few weeks of intense practice and then my audition, and when I hear I've been accepted into LACHSA I'll give myself a break, go back down to my base level of two hours a day for a little while: pre-breakfast, pre-dinner, after dinner. What's a little Advil for a few weeks in the meantime?

I scrap the fifth attempt, prepare to try again with the iPad at a slightly different angle on my nightstand.

"This is never going to work," I say, possibly with a few added expletives of the kind Dad doesn't like me to use around the house.

There's a knock on the door: Ebba's tell-tale three knocks. "Yeah?"

She pushes the door open. "You want some help with taping your audition?"

"You're busy."

"Harry's in bed. Finally." She laughs, like she's making a little joke with herself. "Dishes are in the dishwasher. Rosie's reading. I'm all yours. If you want me."

It's not, obviously, that I want her, exactly. I want Mom and her reassuring confidence in me. Or Dad and his terrible puns. *I don't mind helping you*, he'd say. *It's no treble*. Haha. Good one, Dad. But I do need *someone*, and Ebba is the someone who is available.

"That would be great," I say. "I can't get this iPad to angle right."

We figure it out together and I play the fourth movement of the Telemann concerto, double stops and super-fast eighth notes, with its taped accompaniment, skipping along as effortlessly as I can with the lightest of touches. It would be better to have a live pianist, but no-one in the family is good enough on the piano, and my viola teacher didn't have the extra hours for the extra takes this week. I play it through, and it's good enough, not good *enough*, you know? It's technically damn near perfect. But I don't have it. That extra thing where the music resonates in my bones and in the pit of my stomach.

"I don't think it's happening tonight," I tell Ebba, halfway through the second take that we do together.

"You're not feeling it?"

I shake my head, disappointed in myself.

"It sounded good to me," she says, playing with her necklace like she always does when she's thinking.

"I mean, yeah. It's good enough. To the untrained ear, you know?"

She smiles, sort of, with her mouth but not her eyes. "I feel like my ear is pretty trained," she says. "We've heard you play this for months."

"Sorry if I'm boring you." I don't sound sorry. I sound like a brat. Hashtag sorry not sorry.

"I don't mean it that way," she says, but I'm not convinced. It seems like she's forcing the warmth in her voice. "Want to give it another try?"

I shake my head again. "It's not happening tonight. I'm sorry."

And this time I really am sorry, though I'm not sure what about. Wasting her time? Being meaner to her than she deserves? I don't know, but I must be sorry about something, because I'm crying.

It's embarrassing how much I've cried lately. I am not this pathetic whimpering wimp of a little girl. The embarrassment of it makes me cry more. I don't want Ebba to see me like this. I want her to know I'm strong. That she can't break me. That nothing can break me. Except apparently, it turns out something can after all. Whatever this something is.

I'm still holding my viola in place, under my chin and sticking out in front, which means she can't hug me. I don't want her to, anyway.

"Clara," she says. "Look at me."

My eyes move slowly, across my viola's body and fingerboard and over to Ebba. Her eyes are such a brilliant blue. She's beautiful. I've noticed that before, of course, but I'm struck with it again, suddenly. Dad has great taste, I'll give him that.

"You can do this," she says. "I promise you can do this. Let your fingers do the work. Let the rest go. Remember that time I was watching you from your bedroom door? That time you were so mad at me?"

Like I could have forgotten that.

"What were you thinking about then? Because it was working for you."

I was picturing myself on the stage at Lincoln Center, but I'm not about to tell her that.

"I don't remember," I say.

"Well, whatever it was," she says, like she knows I'm lying, "try that now. You were feeling it down in your bones, the music. I could tell. That's why I couldn't tear myself away. When you play that way, it's impossible for anyone to tear themselves away."

I remember that day, how it felt before I realized Ebba was there, lurking, watching me. I remember it was one of the first times I'd gotten the Glazunov almost right and I remember not caring whether it was perfect, just letting the music carry me the way a wave carries a surfer.

I close my eyes and I start. And when I'm done, I don't have to look at Ebba to know that I nailed it. I felt it as I played. I felt it right in my gut. That was it. My best. But I look at Ebba anyway and her eyes are glistening. She felt it too.

"Atta girl," she says. I don't even mind that she's talking to me like I'm a dog. "That was great. Really. Truly."

"Thank you." I mean thank you for the compliment, and thank you for recording me, but I mean, too, thank you for somehow knowing just the right thing to say to help me do the best I can. Thank you for helping me get there. Thank you for believing in me.

Eighteen

It's Rosie's twelfth birthday on December 9, and what she wants to do is for all of us to sit and watch *The Sound of Music* together. For reasons best known to herself, it's her favorite movie. It's also super-long, and that's hours away from my viola, but she begged me, her blue eyes tearing up right there at the dinner table. "Please, Clara. We never do anything together as a family anymore. You're always up there in your room." I wanted to point out that the reason we never do anything together as a family anymore is that there is no *together as a family*. There's Mom in one house and Dad in the other. Mom with the boyfriends she tries to hide from us and Dad with Ebba and then us, the tag-alongs.

But birthdays have always been sacred in our house. Our houses. Our parents don't work on our birthdays, and they try extra hard to say yes to as many as possible of the things we ask for. So I hold my tongue. And I think that maybe, just possibly, a couple hours without playing through pain might be nice. A couple hours without checking my phone, even. That's a birthday rule, too: we put our phones down and we focus on being together. Mindfulness, or something. Togetherness. Hallmark-movie style. At least Rosie isn't making us watch one of those.

And anyway, I'm so, so sick of having half an eye on my phone at all times just in case it pings with an email notification from LACHSA. Tonight, when I remind Dad that my email could come, as if anyone in the family could possibly have forgotten, he tells me that's highly unlikely since the closing date hasn't passed, and even unlikelier on a Friday night. And also he states the obvious: that the email will still be there two hours later. That I can still have all the emotions and text Madison and Katie and it will still be just as exciting two hours later. Which, on a logical level, makes perfect sense. Logic has always been enough for me. But I'm not myself these days.

I'm on edge. I'm spending a lot of time watching the pre-dawn turn to sunrise through my window, cursing myself for not coming top in math tests anymore, for not being able to get through viola pieces I know like the back of my hand without some major mistakes. My vibrato is uneven. My fingers don't respond as fast as they used to, as fast as they need to if I'm going to play as well as I possibly can at the LACHSA in-person audition in February. Not that I know if I'll get to go to that yet.

The waiting is killing me. No joke: some days I think my heart might just exhaust itself with all its frantic beating and give up. Dad alternates between tiptoeing around me and trying to cheer me up with his terrible puns and *Hamilton* quotes. *Just you wait*, he keeps saying, and I'm like, yes, the waiting is the problem here. Just picking up my viola makes me feel sick to my stomach, which is unhelpful because now is exactly when I can't give up on practice or, in fact, slow down even slightly.

The pain in my wrist is getting worse. I take four Advil instead of two before practice and lessons now, and I experiment with ice, with Icy Hot, with heat patches. I've asked Ebba, pretending to be interested in her ballerina past, how she would dance through pain, what they did to make it bearable. She gave me super-vague answers, so that was totally useless.

On this Friday night, for Rosie's birthday, I make popcorn—real stovetop popcorn, like the kind we have at Mom's. Rosie leans her elbows on the kitchen side and watches with me. I love the building anticipation of moments like this: you think the kernels are never going to explode, and then one does, and then a few seconds another, and then little groups start going at once until they're having a party in there and the smell of them fills the house. We settle under our unnecessary blankets, Dad and Ebba in the middle of the big couch, which I'm sure would be romantic without Harry squirming on Dad's lap. Rosie next to Ebba, Ebba's arm around her. Juliette and me on the other couch, our legs extended and our feet touching, and the big bowl of popcorn on the coffee table. Before this movie is over, there will be popcorn all over the floor and down the sides of the couch cushions. That's just part of the deal.

We keep having to pause the movie to explain it to her and Harry. At this rate, it's never going to end. I've seen it a billion times already though, so it's not like there's any suspense. My favorites are Liesl and Gretl. The oldest and the youngest. Just like in our family, they're the most interesting. Everyone else kind of blends and blurs together. Seven children, though. Seven! Sometimes I think four is crazy. You never get a moment's peace around here. And it's not long before I realize the other cringe-inducing similarities between the story of this family and ours—Maria, the stepmother no-one likes and then learns to love. Except everyone else in this family has always liked Ebba.

I love the thunderstorm scene, I love that Mom and Dad still make us do our own version of *My Favorite Things* when we're scared or sick or nervous. Maybe I should try listing them myself when I can't sleep. The crisp white of new viola music before I mark it. My feet in the warm sand of Coronado beach. My mom's hands in my hair when she's French braiding it. The sweet smell of rosin. The applause of an audience after a solo at a concert. Harry's giggles when I tickle him. Those are a few of my favorite things.

Just before that song, there's the part where Liesl climbs up the drainpipe and tries to make it through Maria's room before she notices. Maria's praying, but really she's talking to Liesl. "Help her to know I just want to be her friend," she says, or words to that effect. I'm sure I can feel Ebba's eyes on me. I sneak a look in her direction and for the splittest of split seconds our eyes meet and I can tell she's trying not to smile and pretty soon I'm trying and failing too. It's the shortest moment. It's over before any of the others notices, probably. But something passes between us. Does she really care about me, the way Maria cares about Liesl? Or does she make herself care because she loves Dad and we're a package deal? I'd ask her someday, if I wasn't so scared of the answer.

I don't know why I'm afraid. I don't *need* Ebba. Liesl didn't have a mom. I do, and she's great, and sometimes I wish I could live with her all the time. It doesn't matter if Ebba doesn't actually love me. If, like almost everyone else, she only loves me because of Dad. But sometimes, like when she just looked at me, I feel like maybe she does actually care. That I might be hurting her by pushing her away. I guess I didn't care about that before. I maybe even wanted to hurt her. But I don't know now. Sitting on the blue couch with Dad's arm around her and Rosie's head on her shoulder, she kind of looks like she belongs there. And Dad looks happy, not in a delirious, going-to-break-into-song-and-dance-any-minute kind of way, but in that super-peaceful, content kind of way. Like sitting on the couch surrounded by his kids and his new wife is one of *his* favorite things. And why shouldn't it be? It's nice. Even I can admit that. Being so angry all the time is exhausting. It's good to have a break from that, too.

♪ ♪ ♪ ♪ ♪ ♪

Juliette's favorite scene, of course, is the dancing-in-the-gazebo scene. I like it too. I wonder if swoopy-haired Tim can dance like Rolf. I already know Tim's not a Nazi, though, so he definitely wins over Rolf in the potential-boyfriend Hunger Games.

I hope he kisses me on the ski trip. Not just a peck on the lips like Liesl and Rolf, a proper kiss, long and deep, with tongues. As far as I know, nobody has yet died asphyxiated from kissing, so people must figure out where to put their noses when the time comes. I hope I'm a good kisser. Or does that come with practice, too? I sort of hope not, because that would make me a beginner, and beginners are painful to experience. I feel sort of bad for what I made my parents endure when I was just a baby violinist, though I'm sure I was better than most. Maybe that's what I'll be like at kissing. Really good for a beginner. Good enough that Tim will forget about Madison Harper and the parties he thinks I can get him into (but which I probably can't) and instead he'll just be thinking about me and how hot I am, even though I'm actually not hot at all.

The thought of it makes me blush. I can feel my cheeks getting red and Ebba's eyes on me again. (How do we feel these things, anyway? Or is not a feeling at all—is it the fact that my peripheral vision catches her, not enough for me to consciously see it, but enough for it to register in my brain?) I think about how nice it would be to talk to someone about Tim, really talk. Not to Katie, because I don't want to draw attention to the fact that he hasn't kissed me yet. Not to Libby, because I don't want to do it by text and even FaceTime is cringe. And not to Mom, because, I don't know, that feels weird sometimes. But to someone who's more like a big sister, and who's actually here with me in my everyday life, not just in my phone. Like Ebba. But she's not my sister, and this isn't *Gilmore Girls*, either. She's the person on the couch next to my dad, where my mom should be.

"Did you know," Juliette starts, breaking into my thoughts. I already know what she's going to say. "Liesl had a sprained ankle when they filmed that scene. How do you dance like that on a sprained ankle?"

It's not really dancing, let's be honest, more like prancing around, but still, it's a valid question.

"Adrenaline," Ebba says. "Painkiller injections. Plain old teeth gritting."

"But she's not even wobbling," I say, helping myself to a fistful of popcorn, without spilling any on the floor. "You can't tell."

"Acting," Dad says.

"I still don't get it," Juliette says, furrowing her brow, like she's trying to figure it out because one day she might have to do it too. "I don't get how it's physically possible."

"You'd be surprised," I say, despite myself. I realize I'm holding one wrist with the other. "When you're really determined, you can do anything."

"Shhh," Rosie says, displeased. We sit back and watch and retreat back into our own private thoughts. It strikes me then that no-one in this room really knows what the others are thinking about, even though we're all watching the same movie. Trippy.

Nineteen

Katie's been skiing, like, a bazillion times, so I've enlisted her help and she's coming shopping with me. She was horrified when I let slip that all I knew about was the ski pants and jackets. *You have GOT to let me help you!!!* she said in her text. *You have to have the right stuff!* The first Saturday she was free was today, and it's only a week till we leave, which is much closer to the wire than I'd like, but whatever. The trip starts on the first day of winter break and we're back the day before Christmas Eve—seven days in total.

Dad drops us off outside Patagonia, the redbrick building on the corner of Union and Fair Oaks, and once we're inside I see it right away: the ski jacket I want, red and white, hanging at the front of a clothes rack.

"We'll do the pants and jacket last," Katie says. "As a reward for doing the boring stuff."

I open my mouth to argue, but she's right. It's a good strategy in life. That's why nobody ends their viola practice with their scales.

"Boring?" I repeat, instead of arguing. Everything about this ski trip is exciting to me. Obviously, there's the prospect of Tim and maybe kissing him. But there will also be mountains. There will also be snow, thick as icing on a cupcake. I've only really seen snow in New York City when Mom or Dad has taken us there for the holiday lights and a Broadway show. (They're both from the Midwest and they say Christmas isn't Christmas if you're surrounded by palm trees and surfers, even though surfers don't tend to hang out in Pasadena since we're an hour from the beach.) And skiing always looks fun in the Winter Olympics.

"Well, you know," Katie says. "Boring in comparison."

We go through the store, picking up a million things and putting them in our baskets. Good thing I've got Dad's credit card. I pick out a couple fleeces—a black one and a white one—and there's the base layer. It's pretty unsexy—a horrible salmon color, but apparently the material it's made of absorbs sweat or prevents sweat or something else good to do with sweat, I'm not really listening, but it seems like essentially it will stop me smelling of sweat, which is obviously a good thing.

"Why would I be sweating, anyway?" I ask. "Isn't it pretty cold in the mountains?"

Katie looks at me pityingly. How is it possible, she is probably wondering, to get to be 14½ and not know this obvious stuff? I guess it's possible the same way it's possible to get to be 14½ and have never kissed a boy.

"You'll be working hard," she says. "Working *out* hard. Also, it can get surprisingly warm with the sun beating down on you and reflecting off the snow. Which reminds me. Goggles."

"Well then why wear so many layers to start with?"

This is honestly a little confusing.

Katie looks kind of exasperated now. "Because you'll also be really cold at the beginning of the day. And when the sun's not out, you'll be freezing. Literally freezing. And then when you're mid-air on the chairlifts …"

"Okay, okay." I sound mad, and I guess I am a little, but I don't exactly know why.

"What is *up* with you?" Katie asks me. We're in front of a sock display now, piles of them laid next to each other, and she picks up a few pairs of the least boring ones. She doesn't have to ask my size. This is the kind of thing that best friends know about each other. I shrug, which is useless, since she isn't looking at me.

"Are you just annoyed that I know something you don't, for once?"

Yes. That's it. That's exactly what I'm mad about. But it has nothing to do with the skiing, not really.

"That would be stupid," I say. "Since you knowing something I don't is the whole reason for you being with me right now in this store in the first place."

"Right."

We're in the gloves section now. She considers them. "These or those?" They're so enormous, they practically look like baseball mitts.

"The red ones." Has she forgotten what my favorite color is? "To go with my ski jacket, remember?"

"Makes sense," she says.

Well, yes. I am nothing if not logical.

We've got everything in our baskets now and we head to the fitting rooms. I don't need to try on the socks, the goggles, the gaiter, the hat, or the gloves—I've tried those on already—but I do need to try on the base layer and thermal pants, the fleeces, the ski pants and the jacket. We're going to be here a while, Katie watching me do twirls in this outfit that looks ridiculous in the middle of Southern California. I should probably be nicer to her.

"How's Jason?" I ask her through the fitting room door.

"He's good," she says. I can hear the smile in her voice, but I can't see her blush, and that's half the fun of these conversations. They can also be fun in the pitch dark of slumber parties, where you can't see blushing either, but those have the added advantage of not being overheard by a dozen strangers. I open the fitting room door dressed in my base layer and thermal pants and tell her to come in with me.

"How's the kissing?" I ask.

She grins. "I still like it," she says.

"Yeah?"

"Yeah." She points at the ski pants, still on their hanger. "C'mon, don't get sidetracked."

I ignore her. "Just kissing?"

I look down at the pile of clothes on the chair. I figure it might be easier for her to tell me the whole truth if she's not having to look right at me, so I start putting on one of the fleeces.

"I let him put his hand up my shirt," she whispers. And then, even more quietly, "Last night he took my shirt and bra off and he took off his shirt and lay on top of me." She's bright red now, and I begin to worry that she might actually implode. "It was kind of amazing. Super-hot. It made me want to take the rest of my clothes off and feel all of him on me."

I raise an eyebrow. Or at least I try to. I haven't perfected that yet. One day maybe I'll get Ebba to teach me.

"All of him, huh?" The ski pants rustle when I put them on.

"Not like that. I'm not sure I'm ready for that."

"Does he have a hairy chest?" The idea of hairy chests is gross. I hope Tim doesn't have one. We probably won't go far enough for me to find out on this trip, but I should be prepared.

Prepared! I know. A girls' trip to Tres Jolie is in order. I'll tell Dad I bought pajamas when it shows up on his credit card bill. Come to think of it, I should get some of those, too.

"Super-smooth," Katie says. "Just a few hairs around his belly button. And then, you know. Below that."

"Boys are so weird." I zip up my jacket, and twirl. Katie nods, like, *you look good.* Actual words are reserved for this far more important conversation we're having.

"Weird and wonderful, though," she says, with a kind of sly grin I've never seen on her before. I'm so behind. I have *got* to catch up.

"You know what we should do?"

"Pay for these clothes and go get lunch somewhere?"

"Yes," I say. I sit down on the wooden stool and stand up, just to check the give in the ski pants. I do another twirl in the mirror. I look ridiculous. But if I squint and imagine myself gracefully sliding down a snowy mountain, it's not so bad. The jacket is a really nice red, almost cherry. "We should definitely do those things. But first we should pay a visit to Tres Jolie."

Her eyes widen. I don't know if it's shock or excitement, or admiration of my French accent. I'd reached deep into my throat for that phlegmy R sound.

"Why?" she asks, like there are a million different reasons to go to Tres Jolie.

"So we can be prepared. Just in case."

"We?"

I'm not a fan of how incredulous she sounds. Does she think I can't get a boyfriend? I can totally get a boyfriend. I just haven't been interested till now, is all. I've had more important things to do with my time. Priorities, you know. But now that everyone else is getting boyfriends, I should probably get one before all the best ones are taken.

Also, Tim has those eyelashes.

"You have Jason. I have Tim."

"You *have* Tim?"

This lie just sort of slips out without me noticing it. I whisper it conspiratorially as I shimmy out of the ski pants. "He kissed me behind the bike sheds yesterday."

Katie laughs! Actually laughs. "The bike sheds?"

"Yeah, I know. So cliché, right?"

"How come you're just mentioning this now?"

She doesn't believe me. She so obviously doesn't believe me. Does she not think I can get a boyfriend? Because I totally can.

"I was waiting for the right moment to tell you." I'm free of the base layer now. Almost back in normal clothes. "And, you know, since our parents won't be on the trip, and since there'll be beds ..."

Katie's eyes widen again. "You're going from a kiss to—to that? In the space of less than two weeks?"

I try to affect nonchalance as I zip up my shorts. "Maybe not that. Maybe just second base." Whatever that is. "But it can't hurt to be prepared, right?"

Nonchalance, even affected, is not something that comes easily to me. Neither is the casualness of this maybe-we-will-maybe-we-won't kind of attitude. If I had thought past kissing, I would have written a list in my bullet journal—the new one I just got, the one with the lock.

1. Kiss a boy
2. Buy sexy underwear
3. Second base
4. Third base
5. Stock up on condoms
or 5b. Go on the Pill
(Ha! Can you imagine my dad's face?) (But wait! I can tell

79

him it's for acne.) (But I don't have acne. What about migraines? There's a girl in my math class who takes it for migraines, or at least that's what I heard her say in the bathroom that one time. I don't get migraines, either, but that should be easier to fake. I live in a house of actors. I should be able to figure this out.)

1. Do the thing
2. Text Katie about doing the thing
3. Take a pregnancy test just to be absolutely and completely sure
4. Meticulously record thoughts and feelings and what can be improved on for next time
5. Do the thing again
6. And again
7. And again

But obviously, no such list exists outside of my head, and it's only been in my head for approximately fifteen seconds (which is fast to write a list, but I guess brains are faster than my multi-colored selection of FriXion gel pens.)

"Don't you want to be prepared, for Jason?" I put the ski pants and ski jacket back on their hangers and gather them in my arms in a big pile with the thermal pants and base layer and fleeces. I could use some help—it's a lot to carry—but Katie's too preoccupied by this conversation.

"I told you," Katie says. "I don't think I'm ready."

"Sexy underwear works for third base too."

"I guess."

"Unless you're thinking the sexy underwear is going to drive him wild with lust and he won't be able to control himself?" The pitch of my voice has risen, possibly in excitement. Or possibly in panic. Hard to tell.

"Clara! Shhh. What is *wrong* with you?" She nods toward

the cubicle wall, to remind me we're not alone.

"We should probably get out of here," I say.

She's irritated with me, and I don't blame her, not really. I am acting sort of crazy. "C'mon," I say, taking her arm. "I'll buy you cheesecake."

If there's one thing Katie can't resist, it's cheesecake, and she knows that I know this about her. I save treating her at The Cheesecake Factory as the nuclear option for when I've really messed up, like that time in the 8th grade I copied her in a test in history class and she was the one who got in trouble for cheating.

"Okay," she says. "I'm having the Godiva chocolate. We need the carbs if we're going to make it all the way to Tres Jolie."

It's only, like, a half-hour walk away, but whatever. "You're the best."

"Yeah, yeah." She's playing at still being irritated. At least I think she's playing.

♪ ♪ ♪ ♪ ♪ ♪

At Tres Jolie, I help Katie pick first—it's the least I can do. She loves purple, so we choose a satiny set of bra and panties. They're pretty plain, but they're a gorgeous deep eggplant color and super-soft to the touch. They're very understated—exactly what I'd imagine sweet-natured Katie to wear the first time she has sex. Or, you know, not wear. Take off. Is it weird to think those thoughts about your best friend? I guess it is kind of weird. Not as weird as imagining myself doing it, though. I'm still not quite clear on how everything is supposed to fit, and also how do you breathe with a guy on top of you? Seems like that would be suffocating. Anyway. I should probably work on figuring out where noses fit when you kiss before I get too deep into this.

We walk around the pink-walled store some more, looking at different things, touching the different fabrics. I'm embarrassed about being here, suddenly. What would Tim think if he knew? He'd freak out, probably. *Chill,* he'd say. *I really just wanted an invitation to Madison Harper's Sweet Sixteen.* Although maybe he wouldn't hate the idea of sex, even if it's just sex with me. If there's one thing better than an invitation to Madison Harper's Sweet Sixteen, it's sex and an invitation to Madison Harper's Sweet Sixteen, or, even better, sex with the daughter of a vaguely famous actor and an invitation to Madison Harper's Sweet Sixteen. There *is* one thing that's clearly even better than that: sex with Madison Harper and an invitation to Madison Harper's Sweet Sixteen, but he's out of luck on that one. She's really into the whole Christian saving yourself for marriage thing. Which, each to their own, I guess?

But right here, right now, in Tres Jolie, Katie is trying to be helpful.

"These?" she says, holding up a red thong and lacy bra.

"Not red," I say.

"I thought—"

"Not for *lingerie,*" I say, because *underwear* sounds like something Mom tells Harry to remember to put on. *Lingerie* is much sexier. "Red *lingerie* is tacky."

"Okay," Katie says. If she was less sweet, she might say, *tacky like kissing behind the bike sheds and then having sex two weeks later?* But she's Katie, and there's a reason we're friends. A reason beyond our shared inability in our first and only ballet class when we were six.

I'm a little grossed out, suddenly, by all the lace and the

colors. All the blatant sexuality in here. Kind of like how at Halloween, I'm like, *candy corn! I always forget how much I like candy corn!* But what I also always forget is that after I've pigged out on candy corn to make up for how much I suddenly realize I've missed it all year, I feel sick to my stomach, and vow never to touch it again, except that by the next year I've forgotten all about that and I make the same mistake over again. Kind of like that. Too much of everything here, and I feel a little sick.

"What about these?" Katie says. She's pointing to a bra and thong set, a teal color, with a little bit of lace around the edges. Baby's First Lacy Underwear? Ugh. Gross. What is *wrong* with me?

"I like that." The bra is padded, which is necessary, and sure, once he takes it off me he'll see he's been lied to but by then I doubt either of us will care. The tops of my legs feel Jello-like and weird when I think about that. I'm not sure about thongs, though. I asked Mom about them years ago, and she said they're a lot more comfortable than they look, but I'm skeptical. Wouldn't it feel like a permanent wedgie?

"A thong, though?"

Katie shrugs. "They're actually pretty comfortable."

"Wait," I say. "Are you wearing one right now?"

She blushes. I can't believe there is so much about each other's lives that we don't know these days. If Katie can wear a thong, I can for sure wear a thong. *Let's do this*, I tell Tim in my mind. *You might not think you want me apart from those selfies and those party invitations, but I'll show you.*

Twenty

I'm packing for the ski trip on Sunday afternoon, almost a week before we leave, when Ebba knocks on my bedroom door. The door's ajar, since I keep running out to go get stuff, clothes from the dryer or sunscreen from my bathroom cabinet (you have to be careful with the glare off the snow, apparently) or my dad's old Taboo for game night. Ebba's learned her lesson about privacy, though. Good.

"Come in," I say, and then I wince. I've noticed too late that the Tres Jolie *lingerie* is lying at the bottom of my otherwise empty suitcase.

Any chance she won't see it?

No, you're right. There's absolutely zero chance she won't see it.

The best thing is to act like it's no big deal. Like I wear underwear—*lingerie*—like that every day. (Though she sees my laundry, so I'm not sure how effective that strategy will be.) I'm really getting a lot of practice at this nonchalance thing.

"I got you that new book of *études* you asked for," Ebba says. "Plus some extra rosin."

"Thanks," I say. I was running low on rosin, but I kept forgetting to get more. Turns out she's remembered for me.

"You got everything you need for the trip?" She is trying not to smile. I can tell.

"Yeah," I say. And I rattle off the list, counting off each item on my fingers—gloves goggles ski pants ski jacket base layer thermal pants fleece hat gaiter sunscreen snow boots regular clothes. I even had to buy extra regular clothes, because I only have enough wool sweaters and Ugg boots for a Pasadena winter, which my midwestern dad doesn't even consider proper winter.

I have to remember to pack my music and my music stand, too, but I'll do that at the last minute after the last pre-ski practice. My viola will be carry-on. No way am I letting them take it from me and stow it away in the too-cold hold where it will be bashed around and lonely, wondering why I've left it. It'd probably sulk and pay me back with wrong notes when I try to tune it. (Yes, I'm aware of how ridiculous this sounds, but remember when I said my viola was an extension of me? This is the kind of thing I meant.)

"Okay," Ebba says. "Good. Let me know if you need anything else, okay?"

"Yeah." And I'm so grateful that she hasn't referenced the teal bra and thong that I add, "Thanks."

"You're welcome," she says. She is out of the door and I'm letting out a sigh of relief and then she pushes it back open and lowers her voice.

"Word of advice," she says, and she nods toward the suitcase. I brace myself for a lecture, formulate an argument about how I really don't think she should be the one having this conversation with me. *That's more the job of an actual parent, don't you think?* But she doesn't lecture me. Instead, with something like sparkle in her eyes, she says, "Save those for the evenings. They can get uncomfortable under ski clothes." She winks, closes the door, and leaves me standing there, relieved and flabbergasted.

Twenty-One

"Okay if I sit here?"

I'm leaning against the foggy school-bus window, still half asleep. I don't even want to think about how early it is. It's the first day of winter break and I should be in bed, recovering from the semester, for several more hours. Still, I guess it's worth it: kissing! Also: snow! Mountains!

I'm thinking, suddenly, about the actual skiing part of this ski trip. The part where we attach pieces of—what? Metal? Plastic? Wood? Whatever—to our feet and hurl ourselves down mountains. Libby keeps excitedly sending me GIFs and tells me I'll love it, and I'm up for the challenge—of course I am, I'm always up for every challenge—but what will it be like? How will it feel? I've wondered plenty about the other stuff: who my roommate will be, whether she'll be sneaking out at night to kiss someone too, whether anybody besides me thought to bring popcorn because it seems like that would be the perfect post-ski snack.

I'm looking forward to the cold, to having to snuggle under blankets or multiple layers of clothing. Cold, to me, means happy. Cold is New York trips and Central Park in the snow and the ballet at Lincoln Center and listening to Dad's endless Juilliard stories and thinking about being there one day too, being one of those people who sits by the fountain with a viola case between my knees. Cold means the sweet smell of roasted chestnuts and the Christmas lights on Fifth Avenue and skating at the Rockefeller Center. All the things from the movies, basically. Cold is dreamy. I'm excited to be heading into it, first this bus and then the flight from LAX to Salt Lake City.

I'm bleary-eyed, too: I'm used to getting up early for viola practice, but four a.m. is kind of ridiculous. The plan is that we make it to Alta in time to settle in, go rent all our equipment and get out onto the snow for at least some of the afternoon. I'm going to need coffee. I'm probably also going to need a snooze, but that's not going to happen on this bus, because apparently Tim is going to sit next to me, and if I'm going to want him to kiss me I probably don't want him to see me dozing with my mouth half-open as I drool and snore. Not that I know if I do either of those things, but it seems preferable not to risk it. I'll also need to chew gum at all times so I can be ready with fresh breath. Imagine how embarrassing it would be to not have fresh breath. Probably worse than passing out because you haven't figured out the nose-and-breathing thing.

"Sure, you can sit there," I tell him. Cool and nonchalant. Good job, Clara. Going well so far.

"You brought your viola?" he asks me, as soon as he sits down. I guess there's not going to be any companionable silence on this trip.

"I have an audition in exactly two months," I say. "I can't afford to slack."

I'll actually be slacking pretty majorly, since there's no way I'll be getting in anything close to my daily three hours of playing. But I've practiced harder than ever these last few weeks, and I've got the pieces down damn near perfect. I'm hoping for half an hour after dinner or something—just enough to make sure my muscle memory is intact. I really wasn't sure about going away, and maybe I should have stayed home, but then there was Katie with all her talk of kissing so here I am, sitting next to Tim on this ski trip. Except that now that I actually am sitting next to Tim on this ski trip, he's not just a concept anymore. Not just the potential provider of first kisses (and uses for the teal lingerie). He's an actual real person whose breath, thankfully, smells like toothpaste, and I'm not entirely sure how we go from sitting on this bus having conversations about my viola to his mouth on mine and our tongues dancing the tango. I can feel myself blushing. This is weird.

"An audition for what? You're trying for LACHSA again?"

"Yup."

"That's too bad. We're only just going to know each other."

"I might not get in," I say. Crazy talk. Of course I'm going to get in—watch me, doubters. But I can't have him thinking there's no point kissing me if I'm going to be leaving anyway.

"You'll get in," he says, bumping my arm with his. It feels like someone's turned the thermostat way up in my body when he says that. I could kiss him right now. That might be weird, though. He wouldn't have time to prepare himself. To decide he really likes me enough to stick his tongue in my mouth and leave it there for a while. Plus, there are way too many people around.

"We'll see," I say. The bus rumbles into life. The kids in the last row cheer.

"We will," he says. Then there's a pause, but this isn't companionable silence either. This is the oh-crap-I-think-we've-run-out-of-things-to-say-to-each-other kind of silence.

"Who's your favorite composer?"

I mull this over in my head, but really I've always known the answer. "Brahms," I say. At orchestra camp we play a lot of Dohnanyi and I like him too, but he's really just an easier Brahms and why do what's easy when you can conquer what's hard? "How about you?"

"Classical music's not really my thing," he says. Actually, as soon as he says *classical music* I know it's not his thing. Because people who know about music don't call it that.

"Classical music's actually not really the right term," I tell him. "Brahms is a Romantic. And then there's Baroque, too, like Bach. Classical is just one of the periods of music."

"Oh," swoopy-haired Tim says. "Okay. Teaching me things already. I like it."

I'm not sure what he expected when he sat next to me. I'm smart and I know things and I consider it my duty to correct people when they're wrong, because who wants to go through life being wrong? But then, Tim wouldn't know that. He doesn't know anything about me except whose daughter I am.

"What's your thing?" I ask him. Because I don't know him, either. I only know he's the one who's going to end the kissing drought and give me things to report back to Katie.

"My thing?"

"You know. The thing you're into. Your passion." My face boils up when I say *passion*. I wasn't trying to come on to him, I swear. Not yet, anyway. He smiles, an embarrassed little smile. Is he embarrassed for *me*? This is excruciating. Get me off this bus.

"Promise not to laugh?"

"I promise."

"Scrabble," he says.

I know I promised, but I can't help it: I laugh anyway.

"What?" he says. He looks mildly offended. Or maybe more than mildly.

"Scrabble the board game?"

"Yes, the board game. What other kind of Scrabble is there?"

I shrug. "I didn't know it was a thing you could be into."
What I mean is, he doesn't look like a nerd. He's way too cute.
He doesn't even wear glasses.

"I play in competitions," he says. "I'm pretty good, actually.
LA County Youth Champion last year."

Okay. Well. Now he has my attention. Or he would have it
if he didn't have it already. What I mean is: he's competitive.
And he's a winner. These are things I can relate to. Things I
can admire.

"Wow," I say.

"I'm pretty impressive." He does this toothy grin that tells
me he only half believes that I believe it, though. He's cool
enough to be into all the regular things that guys are into, but
instead: Scrabble? I think that's kind of impressive. Forging
his own path.

"What's your favorite word?" I ask him.

"*Zyzzyva*. It's a South American weevil. Even without any
double or triple word scores it's worth 43 points. It's also the
name of one of the apps I use to train."

Is it weird that I find it so attractive that Tim is obsessed
with vocabulary? Probably. Or maybe I'm just excited to meet
someone who won't make fun of my big words. But I'm also
intrigued by something else Tim's just said.

"You train?"

"Yep. Serious stuff. I can't afford to slack either, you know."

I laugh, without knowing why, and this time he laughs too.
He digs his phone out of his jeans pocket to show me the app,
but instead of giving me his phone, he moves it toward me
slightly, so that I have to lean into him. His face is so close

to mine it feels like we're touching even though we're not. A kind of phantom touch. I can hear him breathe. I try to make my own breathing even and pretend I'm listening to what he's saying about the app, about Scrabble, about how to get the most points. I wonder if he can hear my heart. It's beating way too loudly. I can feel it everywhere, like right before a performance: in my neck, in my wrists, in my ears. Maybe even in the tips of my fingers.

It usually takes forever to get from Pasadena to LAX, but we're there far too quickly. Maybe it's the early morning and the comparatively low levels of traffic. Or maybe it just feels quick because I wanted to sit like this for hours and hours.

Twenty-Two

Skiing, it turns out, is a lot of hard work. Just getting dressed seems to take forever, and then you feel like the Stay Puft Marshmallow Man walking around with ski pants and ski jacket, all that padding designed not just to keep you warm but, Tim says, also to break your fall. He tells me falling is part of the deal. It's important not to be afraid of it. If you're afraid you'll be tense and actually more likely to hurt yourself. Being told to relax has never really worked for me, but okay.

"The trick," Tim says before we go to our different lessons on the first afternoon, "is to learn to fall right. Like this." He lets himself fall onto his side on the snow, there at the bottom of the slope. "Then you make sure your skis are across the hill, perpendicular to it, and you push on your poles, and you're up in no time. See?" He stands up effortlessly, or as effortlessly as you can do anything with all those layers on.

"Well, yeah. It's easy when you're not actually wearing skis."

He shakes his bangs out of his eyes and looks at me. "Trust me," he says.

"Okay," I say, trying not to let my voice wobble.

If I thought it was hard to walk with my base layer and thermal pants and fleece and ski jacket and ski pants, it was nothing compared to walking in ski boots, aka torture instruments. They're these big heavy clumpy things that make it impossible to move your ankle.

"That's kind of the point," the guy who fit me with them said. "They're supposed to protect your ankles. The last thing you want is for them to turn."

That's when it hit me, how dangerous this all is. It seems, suddenly, like not the best of ideas. Like maybe I should have stayed home this week and practiced my viola for my LACHSA audition, as per original plan. But I'm here now. Tim is here with his swoopy hair and his unnaturally yet sexily long eyelashes. And the mountains are beautiful. Breathtakingly beautiful. More beautiful even than Tim's eyelashes.

Everything is so white. I mean, obviously, snow is white. It's not like I've never seen snow before. Just never this much of it all in one place. And never in New York, where it starts to turn grey fifteen seconds after it lands, except maybe in Central Park, which is beautiful in its own way, but not like this. There are mountains and more mountains and behind those there are more mountains, all of them dotted with people in blue and red and purple and yellow being dragged up on ski lifts or looking down from chair lifts or curving their way down slopes with varying degrees of gracefulness. There's something so beautiful about this, about the real world not intruding. Well, aside from Tim. Tim is real. I know this because every now and then my stomach flips over itself in an effort to remind me.

Twenty-Three

After skiing the first full day, we're all pretty sore. I spent a lot of the day with my body clenched from the effort of trying to do everything right, to get my skis to go parallel and then at the pizza wedge angle when I needed to slow down or stop. "Clara," the group instructor kept calling out to me from further down the mountain. "Straighten your back." Or, "Don't grip the ski poles so hard." Or, "Bend your knees slightly." Or, "Relax your shoulders." There's so much to remember, and on top of it of it all I'm supposed to relax? Relaxing and getting things right are usually not compatible. I've fallen a few times, too, and I can feel a bruise forming on my outer left thigh from falling sideways the way Tim showed me.

Hot baths are apparently really good for this kind of muscle pain, but I don't get a chance to take one before dinner because Abigail was in our bathroom for so long. Just a quick shower, and a dab of perfume, a quick look in the misted-up mirror, and by the time I'm out of the bathroom and down at dinner everyone's deep in conversation that's echoing around the room. There's nowhere to sit except at the end of the table, far away from Tim, who's surrounded on all sides by girls. Including the girl who ended up sitting next to him on the plane—Vanessa, a sophomore with pale skin and long black hair. Oh, and look: she's leaning in close to him now, showing him a bruise on her forearm. (How did she get a bruise on her *forearm*? Maybe that's what he's asking her. That's why he's laughing. The implausibility of it.)

"Hey," I say to nobody in particular as I pull out my chair and plop myself down, but Nguyet and Alicia don't register it. I'm hungrier than I've maybe ever been in my life, my stomach rumbling for mercy, so I focus on my cheeseburger and fries, and I sneak glances at Tim, willing him to look for me, to look at me. But he doesn't, and his laughter gets louder, and I finish my food as fast I can and leave the room as soon as I've swallowed the last bite of airy chocolate mousse. We're probably supposed to wait in case there are announcements from the teachers or whatever, but I can't stand this anymore. My chair scrapes along the floor as I pull back, and finally Alicia looks at me, screwing up her face up in disapproval at the disturbance.

Still, it's good I'm not entangled in conversation. I have responsibilities, after all. Back in our room, I unfold my metal music stand next to my bed, take my viola out of its case, unfold my music and bend it back so it doesn't keep closing, twizzle the end of my bow. I choose an *étude* I can play almost perfectly, position my viola under my chin, and take a deep breath—all of these are reassuring movements that make me feel like myself again, at home in my own body. I'm lifting my bow to play the first note when the door swings open.

"Oh, *hi*," Abigail says, surprised and disappointed to see me there, like she's forgotten I exist and would prefer not to be reminded. "Whatcha doing?"

I try not to roll my eyes. It is blindingly obvious what I am doing. But we have six more nights together and I don't want her to hate me. So I don't say, *what does it look like, genius?* Instead, despite the tone of her voice that clearly communicates that she thinks I'm a weirdo, I smile sweetly.

"Practicing my viola," I say. "I have an audition soon."

"Oh," she says, tossing her blond hair over her shoulder. "Okay."

She flops onto her back on her bed, fishes for her phone in her pocket, and puts her earphones in. She might not be able to hear me now, but, as you know, I don't practice in front of people.

I feel a pang of guilt as I lay my viola back down in its case. Believe it or not, there are days when I don't feel like practicing, but I make myself take it step by step. *Go up to your room, Clara. Close the door. Open your viola case. Take out the instrument.* And once my viola's in my hand, I remember all the reasons I love it, and I'd feel guilty not playing it then, like I'm some kind of tease. That's what I'm feeling now. It's not that different from Tim seeming like he liked me enough to sit next to me on the bus and give me a small sad smile when I walked past him on the plane to go find my own seat six rows back, and then not looking for me at dinner. *I'm sorry*, I mouth to my viola, running my finger along its D string. *Circumstances beyond my control.*

♫ ♫ ♫ ♫ ♫ ♫

It's only fifteen minutes until evening activities, and I don't want to be stuck with a bad seat again, so I wander to the game room, where people have started to gather. On the orange couch, Vanessa and another sophomore girl are comparing injuries. As is customary by now, the butterflies in my stomach register Tim before I consciously see him, sitting on the floor, leaning against the wall, his knees tucked under his chin, scrolling through his phone. It would be so easy for me to walk over, plop down next to him, and casually say

Hey. Or at least, it would be easy if I was smarting less over the fact that he seems to have forgotten about me.

Instead, since the purple couch is free, I grab the corner and nestle there, with my legs tucked under me, making myself as small as possible. I'm about to take my own phone out when Tim looks up from his.

He cracks his neck and rolls his shoulder. "Ouch," he says.

"This is what I'm talking about," Vanessa says, breaking her conversation mid-sentence. "Everything hurts. Necks, shoulders, everything."

"Worth it, though." He smiles, and that's enough for my stupid face to start getting warm.

"I mean," Vanessa says. "If you want a massage—"

"You can do massages?" Tim asks, hope in his voice along with disbelief at the happy coincidence. "I didn't know that."

"There's a lot you don't know about me," she says. I wish Katie was here so I could make a gagging face at her. "Come sit in front of me."

She nods toward the patch of floor in front of her, beckoning him like he's a dog or something. And in that split second, she also makes eye contact with me. *He's mine,* her eyes seem to tell me. *Look at him, practically eating out of my hand. I saw him first. Deal with it.* And also, there's a warning there: *Don't even think about trying anything, little freshman girl.* I hold her gaze, even though I'm a little scared of her. I hope my eyes are saying something cool back, like *Tim who? I barely know who he is, but even if I did like him, I wouldn't let* you *stop me.* That's a lot for eyes to communicate, though. Most likely, mine are just saying, *please, don't hurt me.*

Tim sits in front of Vanessa, stretching out his legs. My feet escape from under me and land on the floor, a breath's width from his, like every part of my body is steel and he's the most powerful magnet ever. As Vanessa kneels up behind him and gets to work on his shoulders, he wriggles and adjusts his position, so that his feet are brushing mine. If I didn't know better, I'd say that he had a little of the steel-and-magnet thing happening himself. But I do know better, because he's barely acknowledged me since this morning. And now he's closing his eyes and making noises that sound way too appreciative for a public setting. Noises I was kind of hoping he'd be making with me by now. Vanessa's hands work his neck, his scalp, his shoulders. I move my foot away. He doesn't open his eyes. His face registers nothing. He doesn't even notice.

Twenty-Four

The designated evening activity on the second evening is board games. We were all supposed to bring one from home, and I'd rooted around and found my dad's Taboo, which as board games go is my favorite because for one minute you talk and everyone has to listen. That's the rule. Plus, I love the purple squeaker that you squeeze when someone else makes a mistake. It's so satisfying.

Tim, of course, brought Scrabble, but that gets vetoed immediately. "Bo-ring," some sophomore guy I don't know groans. Tim's shoulders slump and his face falls, but only a little, as if he's used to this. I know how that feels, for the thing you're passionate about to be mocked or just misunderstood by people around you. From the floor across from him, I try to catch his eye to somehow tell him so without words, but he won't look at me. We haven't spoken since the massage incident last night, since I pulled my foot away from his. We weren't on the same team for those stupid icebreaker games they made us do afterward and every time since then that I've seen him—toasting bagels at breakfast, waiting for the first ski lift of the day at the bottom of the slopes, helping himself to extra potatoes at dinner—he's been with Vanessa.

He doesn't exactly seem like he's not enjoying himself with her, either. Last night as I was finally drifting off to sleep I kept hearing echoes of the sounds he was making during Vanessa's so-called massage. Things like this, I realize all over again, are why I don't bother with boys. So much time and energy, and for what? For the hope of catching his beautiful blue eyes for a few seconds? Please. I've got bigger fish to fry.

To my shock, the popular girls looking through the games piled high on the table choose Taboo. We take a vote, and of course nobody wants to argue with the popular girls.

"Boys against girls," Vanessa decrees, and even though that's very cisnormative of her I don't argue, because all the girls I know are better at Taboo than all the boys I know and I'm all for being on the winning team. People on opposite teams also have to alternate places, so this also means she gets to sit next to Tim on the floor, her long black apple-scented hair brushing his shoulder as she leans close to look at the card. It's her job to check he doesn't say *Sandra Dee* or *cooking* or *hair* or *bicycle* when he's trying to get the guys to guess the word *Grease*.

"Squeak," she says, when he accidentally says *school*. "Squeak! Squeak! Squeak!"

Her voice is high-pitched and discordant. I can't take it.

"You don't actually have to say *squeak*," I say. "You squeeze the squeaker, and it says *squeak* for you."

"*You're* the squeaker," she says.

Her gaggle of skinny sophomores snickers. She presses the purple thing over and over again. I want to say she's going to break it, but I also don't want to let her see that she's getting to me. Besides, there's a game to win, and while we are clearly going to beat the boys, it's important not to get sidetracked. I do a little, though. Sitting in this circle on the floor, it's easy to steal glances at Tim from time to time—or, like, every few seconds. You know how if you look at the sun too directly, you close your eyes afterward and it's still there? I sneak a look at his chin dimple, his swoopy hair, his eyelashes, and when I look away they're imprinted on the inside of my eyelids—maybe forever.

Obviously, though, when it's someone on my team speaking, I'm focused on them, leaning forward, trying to guess the word, often succeeding. When it's my turn to describe a phrase, the first card says *Stuck up.*

"Snob," I say.

"Viola player," Abigail says. I stay focused. You have to, in this game, if you want to stay ahead.

"Loner," Vanessa says, which clearly has nothing to do with my original word and everything to do with her wanting me to feel like *I'm* the loner. "Squeaker," she adds, and it's kind of a weird insult, but I feel the sting of it—the squeak of it—anyway.

Wilson, the guy next to me who has the purple thing, squeaks it, which throws me, because I didn't make a mistake, I know I didn't, but I scan the card up and down, up and down, just to make sure, and they're blurrier and blurrier. This was my moment to shine, to make everyone like me by winning points for the team, and I'm blowing it.

"Sounds like a word for if you're trying to get a teacher to like you," I say, controlling my voice. "Or if you're trying to get a guy to like you." That last part was a stroke of genius. Even I can admit that.

"Suck up," Tim shouts, then puts his hand over his mouth.

"Shut up," Vanessa says, cuffing him on the back of the head, taking any opportunity for physical contact. "You're not on our team."

"Hey," Abigail says. "If he wants to help …"

"Not the point," Vanessa says, wasting more valuable seconds, and I know what the point is. Taboo is a weird kind of test to see if your minds are in sync, and Tim and I just passed it, and she doesn't like it.

"Anyway, it sounds like the phrase Tim just said." His name tingles and hums on my tongue. "But with a T in it."

"Time's up!" someone yells, and my turn is over. Zero points. I'm mortified. I'm usually excellent at this game. Vanessa squeaks the squeaker, and its message this time is clear: LOSER.

Obviously, we still win, because girls always do, but when I come to pack up the game, I can't find the purple thing. I need it—it's Dad's game, he'll want it all back in one piece.

"Has anyone seen the squeaker?" I ask into the hubbub of voices, but nobody pays attention. I look under the couches and the tables. Nothing.

"Looking for something?" Vanessa says, and then she squeaks it in my ear. I try to snatch it from her, but she snaps her hand back, and then she's gone.

♫ ♫ ♫ ♫ ♫ ♫

I'm proud of myself for making it through the evening without crying. It might feel good to let it out now that I'm in bed, might get rid of this lump in my throat, but it's not worth it, not worth Abigail hearing me and getting to report back tomorrow to the others, to Vanessa's delight and satisfaction. Do they really think I'm stuck up? I keep myself to myself, is all. There's no point making friends since I'm going to be gone in a few months. And besides, who *would* want to be friends with these people?

I'm reaching for my phone on the nightstand to text Katie when there's the quietest knock on the door. I push back my covers, tiptoe to the peephole, and hold back a gasp. It's Tim.

I creak the door open. Abigail turns toward the opposite wall and moans incoherently, clearly displeased. I slip into the hallway, crossing my arms over my bra-less chest and hoping the bun I've quickly put my hair into is messy in a semi-glamorous way rather than a bed-head way.

"Hey," I say, like my heart isn't pounding. "What's up?"

"I have this for you," he says, holding out the Taboo squeaker in his hand. I feel my eyes widen. I never expected to see that thing again.

"Thanks." I'm not sure what else to say. I try not to touch him as I take the squeaker back, because I know that will fog up my brain, but my fingers brush his palm and my knees feel suddenly wobbly.

"I'm sorry about Vanessa," he says, his eyes full of earnestness. "She can be—" He doesn't finish the sentence, and let's face it: he doesn't need to. We both know exactly how she can be. "We've been friends since pre-K."

I think for some reason about *Bridget Jones's Diary*, and wonder if they used to play naked in a paddling pool.

"She's suffocating sometimes," he adds.

It's dark in this hallway, and that emboldens me. "Just friends?"

He breathes in, puffs his cheeks out, and sighs. "She wants to be more. I really don't. So she tries to guard me with her life to make sure I don't get to be with anyone else."

"She's a pretty effective repellent."

"I know," Tim says. "I'm sorry. I'm sorry about how tonight was, and how we haven't gotten to talk to each other much. Because I really—"

A flashlight comes on in the hallway and shines almost directly into our faces.

"Back to your rooms," the sophomore mom who's come on the trip as a chaperone says. "Now."

"We were only talking," I say. I don't break rules. And the rule was clearly: no boys in girls' rooms, and vice versa. He's not in my room. We're in the clear.

"We weren't doing anything," Tim says.

"Not the point," she says, shaking her head. "Scoot. Back to bed."

He squeezes my hand before he goes, and I feel my face redden. *We weren't doing anything.* I wonder if there was an unspoken *yet* on the end of Tim's sentence. I wonder what things he has been thinking of doing with me. I can still feel his phantom touch on my hand.

Operation Tim ready for lift off, I text to Katie once I'm back in bed, the lump in my throat well and truly gone now.

Twenty-Five

Tim's right about skiing. It *is* fun. The next day, he finds me at the bottom of the mountain after our lessons, my nose pink with cold. He's in a different group, for more advanced skiers. It's probably for the best that he doesn't see too much of my stumbling efforts. I don't always look as elegant as I'd like to.

"So, you're getting the hang of it?" he asks.

"Yeah." We skied our first blue run in our lesson today, after working our way up from bunny slopes to greens. I tried to relax, like Tim told me to, and weirdly, even though I didn't think I really knew *how* to relax, it helped. My pizza wedge looked good, apparently. *Pizza wedge* is such a ridiculous name for putting your skis into that upside-down V shape. We're not babies. I asked our instructor for the real word for it: it's *snowplow*. Which makes sense—when you put your skis out in a pizza wedge shape you're kind of plowing the snow. Our instructor said in French it's called a snow-chaser. I like that.

"Want to ski a blue run with me before lunch?"

We have a half hour of free time now. Most people huddle in the lodge around hot chocolates after their group lessons. And honestly, I've earned that. It was kind of exhilarating, this morning. The instructor taught us that if a slope looks too steep, the thing to do is ski all the way across, make a turn, and then ski all the way back. It takes longer that way, but you also don't break your neck.

"Then what's the point?" I joked, when the instructor said that, and he looked at me the way Dad does when I'm about to be grounded.

"We don't take unnecessary risks," the instructor said. It seems to me that the whole hurling yourself down a mountain on two planks of whatever is one big unnecessary risk to begin with, when I could be curled up with a mug of cocoa in front of the fire place with Tim massaging my feet. If you're going to risk it, you might as well risk it.

"Let's do it," I say to Tim. We're not technically allowed to go off unaccompanied like this, and I don't break rules, but Tim asked me. Me. Just me. Finally it's going to be just the two of us.

My ski pole is attached to my wrist and I lift it and use it to point to the chairlift I went on earlier with my instructor.

"Careful," Tim says. "You'll take someone's eye out with that."

I dig my poles in the snow and push myself off. It's hard work on the flatter parts, you really have to put as much of your weight as possible on the poles and push ridiculously hard to move just a tiny bit. It takes your breath away, not in a romantic isn't-that-beautiful-way, but actually, physically. But still, it isn't so long before we're on the gentle slope that leads down to the chairlift line.

We wait our turn behind a group of schoolkids and a couple families, and when it comes time to position ourselves for the chairlift to come around and scoop us up I try to surreptitiously shuffle as close to Tim as I can so that our legs will be touching when we sit down. Or, you know, his blue ski pants which are on top of his thermal pants which are on top of his boxer shorts (or whatever, I obviously haven't asked him what he wears) will be touching my red ski pants which are on top of my thermal pants which are on top of my very plain cotton underwear. We're not exactly talking skin-to-skin contact.

When we do sit—or, rather, when we're whacked into place by the not-exactly-gentle contraption that's probably going to give me a bruise—I'm not sure I can even feel his leg against mine. Such a waste of an opportunity and of carefully planned maneuvering. Still, it feels good up here. The air is so clean it hurts my nostrils to breathe it. Or maybe that's just the cold. Regardless, I want to bottle this air and sprinkle it over Los Angeles. They should make scented candles with this air. I don't know what it would smell of—clean laundry, maybe? And maybe it's the clean air or maybe it's the fact that I haven't eaten since breakfast and I forgot to bring energy bars or maybe it's just being next to Tim—I wouldn't call it touching, not with all these layers, but I *am* very, very close to him, breathing this same tingly clean air—but I feel a little light-headed. Is this what being drunk feels like? If it is, I totally get why people get addicted to it.

"So you're glad you came?" Tim asks me. Which is good, because there's always a moment at the beginning of a conversation with him when I'm not quite sure how to start.

"Yes," I say. And then I worry all over again that it's going to be the end of the conversation, and I scramble to think of something else. "The air is just really clean here."

He laughs. "That's such an old person thing to say. What are you—eighty-five years old?"

"Give or take seventy years."

He laughs again, but this time it feels good. This time he's laughing with me—better still, he's laughing *because* of me, because I've made him laugh. The chairlift takes us up, up, up, and maybe that's why my stomach feels funny. Maybe it's not butterflies. Except, who I am kidding with that?

"What do you like best about skiing?" I ask him.

"I like the sound of my skis across the snow," he says.

I know what he means. It's kind of a whooshing sound and I like it, too. He's a much better skier than me, though, so I bet it's even more satisfying, whoosh, whoosh, turn which still whooshes, just as smoothly, whoosh, whoosh, all the way down to the bottom. I can imagine that feels good, almost like music. Like the first time you play from the beginning to the end of a Mozart concerto without your teacher interrupting to correct your technique. When I ski, it's more like, lazy, half-hearted whoosh that grinds to a halt as I attempt a turn, panicked whoosh as my skis take control and I start going too fast in the part of the turn when I'm pointing down the hill, thump as I land on my hip the way Tim taught me.

"I'm also really enjoying this chairlift ride," he says.

My stomach flips before my brain finishes processing the sentence. He doesn't mean the effortless rise up the mountain, the break for our tired feet, the sun on our faces, or the weird but kind of cool sensation of our skis half-resting on the metal bar below us, half swinging in mid-air.

"It's a great view," I say, which would work much better as a line if we were actually facing each other rather than up the mountain.

"Yes," he says, and I hear from the swoosh of his ski jacket that he's turned to look at me, so I do the same thing. Are we actually going to kiss here on this chairlift? That would be so romantic. But we're almost at the top of this mountain, or at least our little section of this mountain, and it's time to move the metal bar that straps us in so we can slide off. Never mind. Next time.

It always feels like I'm a legit skier when I get off a chairlift. I look no different to anyone else. I've got the equipment. I didn't fall off and embarrass myself. I can look down the mountain and convince myself I'm about to ski down just as elegantly as all the other brightly outfitted people, as if I'd been doing this since I was the age of a kid Harry's height who whizzes past us as we stand adjusting gloves and goggles and helmets. Come to think of it, why *did* my parents never take me skiing? Maybe it's to do with Juliette's precious ballet legs. I'll have to remember to ask them.

"Ready?" Tim says. I'm suddenly nervous he's going to whoosh away and leave me here to slide all the way down on my butt. Because, let's face it, I'm actually nothing like those elegant brightly-outfitted people.

"We'll do it in stages, okay?"

He looks at me like I'd be crazy to think otherwise.

"Of course. I'm not going to leave you to fend for yourself up here when you've only been skiing three days."

My hero. Maybe someone else could get away with saying that, but it would sound ridiculous coming out of my mouth. So instead I smile and say thanks. We push off down the mountain with our poles, and I follow in his tracks. He's using the whole width of the slope, like our instructor showed us, like he knows I need reassuring about the steepness. If you ski across and then make a tiny turn, the only scary part is the tiny turn, because you're only facing straight down the slope for a fraction of a second. Or a little longer if you're me, because I do the turn in a pizza wedge position rather than with my skis in parallel like Tim, and that slows me down a little.

The snow feels different than it did when we skied down this slope with our instructor earlier today. Not so much whoosh whoosh as the sound of ice being scraped off a car's windshield in a movie set someplace cold, like Chicago. My skis aren't gripping the snow as well. My turns are happening too fast. There's a lot of slope left, and it looks steeper than I remember. I wonder if this was the best of ideas. But we're here now. We might as well enjoy it, right?

"You okay?" Tim calls. The wind carries his voice back to me. I don't remember it being so windy this morning. My face feels like it's being eaten alive.

"I'm good," I shout back to him. I'm good I'm good I'm good, I repeat to myself, relax relax relax. And then one of my skis catches on snow that's piled up on itself. It happens fast. I don't have time to remember to fall on my hip. I put my left hand out to break my fall. It catches my pole. I hear the crack before I feel it. I'm on the ground. My ski has snapped off and is careening down the mountain. My wrist my wrist my wrist. I think I'm going to black out from the pain. And then I do.

Twenty-Six

I cry sitting on the cold slope waiting for help. I cry and cry when the rescue guys in their orange pants and jackets ski me down the mountain in this big orange canvas coffin, Tim following behind. I can't see, and with every jolt and jerk, pain shoots through my wrist, all the way up to my shoulder. I stop crying when they get me out of there and I walk over to urgent care, because it's hard to walk in these boots and you really have to concentrate. Then after they give me a pain injection I bite my lip and wait for it to kick in. Tim tells me half-hearted jokes to try to take my mind off the pain, but he doesn't know me well enough to know what will actually make me laugh, and anyway, you can't forget about pain this bad. And you also can't forget about a bungled LACHSA audition. My wrist will be fine by February 28—it has to be, right?—but I can't bear to imagine what a month without practice will do to my playing, to my chances of getting into LACHSA. But mostly I'm not even thinking about that. Mostly I'm just thinking about the pain. It's like a million tiny bombs going off in my wrist, over and over. I hate that Tim is seeing me cry like this. I hate looking weak.

Then again, there's an argument to be made that this is all his fault. So I shouldn't care what he thinks.

♫ ♫ ♫ ♫ ♫ ♫

I cry some more on the phone to Mom that evening, so much that she has to keep asking me to repeat what I've said because it comes out in a garbled, snotty mess. In the end, though, she gives up asking me to repeat myself. She realizes, I think, that the actual words don't matter, that what I really need is for her to just be there, like the phone equivalent of a hug.

I do say one thing loud and clearly though: "I want to go home."

The chaperone says that there's no reason I can't stay. It's only a couple more days, and the lodge we're staying in is cozy, with an open fire with real logs crackling downstairs, and thick hot chocolate practically on tap. And I guess if I was the reading type, I'd curl up there, my splinted wrist resting on the arm of the plush red couch, a little high on painkillers, a book in my good hand. But I'm not, and everybody here hates me, and I can't stand to be around Tim. I'm embarrassed that he saw me fall apart the way I did, and mad at myself for losing my logical head and going up there with him. And then yesterday the door to the game room was shut for a while, with a sign up saying the room was closed for a private meeting, and then I saw him shuffle out of there with his head low. I'm mortified he got in trouble, but I'm also glad he did, and I'm also fearful of what my punishment will be. Right now people are saying things like, "I guess you've learned your lesson" and "I think you've suffered enough," but I'm sure they'll change their minds.

That's a lot of emotion, and emotions make me squicky and uncomfortable, and I just want to be in a room by myself with the door shut, bingeing something on Netflix and not having to care what I look like when I come out for dinner—whether my eyes are red and puffy, or my cheeks are blotchy from crying, or the pattern from my pillowcase is imprinted on my forehead.

Those are some of the things I try to tell Mom, lying face down on my twin bed in the shared room, the scratchy bedspread itching my feet, and I'm pretty sure she doesn't understand any of it but at the same time she understands all of it because she's my mom.

"Okay," she says, "okay," and phone calls are made and forms are signed and someone helps me pack up my luggage and drives me to the airport with its enormous Christmas tree and its twinkling lights, mocking me with its manufactured joy, but I almost don't care because soon I'll be home, home, home.

Twenty-Seven

Ebba's going to be waiting for me at baggage claim at LAX. Mom and Dad are both working today, and acting isn't the kind of work where you can call in sick or with a family emergency. There's a reason why *the show must go on* is a cliché, even if Dad does insist on using it far more than he should.

Anyway, it's not an emergency, as such. My wrist is already broken, already in a splint. (I was lucky, apparently: I don't need surgery or metal plates. I don't feel lucky.) I don't really know what it is that my parents rushing to the airport would achieve at this point. What would have actually made a difference would have been for them to rush to the airport on Saturday to stop me getting on the plane to Utah in the first place. (What was I thinking? I can't believe I allowed the prospect of a kiss to derail my entire life's purpose. This is so unlike me. Love clearly makes people crazy.)

Still, all the way home to California two days before everyone else and hopped up on painkillers, my elbow propped up on the plane's armrest, old episodes of *Parks and Rec* on my iPad to try to take my mind off it, I wish Mom or Dad was coming to get me. Someone who's known me my whole life, who understands that my wrist is not just my wrist. The others on the trip, they totally didn't get it. *At least you're not left-handed!* they said, like I care about writing when we mostly type and use both hands for that, and anyway schoolwork is the very, very least of my worries. Mom and Dad would understand. Mom would make me the carrot and cilantro soup which is my absolute favorite. Dad would tell terrible jokes till I couldn't help but laugh, no matter how hard I'd try not to. (It's best not to encourage him.) *You're in treble now,* he'd say. And then he'd look at my crestfallen face and say, *Uh oh. That joke fell a little flat. I guess the pain must be pretty sharp.*

The puns are working, though—they're making me smile. Apparently I don't even need Dad here in person. I'll always have his terrible jokes. I look around at the gate and Ebba's waiting for me, looking sad. Looking as if *she* is the one with the career-ending injury.

"That's her," I say to the flight attendant who was assigned to look after me. The airline was super-helpful, actually. I was pretty impressed. They helped me with my viola so I didn't have to check it and they had me board the plane before everyone else so I could get settled. The flight attendant, Tracey, told me she has a daughter my age. I guess that's why she was kind to me. "That's my stepmom."

"Honey," Ebba says, standing and walking over to me. She sort of stands there awkwardly, I guess trying to decide whether to hug me. She squeezes my right arm instead.

"How are you holding up?" she asks me, after she signs the paperwork on Tracey's clipboard and I say thanks and bye to her.

My two-hour record of not crying comes to an abrupt end. I feel my face crumple. Ebba opens her arms and I let her hug me afterward. She's less bony than Mom, and she smells faintly of vanilla and almond. The hoodie she's wearing is soft, though it's possibly also now covered in my snot and tears.

"I'm sorry," I say, when I pull away.

"You have nothing to be sorry for," she says, warmth in her voice.

Actually, if I'm honest, I've got two years' worth of things to be sorry for. But I push that thought away. Right now I'm really just sorry for the snot and the tears, and the fact Ebba's had to make the hour-long drive to collect me when everyone else will just get to go on a bus in a couple days' time.

"I was so hoping you'd have a good time," she adds, before I can argue.

"I did, before all this."

She raises an eyebrow. What is it with people who can raise just one eyebrow? They make you want to tell them everything.

"Not like that," I say, clarifying.

"No use for the thing you packed?"

"Nope."

She stretches her arm out and around me. I let her, and we walk to baggage claim that way, through the hubbub of people and noise. I think about Juliette, walking with Ebba like this after *The Nutcracker* back in November. I get it now, the warmth of it. Ebba feels like home.

Twenty-Eight

The doorbell rings during the late morning of Christmas Eve while I'm upstairs, not practicing my viola. I guess I could run down and get the door, but really, what's the point? If it was anyone interesting they'd have texted me first. I turn up my music—a Haydn string quartet—and try to focus on my equations. At least I know I'm still top of the class in math. But there's banging on my bedroom door and I have to turn the music back down to ask what the deal is. "There's someone here for you," Dad says.

"Who?"

"Just come down, will you?"

I'm hoping it's Madison Harper. I haven't seen her in forever. But like I said, if it is her, it's weird she hasn't texted first. Or, you know, it could be Santa, with an early gift. Haha. I crack myself up sometimes. I want Christmas canceled this year, anyway. My early gift was the cast on my wrist: getting that put on yesterday was a barrel of laughs, let me tell you.

I brush my hair with my one good hand and walk down the stairs. The fairy lights on the hand rail seem like they're mocking me. When I get down the hallway I realize why Dad didn't tell me who it was at the door. I never would have come if I'd known. Tim stands there sheepishly, his hair all in his eyes, as Mom would say. He's holding, believe it or not, a bunch of flowers.

"Hi," he says. I've always liked the swoopy hair (you may have picked up on that) but now it feels like it's just a clever tool, something to hide behind.

"Hi," I say. My stomach didn't get the memo about Tim. It's still attempting somersaults. "To what do I owe the pleasure?" I can hear the sarcasm in my voice, which is exactly what I was going for. Good job.

The flowers are giant daisies of all different colors. They're actually really nice, but they're too cheerful. I don't want anything cheerful in my life. Not these flowers, and not that stupid tree with its stupid presents underneath it. It feels wrong.

"Thanks," I say, taking them from him, making sure our hands don't touch. "You've brought them now. You can go."

His face falls and for a second I almost feel bad for him. Almost.

"I'm sorry," he says. "I'm so, so sorry. I wanted you to know that." He already said that a million times in Utah. I get the idea.

"Thanks." I look at the flowers. They really are pretty. Tim is pretty too, but I can't bear to look at him. "You know my audition is in ten weeks and now I can't practice for five of those?"

His shoulders kind of stoop. "I did. I'm sorry. I don't know what else to say."

"Last chance. They only take rising freshmen and sophomores."

He opens his mouth to say he's sorry again, but evidently decides against it.

"I should go," he says, after a while of us just standing there. "My mom is waiting."

"Your mom drove you here?" He's totally old enough to have his own car. Maybe his driving privileges got revoked. Good.

His shoulders stoop even more. "Yeah."

"Was this her idea?"

He nods. Wow. You break a girl's wrist and you can't even come up with the idea of taking her flowers yourself. Pathetic.

"Okay," I say.

"Clara, I'm really sorry," he says again. And then he leaves.

Twenty-Nine

"Wow," Dad says, after the door clicks shut behind Tim. "Way to be gracious, Clara."

"He didn't deserve my graciousness."

"That's the point of graciousness. You take the high road to be kind when the other person doesn't deserve it."

I shrug. "He only came because his mom made him."

"Still," Dad says. "Those are nice flowers." That is objective fact.

"Yes," I say. "They are nice."

"And he sounded really sorry."

Sorry's all well and good and it makes the person saying it feel slightly better about themselves even though they don't deserve to. But it doesn't change what happened. It doesn't fix my wrist. It doesn't give me another shot at a LACHSA audition.

"You know, Clara, your mom and I had an agreement that we wouldn't punish you, because you've been punished enough with the pain and the audition and all. But this is not exactly *not* your own fault."

"That's a double negative."

Even I can hear what a smart-ass I'm being, and not in a good way.

"Yes," Dad says. "It is." He crosses his arms, leans against the wall, and looks at me very seriously. Dad's serious face freaks me out more than him raising his voice would. His eyes are always smiling. He always has a pun on the tip of his tongue. And he always likes movie quotes. It makes me nervous when he's like this, so out of character—even though he's been more serious more frequently since the election.

"You didn't have to go up that mountain with him. In fact, you shouldn't have, and you know it."

What am I supposed to say to that? Am I supposed to tell Dad that I thought Tim might kiss me on the chairlift, and that was the whole point of me being on this stupid ski trip in the first place? To get him to like me just for me, not for the Hollywood parties he thinks I can get him into or the Madison Harpers I can introduce him to? That it would feel good just to be liked for who I am? That I'm nearly fifteen and this never-been-kissed crap is getting kind of embarrassing? That I have some nice lingerie from Tres Jolie that I can't wait to use and then report back to Katie? Yeah, no, I don't think so. I just kind of stand there with tears prickling my eyes and wait for the rest of the lecture.

But there's no rest of the lecture.

"Here," Dad says. "Hand me those."

I give him the flowers and he riffles around in the kitchen for a vase. He arranges them pretty well, for a guy. Ebba would do a better job, if she was here, but she's out teaching a ballet class. I certainly can't do a better job myself, one handed.

"Want them in your room?" Dad asks me.

"No," I say. "Leave them down here. That way we can all enjoy them."

But that's not the real reason. The real reason is that I don't want them up there, reminding me of what I've lost. Reminding me of how stupid I've been.

Thirty

For the first week, I can't look at my viola. *Failure failure failure*, it whispers to me from the corner of my red-accented bedroom as Mariah Carey's dulcet tones drift up from downstairs. *You'll never get into LACHSA now. You'd better stick some washi tape over that list in the front of your bullet journal.* Or: *How could you think skiing was more important than your audition, than your entire life plan? Are you out of your mind?* It wasn't the skiing, I say very quietly, so nobody will catch me talking to an inanimate object. It was Tim. *A boy!* My viola says back. *A boy. You chose a boy over me. How am I supposed to feel about that?* In my head it morphs into a little green cartoon character and crosses its little green cartoon arms and turns away from me and sulks in the corner. And part of me wants to say, *you don't feel things, stop it,* and part of me wants to cradle my viola in my arms and cry and say *I know, I'm sorry, I'm sorry.*

By the second week, when the Christmas decorations are finally gone, my arm almost aches from not being able to play. You know how they say that people who have limbs amputated still feel pain in those limbs after they're gone? It's kind of like that. My viola was an extension of my arm and it isn't there anymore, and it hurts. Sometimes I take my bow and hold it in my right hand, and I put my left arm in as close to a viola-playing position as I can manage, and I play the phantom viola with my bow hand and wiggle my fingers as much as I can in a vague approximation of what those fingers might do if they were still capable of moving on a fingerboard. I think about getting my viola out of its case, feeling it on my shoulder, rubbing under my chin, but I don't want to drop it. The skin under my chin where the curved end of it usually rests against me has started to soften. I don't hate that—it looks better, too—but it probably means it will hurt once I start playing again, and boy am I going to have to start playing again, five or six hours a day to make up for lost time while, I hope, LACHSA will let me have a deferred audition for medical reasons.

When I was little, I used to think it would be cool to have a cast on a broken arm, to have all my classmates sign it in different color marker pens. I thought I'd enjoy being the center of attention. And that part, admittedly, is pretty enjoyable, but it's also over pretty fast. For a day and a half after we're back from winter break, week three of the cast, people keep asking if I need help, or they get me to tell the story of how it happened. By Wednesday, they've all moved on to more interesting pursuits. Meanwhile, my wrist still hurts, my cast still itches me, I can't have a shower without covering myself in plastic, and my viola case sits forlornly and accusingly in the corner of my bedroom.

I'm at my locker trying to find my math book when I notice a shift in the air, something there, something not moving, in a super-awkward way. Tim. Well, he's moving a little: he's chewing gum. But he's standing there, in his jeans and navy shirt, the one that brings out the color in his eyes, waiting for me to acknowledge him. He'll be waiting a while. The first day I saw him last August, right here in this very spot, I knew he was trouble. I knew that, nice as it was of him to show me where the room for orchestra rehearsal was, he wasn't doing it out of the goodness of his heart. I knew it, and I tried to steer clear, but I had something to prove: that I may be my father's daughter, but that's not all I am. I wanted him to pay attention to me for who I am. I wanted the whole world to pay attention to me, or at least the part of the world that cares about symphony orchestras. And now look at me: a cast on my wrist, a pathetic girl who needs other people in order to accomplish the easiest tasks.

"Want help with something?" Tim asks, like he can read my thoughts and is trying to rub it in.

"Not from you."

"Whoa," he says. But he doesn't leave. "I guess I deserve that."

"Yes." I'm still wondering where my math book is and until I have the math book I can't leave. It doesn't look like Tim is going to leave, either. I make a quick calculation: if Tim helps me, Tim can leave. Or I can leave. Either way, this skin-crawlingly horrifying moment can end.

"You know what," I say. "Actually, I could use some help to get my math book. I think it's on the bottom of that pile there, and it's kinda hard to move stuff around with just one hand." I say this without looking at him. It's hard to say mad at someone with those eyelashes for long, and so far, it has taken all of my concentration and a lot of energy. My reserves of both are rapidly depleting.

"Sure," he says.

I move away from my locker so our bodies don't accidentally touch, since that would be bound to confuse me. I smell him, though. He smells like mint, like he's just this minute put the chewing gum in his mouth, and of his own salty skin.

"There you go," he says, giving me the book. His hand brushes mine, which was wholly unnecessary. My stomach lurches. I break my not-looking-at-him resolution to glare at him, like, *dude? Really?* But that, according to the further lurching of my stomach, was a mistake.

"Thanks," I say, because I'm not a monster.

"You're welcome," he says, because he's far too polite. And he's still standing there. Why is he still standing there?

"I've gotta go," I say.

"Okay." Tim looks like he has more to say, but he also looks like he's about to wimp out of saying it.

"Bye," I say, and I clang the locker shut and walk away, math book in my good arm and backpack on my good shoulder, but alas: too good to be true. Just when I think I've successfully made my escape, he calls out to me.

"Clara, wait."

"I'm going to be late for class."

He catches up to me, but has the wisdom not to get too close. "You know I didn't take you up the mountain just to get you injured, right?"

"Just?"

"Or at all. Not even a little bit. It was an accident."

"Yeah."

He kicks one foot against the other. "You didn't have to agree to come with me."

I wanted you to kiss me! is what I should maybe say in response to this. *I wanted you to think I was cool!* But, come on. I have some dignity. Not much, these days, but I'm hanging onto what's left of it.

"Why did you invite me on that stupid ski trip, anyway? Was it just so you could get Madison Harper's phone number from me?"

"Whoa," he says again. He furrows his brow and steps back. I've got him. "Okay. I've got to get to class. I'll see you around."

He has no answer to my question. That's how I know I've struck a nerve. That I've got it right. He finally leaves, and good riddance.

Thirty-One

The next day I stop by my locker before homeroom again, which is turning out to be a mistake when it comes to the whole getting through high school thing. Tim's there, waiting for me, leaning against my locker so I can't get to it without, at the very least, acknowledging him and asking him to move. He's wearing a blue and gray plaid button-down and, damn it, he looks good.

"I googled Madison Harper," he says.

I chew on my spearmint gum a couple times before I answer him. "That's nice for you." What does he want, congratulations on deploying an elementary literacy skill?

"She was in that show with your dad last year."

I nod toward my locker so he knows to get out of the way. "Yes."

"I never watched it," he says.

"Too bad," I say. I move the combination lock to the right code. "If you had, maybe it'd still be on the air. My dad was really disappointed when they canceled it." I'm just spitballing here. I have no idea if Dad even cared.

"Clara, I'm trying to tell you I didn't know who Madison Harper was."

"Don't be an idiot," I say, pulling out the book I need. "Everyone knows who Madison Harper is."

"Everyone in your world, maybe," Tim says, shaking the hair from his eyes.

"We live in the same world, in case you hadn't noticed."

He laughs. "No. We really don't. You live in the glamorous

Hollywood world. I live in the nerdy Scrabble world. I don't even have time for TV."

I spin round and face him as I shut my locker and move the combination lock back. "I know for a fact that's not true. You told my dad you were a big fan of his. At Student Arts Showcase in the fall? Someone who doesn't watch TV doesn't go up to my dad and say that." Does he think I'm some kind of idiot?

"I watched *The Classroom*. Everybody watched *The Classroom*. Even people who don't watch TV watched *The Classroom*."

Seriously, people are obsessed with that show. I should really get around to watching it sometime.

"You could have spoken to me at my own recital," I say.

"You're terrifying," he says.

That is ridiculous. I laugh. "Yet here you are, talking to me right now."

"I've grown a lot in the last few months. I'm very proud of myself." I laugh again. I forgot how easily he can make me do that. "In fact, I've grown so much that I'm not afraid to tell you this." It seems like he *is* a little afraid, though, because he can't quite look me in the eye. "I didn't want to talk to you in front of your parents because I didn't want them to see how much I liked you."

"Huh?" I know what all those words mean but they don't seem to make sense in that order.

"You heard me," he says. He's looking right at me now.

The bell rings. We're going to be late, and I can't afford to get yelled at for that two days in a row. Tim picks up his backpack and leaves. My feet, suddenly, are made of lead. He liked me? He liked me way back then? Despite not even knowing who Madison Harper was? The flutter in my stomach suggests I

CLAIRE HANDSCOMBE

liked him too. That I still like him, despite everything. But he doesn't deserve it. And even if I decide he does, I've probably blown my chances forever.

Or have I? I try to remember what I've said to him since the accident. Have I been *mean*, as such? Or have I just told the truth? And does it matter? I don't want to kiss him anyway. I'm finally able to point my feet in the direction of homeroom and I'm halfway there before I can admit to myself that actually, yes, I do. Very much. Want to be kissed. And not just by anyone. By Tim.

But I should probably get over that, and fast. Because he *liked* me, past tense. English may not be my favorite subject but I can still recognize a past tense when it's staring me in the face. And I'm not going to be that pathetic pining stereotype of a teenage girl. I'm better than that.

Thirty-Two

It's finally Cast Off Day today, January 24, and Dad takes me to the doctor. Doctors are always hot on TV shows, but I've had a lot of experience with doctors of late, and in real life they're usually not. This one is pretty ordinary looking, and his stripy tie clashes with his plaid shirt. I'm not a fan of this saw thing he's going to use on me, either, but I'm determined not to cry today so I brace myself. I'm almost sure it's really well designed so that it will cut the plaster while leaving my arm intact.

"Relax," Dad says, as I hop up onto the blue exam table.

"That's easy for you to say. Look at that thing."

"You're fine," he says, and puts his hand on my good shoulder, my right shoulder, my bow shoulder.

"It's not actually going to cut you," the doctor says. "The vibrations are what breaks the cast apart. Prepare to be tickled, if anything."

I shiver, but that might just be because it's freezing in here. The AC is on way too high. I close my eyes and wait for the knife, and Dad's right, I'm fine, it's fine, it tickles a little as the plaster gets shaved off but that's all. But then I open my eyes and my arm sits there, lifeless, thin, pale as an East Coaster on the first day of her California beach vacation. This is the arm that was going to carry me to LACHSA, to Juilliard, to the First Chair of a symphony orchestra. We have a lot of work to do, my left arm and I. Which is fine. I'm no stranger to hard work. You don't get to be as good at the viola as I am without knowing what hard work is.

"See?" Dad says. "You're fine."

I wiggle my fingers in response. They feel okay. They feel free. Which, believe me, is not nothing. The idea that when my arm itches I will now be able to scratch it makes me want to jump for joy. I guess it's going to have to be the little things that carry me through this.

"I'll just grab my pad to write you a referral for PT," the doctor says.

"PT?"

"Physical therapy. It's going to take a while and a lot of effort to get your strength back up."

"Playing viola can be my PT," I say.

The doctor exchanges a look with my dad. I'm probably not supposed to see it, but I'm also not an idiot.

"You're a viola player?" he asks.

"Yes," I say. "A violist. I have an audition for LACHSA coming up. And Juilliard."

By *coming up*, I mean, obviously, in the next few years. Still, I'm embarrassed that I've said this in front of my dad. He's shuffling on his feet, clearly embarrassed for me, too.

"Not imminently," he says. "Not Juilliard."

"No," I concede. "But some day."

"Yeah," the doctor says. "No viola playing for a while."

"What?"

My dad gives me this pointed look, like being polite matters at a time like this.

"I mean, what do you mean, sir?"

"Some PT first," he says. He's talking to my dad, like I can't hear him, or like I'm a little kid who doesn't understand. "Then we'll see if the viola is a possibility."

"A possibility," I repeat. "What does that mean? How long

till I can play again?"

My dad and the doctor look at each other again. A long look. They're having an entire conversation in that look, I can tell. The doctor is begging to be let off the hook. My dad is begging the same, and he is good at this game of holding someone else's gaze. The doctor looks down first. But still nobody speaks.

"We'll talk about it in the car," Dad says.

"No," I say. "I want to hear it from the doctor."

"It's possible you'll never play as well again," he says. It feels like he speaks very fast, the way air rushes out of a balloon when it's been trapped in there. It takes an age for the words to permeate first my ears and then my brain.

"What?" I say. "That's crazy. I'll be fine."

"You will be fine," Dad says. "Whatever happens, you'll be fine."

"See?" I tell the doctor. I have this overwhelming urge to stick my tongue out at him. I'll show him. I'll show everyone. I always do.

Thirty-Three

We're having steak for dinner the next night, and Dad pours himself some wine. *You can't have steak without a glass of merlot once you're over twenty-one,* he always says, whenever we have steak. *I don't make the rules, that's just the way it is.* He's about to pour some into Ebba's glass when she covers it with her hand.

"I shouldn't," she says.

"Oh," Dad says, like he's just remembered something. "Yes." Then he takes her hand and kisses her palm, which seems an unnecessary reaction to someone not being able to drink wine. I exchange a look with Rosie.

"Are you sick?" she asks Ebba.

Ebba shakes her head. "No. Just tired."

I eat my steak, pink in the middle just the way I like it, tuning out the din around me as Juliette chatters and Rosie scrapes her plate with her silverware in that way that hurts my teeth and Harry asks for help cutting his dinner up. As I chew the steak, appreciating the pepperiness, I chew on something else, too. Ebba's always tired, lately. She's been wearing baggy t-shirts a lot. Case in point: today's ratty old Yale Drama shirt.

And now no wine? I think about every sitcom I've ever seen where women suddenly stop drinking. Oh, my gosh. She's pregnant. She has to be, right? But also, she can't be. Isn't forty-three too old? Or too old without fertility treatment? We'd know about it if she'd been having that, wouldn't we? Isn't Dad done with sleepless nights and diapers? Aren't we—aren't the four of us—enough for him?

No. I must be wrong. Our lives can't possibly be changing again. He wouldn't do that to us. There has to be another explanation. Maybe she *is* sick and just doesn't want to talk about it over dinner. There is tons of medication you can't drink with. After all, who wants to wear anything other than yoga pants and baggy t-shirts when they're sick? I don't want her to be, like, *seriously* sick. Not now that I finally like her a little. But that must be it, something she'll get over when the antibiotics or whatever kick in. Because the other thing is unthinkable.

Thirty-Four

I'm not allowed to have my phone at the dinner table, but lately I've been putting it in my denim shorts pocket and sneaking glances when Dad isn't looking. I don't care too much if Ebba sees. She wouldn't say anything—she's too desperate for me to like her, and betrayal would definitely not help that cause.

With every moment that passes, it becomes more likely that I'll hear from LACHSA. I spend a lot of time doing and redoing the math, first with a pencil and paper, and then over and over in my head, to try to figure out the probability of hearing from them at any given moment. Like, if I'm supposed to hear from them within a month of the video deadline, then on the first day after the deadline I have a one in thirty chance of getting an email. On the second day it's one in twenty-nine. And if I further subdivide each day into hours, minutes, seconds, even, I can basically spend all my time calculating and recalculating, and that somehow steadies my nerves. I tried to explain this to Katie when we went to the Cheesecake Factory last weekend and she looked at me like I was crazy.

"You know that in reality there's basically a ninety-nine percent chance they'll contact you on the last possible day, right?"

That's totally illogical, and I told her so.

"You'll see," she said, licking her spoon then smiling in that way she does when she thinks she's right, though how she can possibly think this, when so few of her predictions are based on logic or have any basis in fact, I do not know. With every day that goes by it is, mathematically and therefore inarguably, more probable that I'll get the email than it was the day before. I'm not as excited as I could be—it'll be an uphill struggle to get my arm back to fighting form in time for the audition. I'll do it, of course I will, but I picked up my viola yesterday after PT and just holding it was hard. I know it's going to hurt. But still: when I get that email, and it's a yes, it's going to feel incredible.

Today, there's a one in three chance, and as it's the end of the day and there aren't many hours of it left, it's actually a higher chance than that. Right now, it's 6:30 p.m., so it's actually an 11 out of 107 chance, or 10.3 percent. That's high. So stuff Dad and his stupid rules. I need to be within vibrating distance of my phone at all times.

We're eating lasagna tonight, my Saturday night favorite. (Dad tells me the secret's in going heavy on the garlic and adding fennel.) Harry is telling us all a very elaborate story about a plot of some movie he's probably invented and Dad and Ebba are nodding between bites and asking questions like they're interested. Rosie and Juliette are low-key fighting about the pink sweater that Juliette is wearing and Rosie says is hers. They're both punctuating what seems like every word with a scrape of their forks on their plates.

"Why would I borrow any of your clothes? Your clothes are boring," Juliette says.

"I'm not saying you borrowed it. I'm saying you stole it."

"We live in the same house. You can take it back anytime."

"So you're admitting you stole it?"

"Borrowed it," Juliette says, dropping her fork, which lands off her plate and splatters sauce everywhere.

"Without permission."

"You'd never give me permission."

"Stole it, then."

I look down and, under the table, slide my phone out of my pocket just a little. Just enough to see that I have no notifications. I have the LACHSA email address set to VIP, so I'll know the instant the message arrives in my inbox.

But right now, there's nothing. Again.

"That sweater's too small for you, anyway," I tell Rosie.

She gives me a look that could cut through ice.

"Dad," she says, still looking at me. But Dad is still pretending to be deeply immersed in whatever it is that Harry is holding forth on. "Dad," she says again, more loudly.

"Just a minute, sweetie," Dad says.

"Fine," Rosie says, huffing a little. She gives me another look, like, *just you wait.* And not in an inspiring Hamiltonian kind of way.

"What is it, sweet pea?" Ebba asks her. For a second, Rosie looks a little annoyed. That's how I know for sure that she intended to rat me out. She knows it will have less of an impact if she tells Ebba than it would if she tells Dad.

"Clara keeps looking at her phone." She sounds defeated, like she already knows she's lost.

I look at Ebba and wait for her verdict.

"I think we can let her off the hook this week," Ebba says. Because of course she does. Pander, pander. "She's waiting for an important email."

I turn, so Ebba doesn't see, and give Rosie my *ha!* look.

"But that's what she always says about having her phone at the table," Rosie whines. "*I'm waiting for something important!*"

"Well," I say. "I usually am. This no-phone rule is BS, anyway."

My dad clears his throat. Getting his attention is easiest to do when you threaten to use curse words.

"It's true," I say. "It is."

He sighs. Harry is still talking, apparently oblivious to the fact that nobody is listening.

"We've been through this," Dad says. "At least at dinner we are going to communicate face to face, like civilized human beings."

"The family that eats together with no screen time stays together," I offer. I admit it's not all that catchy.

"Exactly," he says. He doesn't grasp the irony. It's a bit late for our family staying together. "I like to hear your voice and see your face. Is that so much to ask?"

"Honey," Ebba says to him, quietly. I know what she's communicating with that one word. I know she's taking my side (even if the reason might be that if she gets me to like her, it makes things easier for her and Dad). I know she's basically saying, *let's go easy on her this week, okay?* She puts her hand on his. He looks at her like a lovesick puppy. Gross. But also, I'm off the hook for now. I know she didn't ultimately do it just for my sake, but I'm still grateful. Attention successfully deflected.

And then my phone vibrates in my pocket.

Thirty-Five

"I have to go to the bathroom," I say.

Dad raises an eyebrow. "Halfway through dinner?"

I consider all kinds of responses. I could tell him I have my period. I've noticed it tends to shut guys up when you say that, because they have no clue what to say in response. I don't blame them for being icked out—it *is* icky, let's face it—or even for not really getting it, because I get it but I don't *get* it. Your body destroying itself every month because there's no egg implanted in there? Okay. Rosie's always asking me about it. I think she thought she'd get it before her twelfth birthday, like I did. I gave her my old copy of *Are You There, God? It's Me, Margaret* and she left me alone for a while after that. Even I liked that book, and I don't like books. Maybe I should make Dad read it. If you ask me, that book should be on every middle school curriculum, because we all need to know this stuff, not just girls. Maybe if guys knew how our bodies actually worked they wouldn't be so scared of us and, like Dad is always saying, they'd stop making ridiculous laws trying to control them, and, for the love of everything, maybe they'd even be okay with voting for a super-qualified woman for president instead of … well.

Maybe Judy Blume will save us all. Maybe *she* should be president.

Anyway. My other option for getting excused from the table so I can go read the email from LACHSA in peace is to point out that Harry is always getting up halfway through dinner and nobody says anything to him, but there's a valid argument to be made in response: he's a six-year-old boy.

And I don't have time for any of these conversations.

I need to check my phone immediately.

So instead I look at Dad and answer his question, *halfway through dinner?* with a simple *yes.* My chair scrapes along the wooden floor as I get up as calmly as I can, which isn't very. I don't sprint to the bathroom, exactly, but I don't amble, either. I click the door closed and locked, sit on the cold porcelain edge of the bath, and take out my phone. There it is, the notification: an email from admissions@lachsa.edu. The subject line: your LACHSA application. And then the first few words of the message: *Dear Clara, thank you for your application. We—*

I close my eyes. I can't bring myself to look. I press my phone's home button and leave it down for several seconds, which Siri takes as her call to action. I consider asking her, *Siri, should I read this email?* What if it's *we get many applications every year and after careful consideration we have decided to offer your place to someone who plays a more popular instrument?* What if it's *we regret to inform you that* ... But what if it's *we don't even need to audition you, on the strength of your tape alone we would be delighted to offer you a place?* Given the current state of my wrist, that would be super-helpful. It's not protocol, but you never know. I'm worth making an exception for.

That's terrifying, too. My whole life is about to change. LACHSA, Juilliard, the Symphony: the beginning of the rest of my life. Screw getting my period—this is when I really become a woman. Now that an audition might be on the cards and I am letting myself think about it, it's stomach-clenchingly terrifying. I always throw up before exams and auditions, it's as much a part of the process for me at this point as warming up with scales. And my stomach is clenching right now. Okay. Deep breath. I screw my eyes shut, then open one, then the other. I tap on my email app. I have to really concentrate to focus on the email: the letters have gone all blurry. *Dear Clara*, it says. *Thank you for your application. We received your audition tape and, after reviewing it carefully, we are pleased to invite you for an in-person audition on February 28, 2017. Please prepare—*

I can't read the rest. I lob my phone into the empty sink, lean over the toilet, and throw up my lasagna, pieces of undigested carrot and all. Even as I'm leaning over, heaving my guts out, I'm thinking, *I hope this doesn't put me off lasagna forever.* But it might. I guess it depends how this all ends. I take my phone out of the sink, swirl water from the faucet in my mouth and then mouthwash, spit and brush my teeth, wash my hands. I'm so focused on my body's reaction to the email that my brain hasn't had a chance to react yet. I haven't jumped up and down or texted Katie or Madison or Libby. *Wow*, I say to myself. *Wow*.

So now what? I guess I go back to the table and make a big announcement. Someone knocks on the bathroom door.

"Clara?" It's Rosie. "Dad sent me to check you're okay."

"Tell him I have my period," I say though the door, a kind of in-joke with myself.

"Do you?" I imagine Rosie opening her eyes all wide and desperate for details. I crack the door open and forget to be mean to her. Instead, I have this weird impulse to hug her. But that would freak us both out, so I refrain.

"No," I say. "And I'm fine. Never been better, actually."

I must be grinning, I know I'm grinning, I can feel my cheeks aching with it.

"You got the email?"

I nod. Rosie's eyes widen.

"Girls," Dad calls. "You don't want to miss dessert."

She looks excited for me, which is nice of her. All this time I thought she only cared about characters in books. And about Ebba, of course. Perfect, wonderful Ebba. Rosie wants to be in on the secret, but she also wants to be the one to tell the world.

"Clara got the email from LACHSA," she announces, when we're back in the kitchen. I wanted to play it cooler than that, to have the news come out more slowly, to make the rest of the family guess at it and wait for it, but I'm too dazed and too happy to be mad.

Dad looks like he might throw up, too.

"Well?" Ebba says. She's smiling already. She knows. I'm trying to be deadpan about it, for the element of suspense, but my eyes are probably giving it away.

I let the clock tick a couple times, let the anticipation in the room mount. Even Harry has stopped talking and is looking at me wide-eyed. I kind of want this moment to go on forever.

"I got the audition," I say, leaning against the fridge nonchalantly, as if this couldn't matter less, as if I've been expecting this all along, which, of course, I have. Maybe. And then I say it again because the words feel so good in my mouth and sound so good out in the world. "I got the audition!"

Since I'm still standing it makes it easy for everyone to pile onto me in a family group hug. There's the scraping of chairs and then more and more bodies attached to me, saying things like *so proud* and *congratulations* and *do we get to eat dessert now*. And after a while everyone calms down and we do eat dessert. It's crème brûlée, which I also love. Dad has this little torch thing to crisp up the top of them on special occasions. It's like this whole evening was planned just for me. I tap the sugary top of mine with the back of my spoon, watching it crack. I love that moment.

"I still have to get through the audition," I say, reminding everyone to be calm even though I don't want them to be calm, and even though the email is like that first crack in the crème brûlée topping. A good thing is coming, coming, it's inevitable, you have just to dig your spoon in.

Thirty-Six

I'm in bed, but I don't know how I'm supposed to sleep tonight, after just getting the email from LACHSA. And is it weird that part of me wants to text Tim and tell him? Not even in a gloating, I-did-it-despite-you way, but instead because I know he'd be happy for me. He might even want to celebrate with me. But I don't let myself think about that too hard, because this moment deserves nothing but joy.

I want to jump up and down, to dance around my room, or maybe drive around Pasadena shouting *I got in!* out the window. But I can't drive yet, and I'd probably get yelled at in this sleepy town for causing a disturbance. So instead, here I am, tossing and turning, but in the best possible way. Restless with excitement.

And with relief. Can you be restless with relief? Probably not. Relief should feel calmer than this. But I swear I literally feel lighter, like I've been carrying this big weight in a backpack, and someone's just offered to carry it for me. I've gotten past the stage I stalled at last year. I can stop running my thumb up and down my phone screen to refresh my email every fifteen seconds.

Still, at the same time, this isn't over.

For the next few weeks, I have to work harder than I've ever worked in my life. *Take it easy*, the PT said. Yeah, right. Like that's an option. My wrist will just have to cooperate. No choice. Women give birth, don't they? I heard that's pretty bad. They push through the pain. Not to mention Liesl and the broken ankle.

I've got this.

I start to figure out how many hours a day I can fit in. I can get up a half hour earlier than I usually do, at 5:30. I can play in short bursts, and rest between them if I really have to. I can go right to my room after school and put my phone in my desk drawer so I don't spend half an hour scrolling through Instagram before I get to work. I'll have to skimp on homework, figure out a rotation so that each subject takes a slight knock, but nothing too drastic. Maybe for a while I can be the one who copies someone else's answers in the Spanish vocab tests. I should probably warn Ashley, who sits behind me, that she might need to actually learn the words once in a while. Or maybe I'll copy Isabella in front of me and Ashley can still copy me, telephone style. It'll have to be Ashley who asks Isabella to write bigger and angle her body just right so I can see okay. No point in *me* asking, because she could easily look me up and down, pretend not to recognize me, and say, *I'm sorry, who are you again*, and she wouldn't be completely unjustified, since I don't think we've exchanged more than a couple sentences all year so far.

The idea of cheating makes my pulse race. I'm a rule follower and a hard worker. Maybe I won't cheat in Spanish. Maybe I'll find other places to cut corners. Social studies, maybe. But that's already my worst subject, already threatening to tarnish my otherwise perfect GPA. Not that my GPA matters, no-one asks about a star violist's GPA, they're too wowed by the Juilliard thing but, wait, what GPA do I need for Juilliard? For LACHSA it's 2.0, so I'm obviously way, way in the clear on that. But what if there are two equally good violists applying to Juilliard in 2020, and only one of them has a 4.0 GPA? I'd damn well better be sure that violist is me and not the other one. So no skimping, not even in social studies class. And math, well, I'm way ahead in math, headed for an AP class in fact. I could afford to cut a few corners in math class, except I don't want to, because I love math, and I love being way ahead, and I love the way the teacher looks at me, like I'm a prodigy or something.

Fine.

I'll just have to sleep less.

It's only for a few weeks. I've totally got this.

I'm thirsty, though, what with all that thinking. I forgot to bring a glass of water to bed. Can I sleep without it? I assume the position, lie under my cotton sheets on my back with my arms at my side. I count back from 99 in threes. Usually I'm asleep way before I get to 0, but I get to 0 and I'm still thirsty and awake, so I roll out of bed and shuffle out of my bedroom and down the stairs to the kitchen for some ice water to swallow an Advil PM. I'm getting a glass from the cabinet when I notice Ebba at the table, tapping at her laptop at the kitchen island, her forehead creased, like she's deeply immersed in puzzling something out.

"Oh, hey," I say. "I didn't see you there."

She looks up and smiles. "Couldn't sleep?"

I shrug. "Just thirsty, is all."

"If it was me," she says, "I wouldn't be able to sleep."

Well, yes, I want to say. *Lesser mortals.* But then I remember that she was the one who taped me, who got me to do it right. I was so nervous, and she somehow knew just what to say to get me in the right mental space. To be the best version of my musician self.

"Thank you," I say, though I'm pretty sure I already said it. "For helping me out."

"You're welcome," she says, sounding like she means it. I fill the glass with water from the fridge dispenser then turn to go, but the conversation doesn't feel finished.

"Come sit with me," Ebba says, so she must feel it too. She taps the high wooden chair next to hers. "Come talk to me."

I don't really want to talk to anyone, and if I did it would probably not be to her, but okay. I can be nice. She's earned it.

"How do you feel?" she asks me. "Really."

"Relieved. Excited. Nervous. Terrified." I don't know why I'm suddenly being so honest. There *is* something about late-night heart-to-hearts. Maybe that's it.

"Sounds about right."

We sit in silence for a while. She's looping the chain of her necklace around one finger and sipping at her tea. I'm drinking my water.

"Well," I say. "I should probably—"

"Are you proud of yourself?" she asks me. I consider this. Getting the audition is no more than I'd expected, really. I'm not sure I'm proud of myself, but I know I would have been super-disappointed with myself if I hadn't gotten it.

"I guess," I say.

"You should be. Your dad and me, we're so proud of you."

"Thank you," I say. An automatic reflex, even though I hate the *we*, I hate the *your dad and me*. Like, he can speak for himself. You don't have to do it for him. I wonder if I can go now. I think the Advil PM might be kicking in.

"We love you," she says. The *we* again. How am I supposed to respond to this? She doesn't pause long enough for me to need to respond, thankfully. "And you know our love for you has nothing to do with your achievements, right?"

Where is she going with this? I sip my water.

"We'll still love you just as much if you don't get into LACHSA. You know that, right?"

I almost choke on my water. "You don't think I'll get in?"

"No," she says, shaking her head hard, like an Etch A Sketch that's going to erase the words from the air, from my memory. "That's not what I meant. I know what it's like to want something so badly. To feel like who you are is this thing you do, and do so well, and love doing. But you're not just a viola player, Clara. You're a wonderful young woman. I wish you could see that about yourself."

A lump is forming in my throat. *Don't cry*, I tell myself. *Do not show weakness.*

"I can't believe you don't think I can do it," I say, and I hop off the chair and make it all the way back to my bedroom and under my comforter before I start to cry.

Thirty-Seven

I know the PT said to take it easy, but the PT also doesn't know me and my determination, and she doesn't know what's at stake. When I explain it to her she still doesn't seem to get it. *I know it seems like getting into LACHSA is the most important thing right now, but your long-term well-being is actually more important.* She says this like the two things are separate, like my long-term well-being isn't fundamentally connected to my LACHSA-Juilliard-Symphony plan. What am I supposed to aim for, if I'm not going to aim for that? I need goals in life. Everybody does. And if I'm not the girl who gets into LACHSA, who gets into Juilliard, who is Second Chair in the London Symphony Orchestra and then First Chair in the LA Philharmonic, then who am I? And how are people going to know I have my own worth separate to my dad's mediocre fame?

The PT's given me these exercises to do with a red ball I'm supposed to squeeze. Dad says that apart from anything else, that'll be good for my stress levels.

"You've got to admit it, Clara, you're pretty highly strung," he says in the car on the way to dropping us off at Mom's that last Sunday of January. Then he adds, "No pun intended," which is always what he says when the pun is totally intended but hasn't had the desired effect of making its audience either laugh or groan. It really means, *did you notice my pun back there? Because it seems like you didn't notice.* I turn my head to see if he's doing his so-pleased-with-himself smile, and yup.

"Haha," I say, like the dutiful daughter I am. In the back,

Rosie and Juliette are singing 'How Far I'll Go' from *Moana* for the eleventy billionth time this week. Harry has his hands over his ears and is begging them, on behalf of all of us, to stop. It feels good to stay out of that and have this semi-adult conversation with Dad instead.

"Glad you appreciate the pun," he says.

"*Appreciate* is a little strong," I say, trying to not get too forceful about it, in case I accidentally prove him right about me being highly strung.

"Nonetheless," he says. "You heard the PT. Take it easy with the viola playing, okay?"

"Or else there'll be treble?"

"That's my girl," he says, putting the blinker on to turn into Mom's street, so proud of my punning that he completely missed that I haven't actually agreed to take it easy at all. Then again, he's been telling me to take it easy my whole life. My whole life, I've been ignoring him. I don't know why he'd think this time would be any different. It's quite possible that he realizes full well I am going to ignore him, and he is just doing his due diligence, that he realizes that as soon as his or Mom's backs are turned I'll be in my room coaxing my left hand into the long-familiar shapes and my wizened arm into holding my viola up.

It hurts, though. Holding my viola up for more than about a minute feels like a huge accomplishment. My arm starts to hurt the way my stomach did last summer when Katie and I got obsessed with doing sit-ups so we'd have perfectly flat stomachs for the beach. It feels kind of trembly. My wrist spasms a little sometimes, too, and then I have to put my viola down and practice with just the fingering and the bow.

Dad said he'd speak to the LACHSA people about getting

me a deferred audition date, and you know what, unfair advantage or not, I'll take it. But I'm so behind, so behind. I don't know how to make my arm get better faster. My fingers know what they're supposed to be doing, but they don't seem to respond as fast. My vibrato is shaky, and not in a good way. And now I have to be doubly careful about practicing because my parents need to not realize how much of it I'm doing. It helps to put viola music on really loudly and either play so softly they can't hear it over the recording, or just to sit, miming with my left elbow resting on my leg so it gets used to more-or-less the right position again.

I do some variation on these things for four hours a day, and it's boring and joyless, because I can't hear what I'm "playing" and I can't feel the strings vibrating below my fingers and reverberating through my body. But I have to bear in mind the end result, like I always have with practice. It isn't always joy-filled and fun, but that's not what it's ultimately about. It's about hard work, so you can get to where it is you want to go. LACHSA-Juilliard-Symphony. So it hurts. When I rotate my wrist to reach for the C string, pain shoots up my arm and into my fingertips. But like the actress who played Liesl von Trapp, I have to grit my teeth and play through it. The people making the movie were above budget and behind schedule and there's no budget for me but there is a schedule and I'm really, really behind. I have to make this work somehow. Pain or no pain.

Thirty-Eight

Somewhere in this house there have got to be some painkillers. Actual, real painkillers, like the ones I was prescribed after the accident, not just Advil.

Percocet.

Something.

I can't believe I used up all of my prescription when I was just sitting around with a cast on. Sure, it hurt, but I shouldn't have been such a wimp about it. Maybe the fall affected my usually more-than-capable brain, too. I should probably get checked for long-term concussion. Now's when I really need the pills, now that I can't just distract myself from the pain by calling Katie or watching *Crazy Ex-Girlfriend*—now that I need to lean into the pain, to play through it. I've had one pathetic week of "taking it easy," and I only have 22 days till the audition, and I have to do whatever it takes.

I've looked through the downstairs bathroom cabinet. I've searched every corner of my bathroom in case I dropped something somewhere, even though of course I already know I didn't. This is why being organized is so important. Obviously, it's part of being a civilized human, but it also helps you keep track of things. It helps you feel in control of your life. You're not late to things because you couldn't find your hairbrush, since your hairbrush is where it always is. When you want to paint your nails, it's easy to find the exact shade of red, because there they are, lined up in color order. I've tried to explain this to Juliette and Rosie, but they roll their eyes and keep throwing things around wherever.

Well, good luck to them when they're trying to find a stray Percocet pill.

There's nothing for it now but to sneak into Dad and Ebba's bathroom, and hope that Ebba's Achilles tendon still hurts enough sometimes from when she snapped it years ago for them to have a stockpile of something strong. I'm not proud of this, but desperate times, desperate measures. Besides, I'm pretty stealthy. They'll never know I was here. I won't do anything stupid like steal the whole little orange bottle. That's way too obvious. I'll just take a couple pills at a time, so the bottle will dwindle gradually, like it would if you were taking them normally, just maybe a bit faster, but who knows, maybe you weren't paying attention so you can't be sure.

I wait for them to leave—Ebba to a ballet class, Dad to a work function, which is what he calls Hollywood parties to make them sound like Serious Work—and I sneak in. The little kids are watching something on TV, and Rosie, obviously, is reading. Nobody will ever know.

I don't love going into Dad and Ebba's room at the best of times, even though it has windows on two sides and tons of light, and a beautiful brown rug with blue squiggly patterns, and objectively it's a nice bedroom under any other circumstances. I've gotten used to having Ebba around the house, but bedrooms are squicky. Bedrooms are where babies get made. I can't look at their bed without thinking about that. I want to believe that I'm wrong about the whole pregnancy thing, or that if I'm not then they did it just that one time, but I know that adults have sex all the time. Gross, gross, gross. They're too old for this stuff.

And I'm definitely too old to be a big sister again. I'll be fifteen by the time the baby's born. I'll probably be made to feed and burp it and it won't do anything for my social status at school if I come in smelling of spit-up. And what if they want to use the guest room next to my room for the baby? I can't be woken up three times every night. I need to wake up fresh and rested every day, ready for my first installment of viola practice. And what if I'm not allowed viola practice after dinner, so the baby doesn't wake up?

Has Dad seriously thought any of this through? I'm guessing probably not, since this baby is Ebba's, and he loves Ebba now, so it follows that he'll love this baby more than he loves us. Ugh. It was bad enough when their bed just made me think of sex.

This is so much worse.

Forget the Percocet. I'm going to need some Xanax.

I've made it through the emotional assault course that is the bedroom, and I'm in their bathroom now, trying to be as quiet as I can as I open and close drawers and cabinets. It smells like Ebba's shampoo in here, and like her perfume, hints of jasmine and vanilla, almond and rose. There's *got* to be something here. Dad threw his shoulder out during a play a couple years ago. Does Percocet last that long? I don't know. I find some, finally, behind the other, crappier painkillers. The use-by date on it is a year from now. The name on the label is Ebba's. I guess her heel does still hurt sometimes, that she has to dance through it. I admire her for that. We're a family of hard workers, of survivors. We don't let a little difficulty stand in our way. So I guess, in a way, she does fit in with us after all. And she'll understand if she does figure out I'm taking them, or if I have to ask for more once the bottle is done. The show must go on, after all. It always does.

I'm almost out of the bedroom when Juliette bounds up the stairs. "Hey," she says, her ponytail still swinging. "What are you snooping around in here for?"

"Nothing." I close my fist tighter around the two pink pills. "I'm not snooping."

"I'm here because Ebba said I can borrow one of her ballet books," she announces self-importantly, as if I'd care.

"Okay."

"But you're holding something." The Cassidy persistence trait in evidence once more. I guess it's not always a good thing. I think quickly. Juliette is a goody two-shoes, and therefore also a tattle-tale. She plays by the rules and she makes sure everyone else does too. A commendable quality, but also one that, right now, is mightily inconvenient. Instead of begging her not to tell, because she'll *totally* tell if I do that, I make it seem like it's no big deal.

"I'm just getting some Advil from their bathroom cabinet," I say. I open my hand and show her.

"Oh." She looks at me with her big, beautiful eyes, her blue eyes like Mom's and Ebba's, and she asks me, "Does your wrist still hurt when you play?"

"Only a little," I say, which might be the biggest lie I've told so far in this conversation.

"That's too bad," she says. She walks over to the bookshelf and I make my escape.

Thirty-Nine

The next day, Dad texts to say he'll be waiting for me after school, which never happens, since his house is only ten minutes away on foot and he claims it's good for us to walk, no matter how much I point out that we're the only people in Pasadena who ever walk places.

Cool, I reply. *Are we going on an adventure?*

I know from the read receipt that he's seen it, but he doesn't reply. I've got nothing to be nervous about—almost nothing—but still, I feel a little sick to my stomach, the way I do when Mom uses my full name to call me. I know I'm about to be in trouble, even if I'm not 100 percent sure what for.

"Hello, Father," I say when I open the Prius door. (My parents have the exact same cars, Mom in blue and Dad in gray. It's kind of ridiculous.) "To what do I owe the pleasure?"

His face is giving nothing away. He doesn't even crack a smile at my sudden and unaccountable formality.

"Get in the car," he says.

I throw my backpack on the floor, sit, buckle my seatbelt, and shut the door, all in silence, no music, nothing, and my stomach tightens when we fly past the turning for home. Only once we're on the freeway does Dad speak.

"What were you getting from our room when Juliette saw you?"

Damn it. The little snitch. Unlike Mom when she does this, Dad takes his eyes off the road long enough to make glancing eye contact with me. I don't look away, because only the guilty do that.

CLAIRE HANDSCOMBE

"Just some Advil," I say, forcing myself to sound breezy. "Why?"

He doesn't answer. I'm seriously nervous now. My palms are sweating in that way they normally reserve for a Tim sighting or a viola recital.

We've been in the car not even ten minutes when we turn off and then pull into a driveway. A doctor's driveway.

"I'm going to ask you one more time," Dad says, slowing to a stop. "What were you looking for in our bathroom cabinet?"

He knows. He has to know.

"Something stronger than Advil," I mumble. Looking at the dashboard, at my nails (red, because it's February), anywhere but at my Dad's disappointed face. In our family, we snipe and snark and sometimes yell. But we don't lie. Or at least not with impunity. Lying is the unforgivable sin.

"Why?"

"So I can keep playing."

"Okay," he says.

I hate that he isn't losing his cool, or at least not outwardly. He gets out the car, closes the door. It's more of a slam. I do the same, only I slam it a little harder.

We don't have to wait long for the doctor. My dad has obviously pulled some strings. (Ha. Now's not the moment for a pun, though.) Getting to see a doctor at a moment's notice should probably be filed under Things That Are Great When You're Famous! but in this particular case, I think I'll take it as yet another example of how much it also sucks to be the daughter of a famous(ish) actor.

Dad comes in with me and sits silently as I'm prodded and poked and interrogated. It smells so strongly of disinfectant in here that I'm almost distracted.

"How many hours do you practice?" the doctor asks. It's a woman this time, which I'm thankful for. I bring out the maternal instinct in women my mom's age. It must be the clump of freckles. At least they're good for something.

"Two," I say. Conservative estimate so she doesn't think I'm crazy. High enough that she is still suitably impressed by my dedication.

"And have you noticed anything different since the accident?"

Um. Yes. Plenty. My arm gets tired quickly from holding my viola. My fingers don't seem to do exactly what I want them to. And then there's the pain.

I shrug.

"Clara," Dad says. Just that one word, my name, said right.

"My arm is weak." So is my voice. It's about to break. "My fingers don't respond as fast. And of course my wrist. It—" I'm crying now, but I get the last word out. "It hurts."

"Weakness in your arm is probably nothing to worry about," the doctor says. She's speaking softly, reassuringly. "That's pretty usual after four weeks in plaster. Responsiveness issues might be due to nerve damage, though. We'll run some tests."

The word *clinical* comes to my mind, and I realize I understand it better than I ever have. She's delivering her verdict like it's purely scientific. Like it doesn't have a destructive impact on my life, when actually everything is coming crashing down around me.

Dad hands me a tissue from a box in the corner and I wipe my nose. "That's not permanent, though, right?" I ask the doctor.

"We won't know until we've run the tests. And it looks like you have the beginnings of RSI in your wrist."

Repetitive Strain Injury. The dreaded destroyer of string players. It eats them alive. Us. Eats us alive. I didn't know that was what this was.

"No," I say.

"Remember when the PT told you to take it easy?" Dad says. "This is why."

I can't hold it together anymore. I'm a mess. Dad can't hand me tissues fast enough.

"No more viola for a month," the doctor says. "None at all, strictly, if you ever want to play again. And to have a functioning wrist."

"But my audition is supposed to be—"

"I'll take your viola away if I have to," Dad says.

"This is serious," the doctor continues. Like that isn't obvious. I don't say anything. What could I possibly say? She scribbles out a prescription and hands it to Dad. It's probably for Percocet. Not that it matters now anyway.

Forty

I don't talk to Dad in the car on the way home. Not even when, with the keys in the ignition but before he turns it, he says he knows this is hard and he sounds a little bit like he's sorry he had to do this. I'm glad he said it, but I can't look at him. I don't talk to anyone when we get back to the house. I go right up to my room, kick off my shoes, and get into my bed, under my covers, because that's comforting, somehow.

It's over.

Everything I've ever worked for.

Everything I've ever wanted.

No LACHSA, no Juilliard, no Symphony. I cry and I cry till I don't think I have any more tears in me. Then I'm bored of crying but I'm also not ready to go downstairs and face everyone.

So I put on Glazunov's *Elégie* and sit up in bed, because posture doesn't matter when you're playing the air viola. I close my eyes and imagine my left hand is doing what it should be doing for several hours every day, first position fourth position fifth. I sit on my bed, air-bowing, with the Glazunov blaring so loudly that I almost can't hear myself crying. (I did, in fact, still have tears in me.)

Ebba cracks open my bedroom door to call me for dinner. She probably knocked first, but I wouldn't have heard that, either. Her face kind of crumples when she sees me, like she's going to cry too.

"Oh, baby girl," she says, and I don't hate it, I don't hate her calling me that, even though I've hated it for years when anyone has called me that, let alone someone who didn't know me when I was an actual baby girl and therefore has no excuse, no nostalgia, no reason whatsoever to do it. Ebba sits on the edge of my bed, and I don't hate that either, and I extract myself from my covers and scooch over to sit next to her and rest my head on her shoulder and cry some more. I can smell her perfume again, the jasmine of it, like my favorite tea at the Huntington. It's not what I'd wear, but I like it. It suits her. She puts her arm around me and then with her other hand she plays with my hair, tucking the same strand behind my ear over and over. Usually I only like it when Mom plays with my hair, but it's soothing and I let Ebba do it.

"I know," Ebba keeps saying, "I know," and then eventually I stop crying and she says, with her arm still around me, "Did I ever tell you what happened when I was seventeen?" and I know this story, of course I do, but I shake my head because I want her to tell me anyway. I want to know that I'm not alone in feeling what I'm feeling.

"I was a ballerina," she says. "I was good. Really good. And I had all these big dreams. The San Francisco Ballet. We were rehearsing for *Swan Lake* and I was doing the thirty-two pirouettes and I was dizzy and I landed funny and snapped my Achilles tendon."

"Ouch."

"It's so clinical to say it like that. *I snapped my Achilles tendon.* But it sounded to me like the earth being split open. And the pain. I can't even begin to describe the pain."

She looks like she might be about to describe it anyway, but then I guess she realizes she doesn't need to, because I know what pain like that feels like. Not just a part of your body breaking, but your heart breaking, too. Your dreams snapping like an over-tuned string. Just like that. Years of hard work. All of it, gone.

Ebba doesn't try to tell me that it will all work out. It worked out for her in the end, I guess, because she became an actor and a writer and she teaches ballet, but all of that was Plan B, and Plan B is never an adequate substitute for Plan A. That's why you have to work so damn hard to make Plan A work.

"I know," she says again. "I know it feels like your life has ended."

Damn it, just as my eyes are dry, they start to leak again. I'm so grateful that she's said it. I don't want to be the clichéd teen you see on TV, wailing that my life is over. But that *is* what it feels like. I turn my body toward Ebba for a full-on hug. She lets me cry. I don't know how long we sit there for, but I hear footsteps come and go—Dad, to check on us, I guess, then deciding not to interrupt—and we miss dinner and that's okay, I needed this more than I needed food. Plus, that's what microwaves are for, or takeout. For emergencies.

Forty-One

I don't know how I make it through the next month, but somehow I do. I have to learn what life is like without at least three hours a day of viola practice. I don't know how to fill my time. My social media feeds are full of orchestra friends and string player memes. My hands ache from not playing: constant reminders. I watch a lot of TV. I write texts to Tim that I never end up sending. I even text Libby to ask for book recommendations. I do the exercises the PT gives me obsessively, perfectly, squeezing the red ball, putting elastic bands around various parts of my hand and then stretching out my fingers, pushing against the resistance. I want my wrist back. I want to be able to play again.

On week five, the beginning of March, the PT gives me permission to try. Just a few minutes a day, she says, looking at Mom, like, make *sure* she's compliant. (*Compliant*: they use that word to say you've done the exercises they've set you. It sounds so dramatic, like they're going to lock you up if you don't. They don't need to do that to me. Not being able to play already feels like prison. They've already done the worst they can do.) And it feels okay when I try. I start by holding my viola like it's a guitar and go up in increments of five minutes every few days.

By the time I'm packing to go to Libby's in London for spring break the last week of March, I'm up to twenty minutes at a stretch in the right position, the bruise under the left side of my chin where the viola rests purpling nicely. I could probably do more, but I don't want to push it. That's new:

I've always believed in pushing myself. But this time pushing myself might actually destroy me. Not to be dramatic, or anything. Destroy *my ability to play*, is how the PT puts it. But, you know. Same diff.

Libby asked me to bring my viola with me to London, but she didn't really need to ask—I know this might sound weird, but I couldn't bear the thought of leaving it to languish at home without me. Even when I wasn't playing it last month, I could look at it, open the tin of rosin and breathe in the foresty smell of it, imagine myself back at orchestra, hold the bow in my right hand and play the air viola. I've never really been apart from my viola for more than a night at a sleepover, because even on vacation I need to play for a few hours a day.

My mom always jokes that it's my security blanket. Before we go anywhere we have to check that Harry has his stuffed rabbit and I have my viola. Not that anyone needs to check, exactly, because I can look after myself and I'm more than capable of being organized without any help. But still, it's on the list: Harry's stuffed rabbit: check! Rosie's huge pile of novels: check! Juliette's ballet videos: check! My viola and sheet music and music stand: check! Inside my viola case: rosin, bow, extra bow: check, check, check! Okay, kids, let's roll. Somewhere on the list there's underwear and a toothbrush and all that, but all of those things can be replaced on site wherever we're going. Not my viola. And even though I can't play it like I used to, I get cravings for it still, and it's not like Libby's going to have an extra viola kicking around that I can just pick up to (ahem) scratch the itch.

So when it's time to take off for London, I store my viola dutifully in the overhead bin on the plane, adjusting people's jackets around it for extra padding, and pray we don't hit too much turbulence and it doesn't get knocked around up there. The case is pretty sturdy, but still. I worry. It's kind of like my baby, after all.

Libby says she wants to hear me play, so that seems like a plausible reason for taking it with me, much more plausible when I'm talking to my dad to convince him it's a good idea than theories about my viola-as-sentient-being. And he can't really be all, like, *I don't care what Libby thinks*, since he's also used the *you have to like Ebba because Libby does* argument. Either you care what she thinks or you don't. Or, I guess you probably can, but good luck convincing me of the relevance of Libby's opinions ever again.

♫ ♫ ♫ ♫ ♫

We land in London at 4:03 p.m., which is 8:03 a.m. back home. The day is just beginning in California, and it's almost over here. I can't think about that too hard or my brain might explode. It was pretty cool to have a bed in business class, so I slept on and off in between all the announcements and stuff, but I still feel really weird and lethargic even though I'm stoked to be here. I had a window seat and it was so cool to watch London come closer and closer into view, with the rounded roof of the Royal Albert Hall where the London Symphony Orchestra sometimes plays, the river Thames snaking out into the distance, and yes, even the Big Ben tower, looking tall and imposing and in charge of things, and then, right before landing, an amazing sprawling castle, surrounded by greenery. It takes a while to get through customs and baggage claim but finally I'm there, and Libby practically pushes people out of the way so she can run to meet me.

"You're here!" she keeps saying, hugging me. Her brown hair swings around her shoulders. She's grown it to the middle of her back. She looks more relaxed than she did in Pasadena, maybe because she's on her home turf now, or maybe because she's not trying to impress anyone. That summer at our house, she was so in love with my dad. I've seen the way she looked at him in the eyes of a lot of fangirls, and I've also seen it in Ebba's eyes. It's got to have been exhausting to try to impress him all the time.

I know that exhaustion myself from standing by my locker, chewing gum so my breath would smell fresh, taking a bit longer than I needed to grab my books so that Tim would have time to catch up to me. Planning what nonchalant thing I was going to say if he happened to stop by. Sometimes my shoulders ached afterward from the tension.

I miss him.

But, London. *Focus, Clara. You're here now.*

Libby asks me if I want to take the Tube or a taxi, and the Tube sounds kinda cool and Londonish, so I opt for that. My case and backpack and viola are easy enough to manage between the two of us. We hear the train coming way before it gets there, and wind rushes into the station ahead of it, warm on our faces. Inside the train, the blue seats look like they're made of carpet.

With the change at Green Park onto the Victoria Line, where the blue seats are patterned with white crosses and red dots and the poles are light blue instead of dark, it takes well over an hour to get to Pimlico, where Libby lives with Dan, her fiancé.

We climb the steps out of the station, and immediately

I notice how cold it is. When Ebba and I walked out of the airport after I got back from skiing, the wall of LA air, warm and inviting, welcomed me home. And even though of course I knew in my head that England is cold, I guess my body is primed to expect that wall of warmth when I walk out. So it's weird to be cold, but it's also fun, because it reminds me that I really am here, in London. No amount of pictures taped to the inside of my locker can compare to actually being here. As we wait to cross the street, three buses whizz by: red double deckers just like in the movies.

"Hungry?" Libby asks me, as we walk down the alley that leads past a massage parlor and a dry cleaner toward her apartment.

"I could eat."

As I say this, I realize I'm starving.

"Let's drop off your suitcase, and then it's time for your first authentic British experience."

We cross a courtyard surrounded by doors. She holds up her fob to one of them, and it opens. It feels like I'm on the set of a movie about college or something, not a place where real grownups live. I didn't expect a pool or anything, because Libby was clearly very excited about ours, but as we walk into her apartment on the first floor it strikes me that the entire thing is not much bigger than the apartment she lived in above our garage that summer. One extra bedroom, sure, which is where I'll sleep. But the kitchen is tiny and so is the bathroom. The living room looks directly out onto the street. I like watching people walk past, but it's weird that they can look right in at us.

I dump my suitcase next to the twin bed and lay my viola on top of it, then freshen up in the bathroom. A wave of tiredness washes over me, like I need a nap but also like if I lay down now I might sleep forever, and it's too early for that.

Our first adventure awaits.

I look at myself in the mirror as I wash my hands. My eyes are red and my skin looks grey. I have the beginning of a pimple on my chin. I'm so excited to be here, but it's like my body didn't get the memo.

"Clara," Libby calls from just outside the door. "You okay in there?"

I exhale, arrange my face into a smile that matches my mood and not my exhaustion, and reply as I open the door. "I'm a little tired," I tell her truthfully. "But I'm good."

"Let's find you some food. It'll help," she tells me. "Think you can stay awake till 9 p.m.?"

Three hours. I've got this. I nod.

"Jet lag is a killer," she says. "But we want to try and get you on British time as quickly as possible so we can make the most of your week here."

That makes sense. I don't have the energy to brush my hair, so I run my hand through it and hope for the best. It's not like anyone knows me here. We walk out and around the corner, back toward the Tube station.

"I can guarantee you haven't had Indian food this good before," Libby says, pushing open the door to the Millbank Spice. They seat us at a table in the front of the restaurant, on chairs covered in what seems like more carpet, red this time. What is it with carpets on chairs in England? Libby lets me have the seat facing the window so I can watch the red buses go by. It makes me feel like I'm in a movie and Hugh Grant is going to walk by any second.

I tell Libby that, and she laughs.

"That's how I felt about being in LA," she says. "Like I'd
landed in the middle of a film."

The server comes over with the menus.

"We'll take two poppadoms each, please," she tells him.
"This one's starving. And water for now while we decide."

He nods and walks away. I don't think I've ever asked for
water in a sit-down restaurant before. They just bring it to
you, usually.

"I didn't know you were into those Hugh Grant movies,"
Libby says to me. "Which is your favorite?"

I love them all, but sitting here in London, I have to choose
the London-iest of them all.

"*Notting Hill.*"

"My favorite, too." She smiles. "But that probably doesn't
come as a surprise to you."

I think about it, and of course it makes sense. An actor
and a Normal Human getting together? Of course Libby loves
it. When she moved in with us that summer, I'm pretty sure
that was the vibe she was going for. This whole writing-a-
screenplay-with-my-dad thing seemed highly suspicious to
me. I overheard Mom on the phone, too, complaining to one
of her girlfriends: "She's nineteen years younger than him!
I know he's allowed to move on, but come on. She's young
enough to be his daughter!"

I wanted to listen to more of that conversation, but I was
also grossed out by it all, so I went into my room and vowed
to keep a closer eye on Dad and Libby—which paid off pretty
quickly when I caught them kissing. To this day, they both
claim it was just that one time. And my dad did start dating
Ebba pretty soon after that, so maybe it's true.

Even though part of me wants to stay far, far away from any

discussion of my dad's love life, part of me is curious about what really went on that summer. About whether Libby came to Pasadena to try to get my dad to fall in love with her, or if it really was just about the screenplay. I feel a little like it's an unresolved mystery, and maybe, if I figure it out, I won't feel like part of me is stuck in that summer, missing Libby and wishing she was living with us instead of Ebba.

The server brings the poppadoms then, so we don't need to discuss any of this just now. The poppadoms are roundish, crispy, big chip-like things, and I watch and copy Libby as she breaks off chunks and dips them in the chutneys: a yogurt sauce, a mix of diced onion, cucumber and tomato, and mango chutney, which is kind of like jelly. I don't really like raw onion usually, but somehow it works, especially when you alternate it with the mango chutney to calm your mouth down between bites. For drinks, we both order Diet Cokes, and I don't know if it's the taste of the onion, or how tired I am, or what, but it tastes different from how it does back home. Sweet, still, but in a different way. Maybe because I'm drinking it out of a glass. Who knows?

I let Libby order my main dish for me, since I have no idea. She gets me a butter chicken and rice, and a peshwari naan for us to share, whatever that is. I trust her. I don't really have a choice, since I'm totally out of my depth here. There's been so much I've been out of my depth on this year. Apparently, I still have a lot to learn.

"Yeah," I tell her, seeing the opportunity for some real talk about that summer and dragging the conversation back to *Notting Hill*. "It's a beautiful fairy tale, right? You bump into a Hollywood star and fall in love?"

"Indeed." She smiles awkwardly. Maybe even blushes a little.

Outside, the sun is setting, and the lighting is dim enough in here that I can't totally tell. "But the reality is that, when you're not from the same world … you might think you're in love, you might even *be* in love for real, but that's often not enough."

I swallow hard. I think of Tim, even though I know she's talking about her and Dad. We're not from such different worlds, he and I. And at least there isn't a nineteen-year age gap. (Ugh. Gross.)

"How do you know?" I ask her. "If you're in love or just *think* you're in love?"

"Ah," she says. "The 64,000-dollar question."

Our food arrives then, wheeled to us on a cart and covered with rounded silver lids. The mix of spices smells unbelievable. The server moves our plates around on the table and arranges our dishes: my chicken in creamy sauce, Libby's dish still sizzling, and yellow rice, and this incredible looking flatbread. Libby rips it in half and gives me a piece. I take a bite. It's sweet and soft and almondy and I've never tasted anything this good in my entire life. And suddenly the conversation can wait. I want to focus on this amazing food.

"I know I'm in love with this peshwari naan," I tell her. "That's for sure."

Libby laughs. I love making her laugh. I was so caught up in the excitement of seeing London that I'd forgotten how much of this trip is just about spending time with Libby. Mostly, I like being a big sister, being in charge, but it's nice to have a big sister type person of my own, too.

Forty-Two

I ask Libby to wake me up by 10 a.m. the next day, because we have plans. Buckingham Palace, the parks, afternoon tea at a fancy department store called Fortnum & Mason. She also wants to show me this big famous bookstore right down the block from it. I'm not really into bookstores, but okay, whatever. I think she wants to show me her happy places, the places that are meaningful to her, as well as the touristy stuff.

We walk through Pimlico, where the trees are in bloom on Regency Street, and then through St James's Park, where we stand on a bridge with low arches and blue railings and take selfies with Buckingham Palace in the background. We watch as little kids throw bread to the ducks and they all converge on it, quacking, each of them hurrying to be the first to each piece. I mentally store up this ammunition for the next time Mom rolls her eyes at me for my competitiveness. Survival of the fittest, Mom! Even ducks do it.

Buckingham Palace isn't quite what I expected.

"How so?" Libby asks me.

"I thought there'd be more gold."

Libby smiles, like she's got her own private joke about this. "More announcement of its own importance?"

I nod. I guess that's it. There *is* the Queen's Guard, who are guards in red uniforms with weird tall black hats that are made of bearskin from Canada and must be super-heavy and hot in the summer.

"Does it even get hot in the summer here?" I ask.

"Yes. Well, you know. Hot-ish. Once in a while. And we

don't have air con in houses so when it's hot there's nowhere to go to get away from it."

"I can't imagine not having AC."

"People have it in cars now, but no-one really drives in London."

That seems crazy to me. I've never thought it was possible to live without driving or being driven. "How do people get around?"

"The Tube. Nowhere you'd want to go in central London is far from a Tube stop."

Huh. I try to imagine my life without drives to Katie's house and drives to the beach in Coronado or Santa Monica and drives to downtown LA for plays and movies and Hollywood parties and drives to viola lessons and drives to orchestra rehearsal, and my mind is kinda blown. It's the first time I think about how much time we spend in cars.

The sun weaves in and out of the clouds and the light filters through and catches on the water, and I can see why Libby loves St James's Park. We walk through and cross a super quiet avenue (maybe British people actually hate cars?) painted red and called the Mall, but it's nothing like the Mall in DC, which is the only other Mall I know about that isn't built for shopping. We walk through Green Park. The name of it strikes me as funny, like Sandy Beach or Wet Water, but the park *is* pretty green, with a bunch of trees, so I guess at least it's apt.

The other side of the park it feels like we're back in a city—people are walking fast, faster than they did in Pimlico, *definitely* faster than they do in Pasadena, like they all have somewhere to be in a desperate hurry. Maybe they do. Maybe they all have very important appointments at the Ritz, which

I recognize from *Notting Hill*. It's near the beginning of the movie, when Hugh Grant gets on a bus which goes past the hotel and 'How Can You Mend a Broken Heart' is playing. For the millionth time in the last few months, I try not to think about Tim, but have you ever tried not to think about someone? It just makes you think about them more.

"You okay?" Libby asks me. "You seem a bit down."

"Just tired," I say. I wonder if Dad and Ebba pre-warned her to be on the lookout for signs of depression. I've heard them talking about it in low voices, wondering if they should send me to a therapist. But I'm fine. I can get over the one little (gigantic) setback that was not getting into LACHSA. I don't want Libby to think otherwise. Plus, I'm dying to talk to her about Tim. Maybe she has some wisdom about that whole situation, what that was all about. What it means that I still think about him at random moments, like when I've just gotten off the plane in London.

"And thinking about Tim," I add, even though it sounds ridiculous and my face warms up immediately in flushed embarrassment. His name sounds weirdly out of place here, walking down this busy street, weaving around kids wearing backpacks and speaking a million different languages and businessmen with briefcases and wrinkled brows.

"Oh?" Libby says. She's trying to sound casual but I can see in every part of her body, in the way she whips her head round to face me, in the way she walks a little more slowly, that she's desperately interested, that she wants to know everything, that she wants to talk about this from every possible angle and late into the night, with snacks. But there's no way she's waiting until late at night—and, given how tired I am, I'll have passed out by 9 p.m. anyway. Libby wants to start this conversation right now. I can tell.

"Okay, I want to hear all about this," she says. "But wait. Let's get to Fortnum & Mason and get our tea and scones in front of us and then we'll talk."

See? Snacks.

And I'm pretty sure it's late into the night somewhere.

Back home, actually. Huh. Maybe that's why I'm so tired.

We walk in silence for the next couple of minutes, because there's no point starting a different conversation when we know we want to come back to this one as soon as humanly possible and possibly sooner.

Through the heavy wooden doors into Fortnum & Mason, it's like some kind of wonderland. There are displays of tins of candy and a counter where it looks like you can buy toffee and other things piece by piece. There are so many pretty things I want to pick up and look at, like a whole array of teapots I can see further down on the left. But Libby is determined to get us seated with tea and scones and boy talk so I guess all of that will have to wait.

We have time. We've barely begun our explorations, after all.

"So," Libby says. We have a round table by the window. After we ask for afternoon tea, scones and small cakes arrive on stacked Tiffany-blue plates, along with tiny, perfectly symmetrical thin sandwiches made of different kinds of bread, with fillings like cucumber with mint and lemon butter, or ham with English mustard. Libby has ordered Assam for us, and it's redder than any other tea I've seen. She says she wants to teach me about different teas, that the one she and Dan have at home is "bog standard" PG Tips, which is kind of like English Breakfast, but that there are all different types with subtly different flavors.

"We have tea in America," I remind her, blowing on my tea to cool it. "Remember the Huntington? They have great jasmine tea there."

"Yes," Libby says.

She looks wistful for a moment. Does she still think about my dad? She seems really in love with her fiancé, Dan. She and Dan look at each other the way that Dad and Ebba do, like, *you are my whole world*. Except that when it's Dan and Libby, it doesn't make me want to barf. It's kind of sweet, actually. And Libby seems happy with Dan. So she must be over my dad. Right? And if Libby can get over my dad when she was obsessed with him, then I should be able to get over Tim.

"I remember the jasmine tea at the Huntington," Libby says. "I liked it a lot. But I'm talking proper tea. Proper British black tea."

She takes a long, satisfied sip, as if to demonstrate her point. Libby is proud of being British the way I'm proud of being American.

"Anyway," she says. "Tell me about Tim."

I've told her a little about him before, over FaceTime and texts. But it's not the same as real heart-to-heart conversations. If Libby lived in Pasadena, I like to imagine sleepovers at her apartment, long talks about all kinds of things. But FaceTime and texts aren't the same. It takes me a while to open up, to go past the stage where we're just exchanging information, and at that point it's usually time to go do something else. That's part of why I've been excited for this trip. We've got time to settle in and *really* talk. I get to feel like the little sister for once.

I give Libby the quickest rundown about Tim to catch her up. Sophomore, very helpful in my first week of school, cute as all get out with the swoopy hair and the long eyelashes and the chin dimple and the blue eyes. Probably wants something from me, even if he claims not to know who Madison Harper is.

And then the whole ski trip disaster, which she already knows about, though she didn't know the part where the reason I wanted to go was Tim because he was supposed to kiss me, and then I won't get to be fifteen without ever having been kissed, because it's about time, and everyone (mostly Katie) is leaving me behind. And I don't want my first kiss to be some random dude who's not even attractive. At least this way I'd get to have my first kiss with someone impressive, and maybe wow him so much I'd impress him right back, enough for him to forget whose daughter I am and whose friend I am and the many ways in which I can be useful to him, and maybe he'd like me for me. Although, how I was ever going to do that without any prior experience of the kissing thing is unclear.

Once upon a time I might have wowed him with my viola playing and my admission to LACHSA and Juilliard and the Symphony but that's all over now, my chances of impressing him ruined by my attempts to impress him.

And maybe I don't care anymore.

Maybe I'm too mad at him anyway.

And anyway, he said *liked*. Past tense. I've missed my chance. I should have corrected Libby every time she said he *likes* me, but I let it go because it was nice to hear.

"Okay," Libby says. "Take a breath. Have a scone."

I copy what she does—a layer of thick clotted cream and then a layer of jelly, on the cut-in-half scone. I bite into it. Yum. The scone itself isn't as sweet as the ones you get at Starbucks. It's more like a biscuit, but with the clotted cream and the jelly, it's just the right amount of sugariness.

My dad has a theory that a woman can't cry with chocolate in her mouth. I've never been able to prove him wrong. I bet it'd be hard to cry with a mouthful of this scone too, and not just because you'd spit dust everywhere. It's probably helpful, for the purposes of this conversation, if crying is impossible.

"What do you think?" Libby asks me. I can tell by the amused look on her face that she already knows I think it's amazing.

"Scrhphm," I say, through a sticky mouthful. She laughs and pours another tiny bit of milk and then more tea into each of our dainty, gold-flowered cups.

"Tea and scones really are the perfect pairing," she says. "Like red wine and cheese." And then she remembers that I'm fourteen, and that we can't even get all the cheeses she likes in America. "I mean, like fish and chips. Like Ron and Hermione. Or maybe like you and Tim?"

I like the way she circles back like this. I was a little bit afraid we'd gone off topic.

"Maybe?"

"What do you like about him?" Hasn't she been listening? The hair, and— "Apart from his hair and his eyes and his chin? What makes him crush-worthy? Does he play a musical instrument?"

I shake my head. "No. He's kind of a nerd, actually. He plays Scrabble."

Libby smiles. She's into the idea of him. "A nerd. I like it." This is not at all surprising, given her (past?) crush on my dad, who played a nerdy high school English teacher complete with nerdy glasses on *The Classroom*, that show that everyone loved, and also given Dan, who also wears glasses and likes to read books for fun *and* for work. That's a *lot* of books. And if you read them for work, wouldn't you want to do something completely different when you get home? Like, play tennis or videogames?

"And is he kind?"

I think about this as I spread cream on the next scone. "He brought me flowers after I broke my wrist."

"Nice ones?"

"Yeah. But only because his mom made him." I add the strawberry jelly, a thicker layer of it this time.

"Still, it must have taken guts, don't you think?"

"Well, yeah. But he didn't have a choice."

She frowns. "Are you sure you like him? It doesn't sound like you like him that much."

"I have a crew of butterflies in my stomach that think I like him."

"A crew?"

I chew and swallow my bite of scone. "I don't know if that's the right word. A gaggle? Or a flutter. A flutter of butterflies."

"Nice." She laughs. "Okay, so you fancy him."

"Huh?"

"Think he's attractive."

What do you know, it seems the butterflies followed me to London. Or, I guess, since they're inside me, they didn't have the choice in coming too. Well, whatever. They're clearly over their jet lag. They've woken up and they're fluttering, is what I'm saying.

"Yes," I say. "I fancy him. And I want to kiss him."

"I have a question for you," she says, pouring us both yet another cup of tea. "But you have to promise me you won't get mad."

In my experience, it's never a good sign when someone makes you promise that, but I want to know what the question is. "I promise."

"Do you want to kiss him *specifically*? Or is just that you want to kiss someone and he happens to be available?"

"I don't know if he's actually available. To me. As such."

Libby looks at me, stern-teacher-style, over the top of imaginary glasses. It's clear that I'm not going to get away with not answering her question. Behind us, from another table, spoons clink on teacups.

"I don't know," I say again, a real answer to her question this time.

"Because you can't be mad at him for using you to get to Madison Harper if you're using him to get any old kiss."

"Hopefully it wouldn't be any old kiss. Hopefully it would be an amazing kiss."

"I should probably warn you: they're never that amazing the first time," she says, and then lowers her voice like she's about to reveal some great secret. "Everyone just swirls their tongues around and around and it's a bit mechanical."

"What else are you supposed to do?"

"It's hard to describe. I think everyone probably needs to start with the mechanical swishing. Kind of how you have to start with scales when you practice, you know?"

"I do." I get the scales part. The rest is fuzzier than it's ever been. I feel weird asking for detailed instructions from Libby, and I can't ask Katie since she thinks I've already gone way past that base. But now I'm even more nervous about the whole thing.

"But after that," she says. "It's flippin' amazing." She's lost in a daydream, suddenly. Please oh please let her be thinking about Dan and not my dad.

"So anyway," I say quickly, just in case she's thinking thoughts

I don't want anyone thinking in my vicinity. "Back to me and Tim."

"Yes. Back to you and Tim. So, to recap: you're worried he only likes you because you can get him into Hollywood parties. But it seems like maybe you only like him because you want to kiss someone and, well, he'll do."

I think about the theme song to *Crazy Ex-Girlfriend*. Katie and I love that show. We love that all the songs still work if you substitute Pasadena for West Covina. "Well, it's a little more nuanced than that," I say, a defense I've learned from the theme song.

"Well, maybe it's more nuanced for him, too," Libby says, not showing any signs of recognizing the reference, which is too bad. I think she'd like the show. I feel like she probably has a lot in common with the hopeless romanticism of the main character, Becks, who leaves her entire life behind to move to California for a crush on a guy named Josh. But then she meets another guy called Greg, who does this whole song about how he wishes she would drop the idea of the guy she's obsessed with but can't have and settle for him instead. I hope Dan's not the Greg she's settling for because she can't have her Josh, which in this analogy would be my dad. Disturbing thought. Dan deserves better than that. (So does Greg, in the show.) He's sweet.

"Maybe Tim does like you, and maybe he also wants to get into Hollywood parties. The two aren't mutually exclusive."

Like, I want to be kissed, by someone, and also, I want to be kissed by Tim, because he's cute. Those things can both be true and that doesn't make me dishonest or a bad person. The situation actually *is* a lot more nuanced than I thought.

"Huh," I say. "I hadn't considered that."

"That's what an old wise friend like me is for. And for teaching you about scones and real tea. Waterstones next? It's one of my favorite bookshops."

"Sure."

But, after we've paid and left and headed a few doors down, I realize I'm not prepared for *this* bookstore. From the outside, it doesn't look like much: ugly and boring compared to the older, more intricate buildings on either side. But inside, display tables are neatly arranged, with a lot of space to let people browse without it feeling cluttered. Somebody with an ordered and logical brain clearly designed it, and that makes me feel right at home. And it's big: I thought everything was smaller in England than in California, but this bookstore is, what? Ten times the size of Vroman's?

"Pretty cool, isn't it?"

"I didn't even know I cared about bookstores," I say. In my excitement, I forget to filter my lack of enthusiasm for novels, which I know disappoints Libby. "But this one is pretty amazing. It's, what, five stories?"

"Six."

On the first floor, we wander among bestsellers and journals and magazines. The floor for the casual browser, like me, I guess. The real book nerds ride up in elevators to fantasy or classics or non-fiction. Rosie would love it here. I'm standing in one spot, turning to take video to send her when Libby motions me over to one of the themed display tables.

"Hollywood-themed books," she says. "Just for you to feel at home."

"Yeah." It makes me smile that she's thought of this. And then I notice it: her book, a big pile of copies, right in the center.

"Wow!" I pick it up, even though of course I've picked up

copies of it many times before. Is it my imagination, or is it a slightly different size from the one we have at home? What, are even *books* different in England? "You're famous."

She laughs, but I can tell she's pleased. "Yes. That's why there's an orderly queue of fans waiting for my autograph over there."

There's nobody over there. This is just her sense of humor. "Seriously, this is cool." I make her pose with a copy. This is for sure going on my Instagram. "Even if it still creeps me out you were inspired by my dad."

"Your dad is a very charming man," she says, not at all sorry, even if she's blushing a little.

"Which is why you flew over to LA to get him to fall in love with you?"

She laughs again, puts her arm around me. "Yes, that's exactly why." But it's not the same tone as the one she used to joke about the queue of fans. It's a tone that says, *I'm telling you the unvarnished truth.*

"I knew it," I say. "I knew it wasn't just about a screenplay."

"Of course it wasn't," she says. "Not for me, anyway. But if you want to know what your dad was thinking, you'll have to ask *him*."

My turn to laugh. "Okay."

She and I both know I'm not going to ask Dad in a million years, but that's okay. Just knowing I wasn't totally imagining things is a tiny victory. And maybe it's that, or maybe it's the delayed sugar rush from the scones, but for the first time since arriving in London, I feel suddenly wide awake.

Forty-Three

Sunday evening, after the parks and the afternoon tea, Libby asks me to play my viola for her. It's a bit weird, playing for just her and Dan in their tiny apartment, sandwiched between the TV and the squishy red couch, but I've got to get back on the wagon sometime. It would be less weird with a piano accompaniment. They've managed to fit a piano in this living room, too, along the wall, and Dan plays a little piano, he says, but not enough to "do me justice" and certainly not well enough to sight-read a piece.

"But," Dan says, scratching his chin. "Hang on a minute. Do you know Beethoven's Sonatina for Viola and Cello?"

"I do."

I've actually played both parts in the duet before, because cello music is often transposed up an octave for viola, moved into the range of notes that a viola can cover. It's not quite the same when it's two violas playing instead of a viola and a cello, because the tonal difference between the instruments is a big part of what makes the piece, but there's not a ton of music written for solo viola, so we violists are used to making these kinds of compromises.

"I'll play it with you," he says, and that's right, how could I have forgotten? Dan is a cellist. Libby has good taste. The cello is elegant and gracious and the cellists I know tend to be sensitive types, strong in a quiet way. Each instrument has its own stereotype, and they're often backed up by strong anecdotal evidence, though, sadly, not by actual data. Like, trumpet players are often shy little mice who only make noise when they're playing music. Flautists can be a little haughty and attention-seeking, like they know that theirs is the instrument that catches the light on a stage. Oboists can be bossy—not unrelated to the fact that they're the ones who give the all-piercing A note that the whole orchestra tunes to.

Anyway, cellists are lovely and Libby has chosen wisely. She can be a bit of a drama queen, a bit head-in-the-clouds with all her dreaming and idealism and maybe it's good for her to be marrying someone quiet and calm but who also gets her. And if she needs someone even more rational in her life, well: that's what I'm for.

"Playing would be fun," I say to Dan. "I could get on board with that."

We each go to our rooms and free our instruments from their cases, then bring them into the living room with our silver music stands. We twizzle the ends of our bows and run their horsehair across cubes of rosin. Dan's rosin is darker and softer than mine. We unfold our music stands, adjust them to the right height, drag our chairs across the beige carpet, and sit. I feel—I don't know, something. Something in my gut, like anticipation or excitement. Something I haven't felt in a while. It's the feeling I used to get when my teacher would set a new piece on the stand and bend it open, holding the pages with clips because brand new sheet music tends to always want to close itself back up, like it's shy. And it has that new-paper smell, and that crispness, and it all adds up to an invitation to discovery.

I love getting something just right; I love that feeling of having worked and worked on a piece and getting it as close to perfect as humanly possible. But I also love the first run-through, the deciphering. The first time I meet the music. The creation of something I've never created before. It feels like the first time I held a violin or the first time I held a viola. It feels, I guess, like pure joy. Like the look on Mom and Dad's faces in the picture when they're holding me as a tiny baby, full of hope and joy. I've never done anything to disappoint them and they have no-one and nothing to compare me to, they just know that I'm perfect and beautiful and all theirs.

That's how I feel as I sit next to Dan, even though I've played this piece before. I run my eye over the first page of the first movement of Beethoven's Sonatina for Viola and Cello.

"Ready?" he asks me. He has the kindest eyes, and they're dancing too, like he's excited.

"Ready," I say.

"Just pretend I'm not here," Libby says, which is funny, because her being here is why we're playing in the first place.

"Okay," Dan says. We make eye contact and he counts us in, then he visibly breathes in and off we go, our music curling over and around each other's. At times it feels like he's the piano's left hand and I'm the right, my melody soaring over his background hum. At other times we play in unison, and at still others we're echoes of each other. We're at the end of the first movement before I realize I haven't worried about my wrist cramping. Libby claps, even though you're not supposed to clap between movements, so we pause long enough to let her.

"Want us to keep going?" Dan asks Libby, but he's asking me too, and I nod. I'm enjoying myself. I don't remember the last time I truly enjoyed myself like this. Just two of us, reading something familiar enough that there isn't the adrenaline of sight-reading but new enough that there isn't the pressure of performing perfectly. And actually, I don't know if I've ever in my life not felt that pressure. I can hear my playing relax and open itself up. We're playing for someone who loves us both and wants to be impressed by us both and will find every reason to be. Dan's cello has such wonderful, deep tones, and something in his body language, in the way he leans over his cello, tells me how much he is loving this moment too. When we're done we look at each other and smile, but really, even though my wrist is aching a little, I want to jump up and down and shout *Yes! That's what it's supposed to feel like!*

"I could listen to you all day," Libby says. "I know you can't, 'cause of your wrist, Clara, but I'd love to just sit here and read while you play."

And it's weird, but if I could, I wouldn't mind that. It'd be okay not to have her full attention or even that much of it. Today it felt like I was doing this just for me. For the pure joy of it. And it felt good.

Forty-Four

The next day, Monday, Libby wants to play Scrabble, so we sit down with half-drunk cups of tea at the table in the living room, under the mirror that makes the room looks like it extends twice as far as it actually does. She can't believe Scrabble isn't something I'm into. And it's not that I've never played. I know the gist.

School subjects in general don't really do it for me, they're just things that get in the way of viola practice, but if I had to pick one it'd be math. I like the logic of it. I like that you're either right or wrong and nobody can pretend otherwise or say "that's an interesting point of view, but have you considered this other angle?" There are no angles in algebra. (Though, obviously, there are in geometry. Ha.) There are no angles in spelling bees, either. You do your homework, you perform, everyone recognizes your superior preparedness, the end. Sometimes I wish music was more like that.

Libby, on the other hand, is all about the words. Her first novel came out last year and her second one is due to her editor soon, so she has to fit her writing around her teaching. She reads more in a month than I can imagine reading in a year, which is probably why she and Ebba have so much to talk about. Well, that and their shared admiration for my father the not very famous actor.

"Do you still think about him?" I ask her, as we pick off the previous game's Scrabble tiles from the board. It's a travel set, and it's pretty clever how it's made. You can fold it up with the letter tiles still attached to it and they stay there waiting until the next time. And the board opens up, and underneath is a place for the racks where each person lays out their tiles when they're thinking of words, and the cloth pouch from where you draw the letters.

She sips her tea. "Who?" she says.

So maybe that's my answer. In my experience, when you're in love with someone they're all you ever think about. The word "he" can only refer to one "he", because he's the only one that matters, the only one alive for you in the whole world. Like in the *Pride and Prejudice* movie—the actual movie, not the BBC mini-series, which Rosie and Ebba wrongly insist is better and love to sit under their shared blanket and watch over and over while they drink cocoa. (Again: California, people. It's only cold because of the overzealous AC.) Anyway, in the Keira Knightley version, there's this scene where they're all dancing at one of those fancy balls, but the way it's shot, everyone disappears and it's just Elizabeth and Mr. Darcy dancing. That's how it feels when you're in love with someone. Like the whole world could stop and you wouldn't even notice it. Lin-Manuel Miranda himself could have walked past my locker when Tim was talking to me there and all I would have seen was a blur.

So if the word "him" doesn't make Libby think of Dad immediately, then Dan can probably relax. On the other hand, maybe she's bluffing: *what? Who? I don't know who you could possibly be referring to.* But that's not what Libby's like. She's more into wearing her heart on her sleeve at all times. What you see is what you get. WYSIWYG, she calls it.

"My dad," I say. "Do you ever think about him?"

"I think about all of you," she says. The plastic Scrabble tiles make clicky, tapping sounds as we throw them into their pouch, handful by handful, and they all knock against each other. "I think about that summer in Pasadena with you guys, yeah."

But that's not what I'm asking and I know she knows it. Libby is not stupid.

"Yeah," I say. "I mean, I assume that you do since we wouldn't know each other if you hadn't come to stay."

She's still looking at the board instead of at me.

"Do you still," I say, taking a deep breath and going for the cheesy question. "You know. Have feelings for him." I don't know why I want to know this. *Do* I even want to know this?

Libby's hand is deep in the Scrabble pouch now. She's mixing the letters with her hands over and over. Click, click, click.

"You know how some people have crushes on TV characters?" she asks me.

I do. Since, before I let myself get distracted by Tim, I never had time for real boys because of the whole LACHSA-Juilliard-Symphony plan, the only crushes I allowed myself were the ones on Matthew Saracen from *Friday Night Lights* and Bailey from *Party of Five* reruns.

"When I came to California," Libby says, "it was kind of like I was going behind the fourth wall. You know what I mean by the fourth wall?"

You don't grow up with actor parents without knowing what the fourth wall is. It's, like, the thing between you and the audience, the boundary between the real world where the audience is and the imaginary world you're creating. With TV, it's the actual television set that contains the imaginary world. With plays, it's basically the stage. When you break the fourth wall, it means that the actors talk to the audience, when really the characters they're playing aren't supposed to even be aware that the audience exists out in the real world, because if they knew about the real world that would mean they'd also know that they themselves were imaginary and then you wouldn't have characters on the stage so much as you'd have puffs of smoke where their brains have exploded.

"Yes," I say to Libby. "You mean you felt like you were in a play or something?"

"A film, maybe," she says, which is trippy in itself, since writing a film—a movie—was what she was supposed to be doing with my dad. "As if it wasn't really real. Or that's how I think about it now, anyway. Once I was behind the fourth wall, it felt totally real. But now your dad's like a character in a TV show. I'm on the other side of the fourth wall again. He's safe behind glass. Like a fantasy—if that's not a weird thing to hear about your dad."

I shrug. It is, totally weird, but on the other hand, I did ask. And I know what she means. A lot of people who come up to my dad tell him they love him, but they don't even know him. They love the characters he plays, but that's not him. Or maybe they think they know him because they've seen interviews, but that's not really him, either. That's a character he plays, too: charming Thomas Cassidy, funny Thomas Cassidy, slightly flirty Thomas Cassidy. (That makes me a little queasy.) My dad's not real to them. He's behind the fourth wall, and sometimes it feels like we're all there with him, in our imaginary goldfish bowl of a universe, existing just so we can be gawked at.

"So you ship him and Ebba now," I say, thinking about how our lives would play out on TV, like in *The Truman Show*.

"I've always shipped your dad and Ebba," she says. "It just got confusing for a while when I was there behind the fourth wall with them too."

"Why?"

"Because your dad is incredibly charming."

"No." I know *that*. Or at least, I've gathered it from social media. "Why do you ship him and Ebba?"

Libby puts the green Scrabble tile pouch down and disappears into her and Dan's bedroom. Then she comes back with a book I recognize from its cover right away, a man and a woman in shadow against a sunrise. Ebba's memoir. She reads me the lines I've avoided reading in the book I've only pretended to look at.

Ebba's description of Dad is actually, I have to admit it, beautiful. It's all the more beautiful because it's real. She tells us, the readers, how terrible his puns are, how he nearly burned the house down with a frozen pizza, how he couldn't cook. (I'm glad he fixed that.) How he loved it a little bit too much when other people loved him. But also how his terrible puns ended up making her laugh, how he came alive on stage, how his wanting to be great made him somehow charismatic, attractive not in a gross way but in the sense that people wanted to be around him. She loved him: it's obvious, even to me. Even though she left him and broke his heart, which I can't fault her for since it led to my existence after Dad met Mom, unless there's some alternate universe in which I am Ebba's daughter, or maybe fan fic for the TV show that is my family. I think *my* brain is actually going to explode. I swear I can feel smoke beginning to seep out of my ears.

"Yeah," I'm forced to admit when Libby is done reading. "That's beautiful."

"You've read it before, though, right?"

I'm quiet. Somehow I feel like *no* is not going to be an

acceptable answer.

"I'm not really a books person," I say instead, though that's probably even less acceptable. I take a sip of my tea, forgetting it's stone cold by now, and nearly spit it back out. I swallow it down hard instead.

"Oh, Clara," Libby says. Pronouncing it right, because she's the only person in my life who always does. Because she's why I say it that way to start with. "You have to read it. It's one of my very favorite books."

"Because it's about Dad?"

"No," she says. "Not because of that. Or at least not only because of that. It's not really about him, anyway. It's about Ebba, and it's about Ebba and Ethan. It's just—it's a beautiful book. It will help you to understand Ebba. It made me feel like she was worthy of your dad. Like if I couldn't be with him, it would be okay if she was."

I don't know if it's because she's been so honest, but suddenly I feel like I want to be honest too. Even if it's ugly.

"I don't really want to understand her," I blurt out.

Libby shakes the pouch to mix the letters up and looks at me carefully, like she's trying to read something in my face.

I am inscrutable. She should know this by now.

"What are you so afraid of?" she asks me.

From out of nowhere I have that horrible pain in the back of my throat, the pain that means I'm about to cry no matter how much I am determined not to.

"I'm afraid she'll leave us," I blurt out.

I don't think I even knew that until this moment. I'm sniffing now. But that's not all I'm afraid of. I'm afraid that she only loves me because she has to. I'm afraid that I was right about her being pregnant and that she won't care about me once the baby's born. I'm afraid that I'll always be in Dad's shadow. That I'm swimming around in the goldfish bowl but no-one is really looking at me, and if there's one thing worse than being gawked at, it's being ignored. I can't really say any of this, though, because I'm crying now. It won't come out coherently.

Libby disentangles my hands from my cold tea cup and squeezes them in hers.

"I wish I could promise you she won't leave you," she says. "Life is hard sometimes. Things happen that we don't expect, you know? I know she would never deliberately hurt you. I know that your dad loves you very much and she does too."

"That's not very reassuring," I say.

"Okay," she says. "Look. Here's the thing. I was in love with your dad. I was head-over-heels, can't-think-about-anything-else in love with him. It was real to me then. And I thought it was going to work out and when it didn't, it was so incredibly painful. It broke my heart. Love does that, sometimes."

I don't know if I was in love with Tim. I don't know if I'm love with him now. How do you even know you're in love with someone? But what happened still hurts a lot. Every time my wrist twinges, my heart twinges, too. I'm not proud of how mean I was to him after the accident, even though I thought and maybe still think that he deserved it.

It hurts when I catch his eye around school and he gives me a sad, distant smile. It hurts when he doesn't see me at all. It hurts, because I never even got to know him as well as I wanted to. I've picked up my phone so many times to text him, but then I give up because what would I even say? I don't even know him well enough to know which GIF would make him smile the most.

Libby gets up to fetch a tissue and presses it into my hands.

"The thing is," she says. "It was worth it. Even with all the pain I felt. It was worth it, you know? You've got to open yourself up to love. Sometimes it will hurt. I don't think anything hurts as much as the first time you get your heart broken."

"That's a relief," I say. "Because if it gets worse than this, I'm out."

Libby takes a sip of her tea, and aside from the slurp, there's silence for a while. "You know," she says eventually, "it doesn't sound like this story is necessarily over. It sounds like maybe you could think about whether you could forgive him, and maybe you could try to get to know him better? You're both nerdy, in your own ways. You're both competitive. And he sounds like a thoughtful guy who made a mistake and regrets it and wishes he could make it up to you. Maybe he's not meant to be your boyfriend, but maybe he's still a great person to have in your life. Maybe he could be a good friend to you."

I think about this. The butterflies in my stomach are awake, and fluttering, but lazily, like they're considering this, too. Let's face it: Tim is the only person at my school who's ever been kind to me. And now it looks like I'm stuck at this school for the next three and a half years. It would be good to have a friend. Even an attractive friend, which might get confusing since he *liked* me, past tense.

"Where would I even start?"

"Well," Libby says. I've noticed before how many of her sentences start with *well*. It must be a British thing. "You could start with Scrabble."

"Wait a minute. Is this why you wanted to teach me to play?"

She smiles, so I know I'm right. "Scrabble is a basic life skill."

I laugh through my tears. I'm lucky bubbles don't come out of my nose.

"I wish *you* were my stepmom," I say. I'm just realizing this now. Libby is the best. Maybe the reason I'm mad at Ebba is that she's not Libby.

"Oh, Clara," she says. "That's so sweet of you. But I'm here the other side of the fourth wall. Of the Atlantic Ocean. And Ebba is wonderful, I promise you. Read her book."

"She doesn't understand me." I'm grasping at straws now. I know that's not fair. When she sat on my bed and told me about her ballet injury, I remember thinking she might understand me better than anyone. I sound whiny right now, even to myself, like I'm just coming up with excuses. But I'm also thinking of last fall, that time she was watching me play my viola. Who *does* that?

"You've got to give her a chance," Libby says. "Sit with her and be honest. Like you're being honest right now with me."

"What, and tell her I'd rather Dad married you?"

She laughs, through her nose, the way Dad does sometimes. "I wouldn't suggest you lead with that." She's quiet for a while, and the only sound is my sniffing. "You know, I'm not perfect I'm not even close to perfect. Ask Dan sometime to tell you all the ways I'm not perfect. I bet your dad could give you a list. Ebba, too, actually. It's easy to idealize someone when they're not there to let you down. Like a TV character, in fact. Ebba's there, in your world. I would give anything to spend as much time with her as you get to. She's not perfect, either. But she's real. She's in your world. She loves you. And why wouldn't she? You're great. Have faith in yourself, too, Clara. Have faith that people will like you if you let them get close."

Is it possible to somehow feel simultaneously punched

in the gut and enveloped in a warm hug? I guess it must be, because that's what I'm feeling right now.

"I don't think I have the energy for Scrabble tonight," I say.

"That's okay," Libby says. "There's always tomorrow. Want to pick a movie to watch instead?"

I choose *Me and Earl and the Dying Girl* so I can cry some more and Libby will think it's because of the movie. I hate being this pathetic. Also, Thomas Mann is kind of cute.

Forty-Five

On Wednesday, I get up and dressed and ready to visit an old timey palace called Hampton Court, but by the time I come out of the bathroom people are rushing past the apartment huddled under umbrellas and it's raining too hard to go anywhere. So while we wait for the rain to stop, we try Scrabble again. Libby gets the set out and this time there are no playing tiles to remove since we did all it a couple days ago, so I don't have time to think thoughts that lead to heart-to-hearts that lead to tears that lead to a movie that leads to more tears that lead to a splitting headache.

We get right to it. Libby jiggles the bag of letter tiles and we each pick out one to see who's going to start. I get B, so I win that round, since it's closer to the beginning of the alphabet than the Q that Libby gets, even though the Q is worth 8 points to the B's 3 and I think it would be more logical to win the opening turn on the basis of the number of points. But rules are rules, and I'm certainly not about to argue with them, especially when they benefit me.

We listen to a Brahms sonata as we play. Viola music helps me to think. I have this theory that it's because it lights up my brain with dopamine or whatever that happy substance is that lights up people's brains. It lights up my brain with inspiration and creativity and hope.

I'm trying to make the longest words I can with the seven letters I have, to use up as many letters as possible and cover as many special squares on the board as possible: Double word score! Triple letter score! Libby knows a trick or two and I start to take notice of them. Like, say someone puts the word CAT down. You can add an S onto the end of CAT and start a whole new word with it, like this:

```
C A T S
      U
      G
      A
      R
```

Or you can end a word with the S, like this:

```
      B
      A
      S
C A T S
```

That way, you get the points of the new word you made, plus the points of the old word you added the S to. And if the S happens to be on a double word score square, then you double the points for both the words. So it's words, but it's also math, and it's also strategy, and dopamine is firing in my brain, or it's doing whatever it is that dopamine does, and it's not just the viola music. This is fun—the tactics and the scheming. At first I was just doing it because Libby seemed to really want to play, but now I'm genuinely enjoying myself. My proudest moment is adding the X to make *xi* and *ox*, like this:

```
H O B O
      X I
      S
      L
      A
      N
      D
```

It's on a triple letter score and X is worth ten points, so that gets me sixty-two points, thirty-one for each for *xi* and *ox*.

"What's *xi*?" Libby asks me.

"A Greek letter," I tell her, a little disappointed in her. "You didn't know that?"

She smiles. "No, no. I knew. I was just checking that *you* knew. In competitive Scrabble, there's a rule that you can challenge someone's word, and if it's not a real word, they lose the points and have to miss a turn. So I'm just making sure you're not randomly making words up."

When Libby first suggested Scrabble, my mind went straight to Tim. But I was enjoying the game so much that I almost wasn't thinking about him anymore while we played. I can't believe I laughed at him when he said he was into this. I totally get it now. I imagine that Professional Scrabble Player isn't really a thing, so I'm not about to cross out

LACHSA

JUILLIARD

SYMPHONY

in my bullet journal and replace it with

WIN SOME COMPETITIONS

BECOME A PROFESSIONAL SCRABBLE PLAYER

because I want an actual career—and also because I'm still holding out hope that my wrist will heal completely, that I'll be able to get back on track for the original plan somehow even if I have to skip a step or two. I'm not about to give up quite so easily.

Clara Cassidy, Quitter?

I don't think so.

I'm aware that Libby is looking at me as if she's trying to read me, that she's smiling.

"Oh no," she says. "Have I created a monster?"
"A competitive Scrabble-playing monster? Maybe."

♫ ♫ ♫ ♫ ♫

In the evening, I make Libby play three more games until I finally beat her, and then we watch a couple episodes of *Parks and Recreation* before bed. I like the room I'm sleeping in. It's long and thin with a desk at the window that looks out onto a grassy communal courtyard. I call it my room, and Libby says that's fine, it can be my room, but would it be okay if I lent it to other people when I'm not here, like basically fifty-one weeks of the year? I tell her that's fine, though I pretend to have to think about it first. I even tell her that if she and Dan need the space for a baby one day, that would be okay too.

"We're not thinking about that yet," she says, in a way that makes it seem like she has actually thought about it plenty. I'm going to need to come to London a whole lot when that happens, because you can't be an honorary aunt from an eleven-hour plane ride away. Or, I guess you can, but where's the fun in that?

On the desk, in my bedroom, there's an old but still functioning desktop, a pile of textbooks, and Libby's teaching supplies. I've seen a quilt cover like the one I'm using before: white with swirls of lime green and purple and grey. Do they have Ikea in England? That would totally explain it. Dan and Libby use this room to work in as well as for guests to sleep in. It's a pretty small room for all of those uses. Everything in London is pretty small, even the apartment buildings. There are a lot more houses than apartment buildings, all squished together, not like the ones in Pasadena with yards and space around them. And no-one has a swimming pool, which makes sense, because when would it be warm enough to use one? The streets are pretty narrow, like they weren't really designed for cars. And I've only been here four days, but so far it's rained at least a little on all of those days. The sky can go from grey to blue to black several times in one afternoon and you can't leave the house without several layers and an umbrella. It's really true that British people drink hot tea all the time, too.

Dan kind of reminds me of Hugh Grant in all those old movies from the 1990s. He doesn't look anything like him, and he's sandy blond, but he is a little socially awkward and I sometimes feel like he isn't quite saying what he thinks. Libby says that's pretty normal here, as if they're talking in some secret code that they all understand but that we Americans don't have a hope of cracking. Like, for example, *do you want a cup of tea?* seems to translate to *I want a cup of tea* and *Sorry* seems to have a multitude of meanings, including *I'm not even remotely sorry* and *I think you're the one who should be sorry*. Definitely not the hardest word, judging by how often they say it. Sometimes, they just put it at the beginning of a sentence, the way you might say *um* or clear your throat. *Sorry, did you want another drink?* That kind of thing. It's kind of adorable, though. I like England.

"London," Dan corrects me when I say this. "You like London. England as a whole is a different kettle of fish." There's probably a *sorry* in there, but I've learned to screen those out. We're going to Cambridge for the day tomorrow, though, so I'll get to test out this theory.

When I snuggle into my twin bed tonight—right under the comforter, since there's no top sheet, which is a little weird—I spend some time scrolling through Scrabble-related information on my phone. I jump from website to website, Facebook group to Facebook group, Tumblr to Tumblr. There's a lot of intensity about all of this out there. You sort of know there's a Tumblr for everything, like bullet journals and viola playing, but taking a deep dive into this Scrabble world is something else.

I learn a lot through my scrolling, though. For starters, one of the most important things seems to be learning all the two-letter words that are allowed. They're useful for doing the kind of thing I did with *ox* and *xi*, which apparently is something called a hook. And then there are a ton of exercises you can do, online and in special books and on the Zyzzyva app that Tim showed me, to train yourself to be better at seeing words when they're right there in front of you in your rack of seven letters. There are lots of common combinations of letters, because there are a bunch of, say, Ts and Ss and As in the Scrabble game, much more than Xs or Qs. For example, AETSRDL is one of the common hands to be dealt, and so it's a good idea to learn all the words you can make from combinations like that.

I have an excellent memory, and I'm certainly not afraid of practicing. I have the kind of faith in practice that you really only have from repeatedly being given what seems like an impossible piece—maybe with pizzicato or double-stopping—and then three months later being able to play it damn near perfectly. Anything is possible if you really put your mind to it. If you can't do it, you just aren't trying hard enough. If I wanted to do this Scrabble thing, if I wanted to be LA Junior Champion or Southern California Junior Champion, I could totally do it. Practice and determination—that's what it's about, like everything else in life. I just have to decide if I want it.

Forty-Six

On Thursday morning, we get up early, or what Libby calls early, at least during her spring break: 8 a.m. I'd question the term, but my body clock is still a little messed up. Turns out jet lag is not so easy to shake, and melatonin helps me sleep through the night but leaves me a little groggy in the mornings.

The reason for the sort-of-earliness: a train trip to Cambridge, where Libby went to college and met Dan, along with all the other friends she talks about a lot, like Vicky, who lived in this apartment with her before Dan moved in. It's also, years later, where Libby met my dad for the first time, at some debating society event where she handed him her novel with a Post-It note that said "let's write the screenplay together." So, in a way, Cambridge is also part of the origin story of my friendship with her.

I've studied the London Underground map and so I know before Libby tells me that we'll be riding the Victoria Line to King's Cross St Pancras, and then taking a train from there. Libby's underground station is usually pretty quiet—sleepy, even—but it's still rush hour when we get there and we have to let two trains pass us because they're too crowded for us to be able to squeeze on. It's not till the next stop, Victoria, that a lot of people get off, which gives us the chance to shuffle down the car and grab a couple seats.

It's really warm in here. I ask Libby if the AC is broken, and she laughs.

"Air con in these things? You must be joking."

I must look confused, because she explains further. "I

know it's weird to imagine life without it. But the Tube was designed too long ago for anyone to have thought of that, and apparently it's just too complicated to do it retroactively." She leans on the *apparently* pretty hard. I don't think she's convinced.

"But it's not even warm outside."

"Oh, trust me," she says. "I know. It's disgusting down here in August."

By the time I've gotten over my shock about the AC thing, we're at King's Cross, and there's mad scrambling and a lot of pushing to get off here. I'm beginning to see the benefit of cars. But there's something cool about this too, about going up all the many escalators—always standing on the right, so that people with places to be and things to do can rush past us on the left. There's a lot of rushing in London.

When we pop out onto the concourse, this part looks new, like it was built in the last few years and not way back in Olden Times like a lot of London was. We're here in time to get a bacon roll from Costa Coffee, which is what Libby bribed me with to get me out of bed, and it worked even though I didn't totally know what she was talking about. It turns out a roll is just a sandwich on soft round bread and the bacon isn't like our bacon, it's pinker, with less fat, and tastes different—not bad different, maybe even good different. And there's literally nothing else in the sandwich, just bacon, and the sauce we add. I go for ketchup, because when I ask Libby what's in "brown sauce" she shrugs and says "nobody knows," and there's only so much adventure I can take before 10 a.m.

It takes around an hour to get to Cambridge on the train, and Libby brought travel Scrabble with her for us to play, but we end up just talking. I ask her to tell me about Cambridge, and she explains that it's the second oldest university in the country and arguably the best.

"Is that what people who went to Oxford think too?"

She smiles, and I know I've hit home. "They can think what they like," she says.

I look out the window, at the fields rolling past and the names of stations I can't read as we whizz through them, their short platforms in and out of sight within seconds. I think about college, what it'll be like. I think it's pretty different in America.

Libby's explained to me that she used to have just a few hours of class every week—big "lectures" where everyone in the same class studying the same subject sits in a big hall together. Smaller "seminars" where there's maybe twenty of them discussing a text or a theme. And then, what sounds super cool, scary but in a good way, is supervisions: a professor and one or two students going over a paper you've written, in lots of detail. But, get this: no gen ed classes. No sitting through hours of Nineteenth Century American Literature if you want to study math. You choose your major from the beginning and that's all you study. If, say, I majored in music, I'd spend my entire time improving my composition and performance skills, and learning about things like history and politics and psychology and how they all interact with music. Pretty cool. I wouldn't feel like studying was just getting in the way of viola playing, which is how I've felt the last few years of school. I'd feel like it was all working together to help me be a better, more rounded player.

"I was really lucky to get into Cambridge," Libby says now. "Not many people from my kind of school get to go."

I must look confused because she explains. "There are lots

of different kinds of secondary school in the UK. If you have the money and you want your kids to get ahead, you often send them to private school, which prepares them better for Cambridge and Oxford. So most people at Cambridge are from private schools or schools that only take the most intelligent kids to start with, even if they're state schools. Or what you call public schools in America."

This seems really complicated, but I want to try to understand. "Is it really expensive to study at Cambridge?"

"No," she says. "It doesn't work like that here. All universities charge the same amount here, so like, in theory, getting to Cambridge is just based on ability, but in practice it's more complicated than that. If your parents can afford to pay for secondary school, or if they can afford a house where there's a good state school, then you have a massive advantage."

I think about that. It doesn't seem fair to me.

"It should be based on talent and hard work," I say.

"Wouldn't it be great if the world worked that way?"

I realize that I've never thought about my school like this—how much it costs, or the acceptance rate. When I didn't make it into LACHSA, my parents sat me down with options and we went through them. In the end, they kind of chose for me—I was too bummed to care where I ended up. It makes me wonder, do I have unfair advantages too?

By the time we get to Cambridge, I start to realize why we had to get up so "early." We still have to walk into town, past some language schools, and then, on the main street, some cute little stores and a museum that looks like a temple and then, finally, more and more impressive old stone buildings. They're all the different colleges Cambridge is divided into, kind of like how Hogwarts is divided into houses. And then we stop in front of the most impressive one so far, and Libby says, "This is it. This is King's." We pause, and I can tell Libby wants me to take it in, to be awed, and to love it. And I do, because it's not hard to.

King's College takes up an entire city block, a line of Gothic-looking gates and then at the end, the chapel. I've seen photos, of course. I am nothing if not thorough, and I've done my research, but it's something else to see it in real life. So tall and imposing and somehow elegant too. "Chapel" makes me think of a tiny little church but this is ... definitely not that. How did they even build things like this back in 1441?

Once we're through the gates, Libby gives me a tour of every nook and cranny: we sneak into the mail room behind a student and she shows me the cubby where her letters used to arrive, but also, on Valentine's Day, flowers and fresh cookies from her friends. The bar, its walls painted red, where she used to hang out with her friends before and after dinner. The dining hall that also looks like something out of Harry Potter. Outside, she walks me along a path and points up at a window.

"That was my room in my final year," she says. "It was actually Dan's at first, but he let me have it because I loved the view so much."

"Wow. That's nice of him."

I imagine the view from that room: it looks out onto a big, perfect lawn that seems like it's never been touched by humans—apparently, in Cambridge, grass is not for walking on. And the lawn is framed by the chapel on one side, and on the other, the river.

"This is where Dan asked me to marry him," she tells me, standing on the bridge. "Right here."

It seems like a scene from a movie. I can totally imagine it: Dan down on one knee right where the bridge curves up, the chapel in the distance, overlooking them as if in approval. Happy sounds from people in boats on the river. Tourists stopping on the path to let them have their moment, maybe taking pictures for Instagram.

The sun has peeked out of the clouds, and, right on cue, catches on her ring and makes it glisten.

"Wow," I say.

"Yeah. It was pretty great."

She can't stop smiling.

I look down at the river, at people on these things called "punts": long boat-like things with platforms at the ends. Well, kind of boat-like. They're long, thin, flat, and low, and tour guides in ridiculous hats and striped shirts stand on platforms on one end of them with a metal pole, digging down into the riverbed, and pushing them along that way. I don't know how they don't wobble and fall in. I think I definitely would. But they seem perfectly calm and poised, like it's no effort not only to steer the boat, but also to talk about the history of Cambridge at the same time. Libby laughs when she listens in.

"They're making half of that up," she says.

"Maybe they don't have the energy to think of the real facts because they're having to concentrate so hard on not falling in," I say, and she laughs again.

"Maybe. I was always terrified."

On other punts, groups of laughing students pass around a bottle, taking turns to drink from it. Libby makes out that studying at Cambridge was hard work, but from where I'm standing with the sun on my face, it seems like it must've been pretty fun. I wonder if Mom and Dad would let me come here for college.

Further up the path, crocuses grow, purple and white: the college colors and also the color scheme for the wedding. They don't have a date yet, but Libby's thought about a lot of the details already. This place makes me dreamy. Imagine studying somewhere like this! I feel like I'd fall in love with everyone I met.

I think about Tim, how I'd love to bring him here, to share this with him. I want him to be part of my life. Maybe it's time to get over what happened. But I don't know how I'd even begin to be friends with him again. Stand by the lockers and wait to bump into him there? I don't know if I'm brave enough to call him.

I tune back into Libby's chatter: she's telling me about some of her favorite memories: punting on the river, eating strawberries on the lawn after a concert in the chapel, staying up till 2 a.m. discussing linguistics theories. She's such a nerd—but then, so am I, just about different things. Maybe that's why she gets me.

We loop back to the chapel, and when we're inside, it actually takes my breath away. Dad told me about this. He said he tripped over his own feet and nearly fell flat on his face because he couldn't stop looking at the ceiling. I rolled my eyes at him, but now that I'm here, I can totally see why. I crane my neck to look up, so high, at the elaborate pattern of crisscrosses and flowers.

There's almost reverent silence in here, just the occasional high heel clicking on the tiles and people speaking in hushed tones, but then I jump when it's broken by a loud chord from the organ. I'm not a huge fan of organ music, but in this space, it fits. It feels almost ... majestic. And then I realize why: it reminds me of the church where William and Kate got married. King's College Chapel would be a pretty amazing place to get married, too. I wonder if Libby and Dan will get married here. I can already picture myself (because naturally I'll be a bridesmaid) walking down the aisle, backlit against the sunshine streaming in through the stained glass windows. Tim is looking at me, thinking *wow*, even though of course he wouldn't be at the wedding, but a girl can dream, right?

Or, apparently, not: "I wish," Libby says, when I ask her. "Only people who sing in the choir are allowed to get married in the chapel."

"Oh."

"We're considering having the reception in the college dining room, but it's a stretch."

"You're not allowed that either?"

"No, we're allowed. It's just … not cheap."

For the second time today, I realize money is something I never think about. I guess maybe because it's up to my parents to figure that stuff out. But also maybe because we've never had to worry about it. It's not that my parents just give me everything I want—we're still negotiating what car I'll get when I can finally drive—but if I need something, like extra viola lessons, then I just have it. I'm ashamed, suddenly, that it's never occurred to me to wonder about this.

But I shake it off, because I don't want to ruin the day.

And also because I'm distracted by the sweet smell of the fudge shop opposite King's College once we walk out through the gate. Outside the shop, a man stands in a big hat and an apron, offering us a free taste from a tray. I look at Libby, but she's already anticipated my thought.

"Oh, don't worry," she says. "Fudge is definitely on the agenda."

We cross the street.

"Hello," Libby says to the apron man. "My friend has never tried English fudge, so give her your best."

"Then might I recommend the strawberries and cream," he says. His formality makes me smile, but it goes with his outfit and the old timeyness of this place. I pick up a pink and white cube, pop it into my mouth, and instantly suspect I've died and passed on into heaven. I've never tasted anything that compares to this.

Libby watches my face and laughs. "I take it you like it," she says.

"It's unbelievable."

"Want to see how it's made?"

Inside the shop, we watch the process: a viscous substance on a marble table becoming slices of deliciousness before our eyes. It's mesmerizing. I should record it for my dad to watch when he's stressing out about politics, to calm him down. I watch them flip the goop, move it around the marble, until eventually it solidifies. This particular fudge won't be available just yet. It needs to finish cooling and be sliced and packaged, but at the counter there are pre-wrapped slices, grouped together according to flavors.

"Let's pick some out for us," Libby says. "And do you think your family back home would want some?"

"Um, yes." In fact, it would be a pretty great way for me to buy their love and/or bribe Rosie and Juliette for various purposes. "It's nice of you to think of it."

"Of course," she says. "I'd love to treat them."

We take our time picking the flavors: Libby thinks Ebba would like the mint chocolate, Dad the sea salt and caramel. Less subtle chocolaty flavors for my siblings.

I don't say it, but I think it so hard I hope Libby hears it anyway: I'm so glad she's in our lives, part of our family in a way. It was weird, really, the whole thing: how she appeared and how quickly she left again. But I'm really glad she did, because she's the best, and because without her I would not be standing here sampling this delicious fudge, sitting on a stone wall outside one of the prettiest buildings I've ever seen, watching students on bikes and tourists with cameras and feeling lucky to get to be an insider for the day.

Forty-Seven

At breakfast the first Saturday after I get back from London, Ebba sits across from me in silence, stirring sugar round and round in her tea. I've been trying, really trying, since I got back, to think about what Libby said. To let myself warm to Ebba. To push down this nagging feeling I keep getting that maybe the baggy t-shirts from a few weeks ago did mean what I thought they did. Because they wouldn't do that to us, would they? She wouldn't do that to us—throw us off again when things are just starting to get on an even keel, when maybe I'm just starting to accept how things are now, and starting, maybe, to actually want her in my life.

The sound of Ebba's spoon repeatedly hitting the sides of the mug has been getting on my last nerve, and then she scrapes her chair back, stands up, and practically sprints to the downstairs bathroom. I look at Dad and make the *what the heck?* gesture with my hands and he sort of half shrugs and looks at me evenly back. That's the problem with having parents who are actors. They know how to, well, act. I raise my eyebrows in what I hope is an *I'm not fooled, come on, what's going on?* kind of way and he breaks eye contact to look at his Cheerios. Hmm.

Harry's rocking back and forth on two legs of his chair. Rosie, of course, has her nose in a book. (I'm not allowed to have my phone at the table, but somehow she's allowed to read. I don't know what that's about.) Juliette is pouring milk into her bowl and I just know she's about to spill it everywhere.

There's a lot going on.

There's always a lot going on when we're all together.

I'm leaning against the counter, waiting for my two slices of toast to pop up when Ebba comes back. She looks pale. She looks, with those shadows under her eyes, like she hasn't been sleeping much. I turn to her and ask, all kind and concerned-sounding, "Everything okay?"

"Yes," she says, and sits back down, and starts doing that annoying thing with the spoon again.

"So," I say. I come back to the table and scrape a buttered knife across my toast. "What's new with everyone?" It's a weird thing to ask of people you see all the time, but whatever. I was away for a whole week even though I've been back for nearly another, so I might conceivably have missed something important. Anyway, I have to get at this somehow.

"We're starting rehearsals for our end-of-year recital," Juliette says. "It's going to be a good one this year, I can tell."

An end-of-year recital is an end-of-year recital, but okay.

"Sounds great," I say, to keep this ridiculous farce of a conversation going. I try to think what else I can ask about it to make it seem like I care more than I do, but I already know which piece they're doing and I don't know what to ask about the steps. Like, is there a particularly difficult arabesque or something? Do people even talk about this stuff in normal conversation? Ballet's not something you can talk about in the abstract without at least demonstrating it. And as both my parents have frequently had to say over the years, we don't do ballet at the breakfast table.

"It'll be on pointe," Dad says, because of course he does.

Ebba shakes her head and smiles. She's so in love with him that it's a little gross. The way women look at my dad, it's kind of ridiculous. I mean, come on: did you not notice how bad that pun was?

"Anything else?" I say. "Anything new?"

You can always tell when it's Rosie's turn at the toaster because she turns it up too high and before long there's the smell of burning. And yep, sure enough.

"New since when?" my dad asks.

"Oh, you know. The last few weeks." I look at Ebba, who's across from me. "The last—period."

She looks down at her tea and stirs it some more.

"Ebba," I say. "I think it's safe to assume the sugar is stirred in by now."

"You're probably right," she says. She stirs it some more, though, just to be sure, and also possibly because she knows it's irritating me and she wants to irritate me just a tiny bit more.

This was a tactical error on my part, though. What I should have done is left the question hanging in the air. *What's new? In the last period?* Until Ebba couldn't stand it anymore and said, in a small voice, *I'm pregnant.* I can see it now: Harry asking, *what does pregnant mean?* Ebba saying, *it means I'm going to have a baby.* Rosie looking up from her book. *A baby?* she'd ask, the way she always emerges from her book halfway through a conversation so that we all have to tediously repeat it to update her. *Whose baby? What? What are we talking about?* Juliette would sit there with her mouth open, in shock or in her usual awe of Ebba or in fear that she wouldn't be the favorite anymore. And Dad would try to make it look like this was exactly the way he wanted the news to come out, not a problem at all, this was precisely how he planned it, all casual, like there's nothing at all to worry about when it comes to how we'd all react, babies after all are small and unobtrusive and almost completely quiet almost all of the time. And if Harry wants to know where the baby is going to come from and how it got to be in Ebba's belly in the first place, Dad'd be only too delighted to explain to him in front of all of us right there at the breakfast table, maybe he'd even use an actual egg to illustrate. Poke it with a knife or something to represent the sperm entering the egg so that it splits into the cells that eventually make a baby. And then he'd turn to the rest of us, maybe put Juliette on his lap, even though she's almost ten and way too old for that, and explain that this changes nothing, that we'll all always be his favorite children, and now there'll be another favorite child, too. And then maybe Harry would whine, *but I like being the littlest*. And I would take him on my lap and say, *I know, I know, you'll always be my favorite little brother*, and I'd look at Dad and say, *like, the way people actually mean it when they something is their favorite. You're the brother I like best, more than all the others.* Harry would say, *we don't have any other brothers*, and I'd say, *no, but this baby might be a boy, and then we would.* And then his face would go all crumply and Dad would panic but try to cover it and calmly say, *but wouldn't it be fun to have another boy to play with?* And Rosie would say, *that's sexist, Dad*, and Juliette would say, *well boys and girls are different, that's just a fact*, and pretty soon everyone would be arguing and talking over each other and I would lean back and look at Ebba and watch her will the ground to swallow her up and wish she had never come into this family and messed with our lives.

But I made the tactical error with the spoon thing, betraying my irritation too early in the game, and now I'm not sure how to get back on track with the conversational plan.

"I'm learning the Vaughan Williams *Galop*," I say.

"That's great, honey," Dad says, like he even knows what the *Galop* sounds like. Like maybe he is relieved that I had this big announcement (which even when you care about the viola as much as I do and even when you're finally getting back on track with your damaged wrist is not really *that* much of a big announcement) and that's why I started the conversation and it's not at all because I've guessed that Ebba's pregnant.

"Yeah," I say. Nothing else. Ebba takes the spoon out of her mug and lays it on the table. I can't decide if it's a plea or a threat that I see in her eyes.

"Really great," she says, echoing dad. "I have to go. That ballet class isn't going to teach itself."

She stands up, walks over to Dad, and leans down and kisses him, because of course she does.

"You sure you're up to it?" he asks her, quietly, but not so quietly I don't hear.

"I'll be fine," she says.

Like, hello? Is nobody else noticing this stuff? I get Harry being oblivious. He's a six-year-old boy. And even Juliette—she giggles when Dad and Ebba kiss, like it's something delightful. If Rosie was any fun at all, if she wasn't always reading, even at the breakfast table, I could nudge her and exchange sideways speculating looks with her. But she'd have to be a different kind of sister for that to work. You'd think that with two sisters I could have gotten lucky with one of them.

Maybe this baby will turn out to be the kind of sister I've always wanted.

Yeah, right. Likely story.

Forty-Eight

Who was I kidding about having to decide if I wanted the Scrabble thing? Of course I want it. It's killing me that I can't be the best at the viola right now. That I'm not working toward anything. That I'm just drifting through life doing homework and talking about boys with Katie. There's only so much pre-sex speculation I can take without wanting to scream. *Look, Katie, either do it or don't,* I want to tell her, so that at least our conversations can move past what it will be like and whether it will hurt to what it was like and whether it did.

Now at least I know that *sex* is twelve points and that *sext* is also an allowable word, and at least that adds a much-needed new angle to our conversation, something for me to turn over and over in my head while she's off on her usual monologue about all the reasons she wants to and all the reasons she doesn't and what if the condom breaks and then again that's what Plan B is for, but that means her parents will have to know and can you imagine the horror and she'll be grounded for weeks and what if Jason breaks up with her because he gets tired of waiting, which hopefully he wouldn't since he says he loves her, and love is stronger than that, right? Oh my gosh, yes, please give me a list of words with the letter *x* to rehash in my head while I nod and smile so that the boredom doesn't kill me.

My parents are bewildered by my newfound enthusiasm for Scrabble, and I don't blame them. One minute I'm all about the viola, and the next minute I'm back from London and I have word lists on color coded Post-Its stuck on my bathroom mirror, and I'm curling up on the couch with a dictionary in preparation for the Pasadena tournament, the LA-wide tournament, the Southern California and then the national tournament.

But here's the thing: even now that I'm allowed to play the viola again, I can't play anything like as much as I would need to in order to get into LACHSA and it doesn't even matter because I can't get into LACHSA anyway, and I couldn't even if I were the best violist in the world, because they don't reschedule auditions and they don't take rising juniors or seniors. So I have all this spare time and all this competitive energy and if I don't direct it somewhere it's quite possible I will actually go crazy.

And then, of course, there's the thing that happened between the minute I was all about the viola and the minute I became all about Scrabble: Tim. The reason for the whiplash. The reason for my unforgivable distraction. Maybe Libby is right. Maybe Tim and I could be friends. Maybe Scrabble is my way back to him.

Forty-Nine

When I get home to Dad's from school the last Friday of April, the house feels different right away. Something in the air, maybe? And then I realize: no. It's not the air at all. Someone's crying. Ebba. I don't want to have to deal with this, whatever it is, but I can't remember if Dad is working today or where anyone else is. I drop my bag at the foot of the stairs and run up them.

"Ebba," I call, once I've caught my breath. "Ebba, you okay?"

I don't see her anywhere, but I can see through their light-filled bedroom to their closed bathroom door. The crying sounds like it's coming from there.

"Ebba? You need help?"

"I'm okay," she says, but even though she's muffled through the door I can tell that she is clearly not okay. What am I supposed to do, just leave her there? I'm not a monster.

"You're not okay," I say. "What can I do?"

"You can go get my phone from the living room. I should call your dad. I think I'm miscarrying."

I try not to panic, like trying hard is really any match for the knot in my throat or my thumping heartbeat. Now is probably not the time to point out that technically I didn't officially know she was pregnant.

"And then I guess 911," she says. "I don't think I should drive."

Ebba opens the bathroom door. She smells like mouthwash—the tell-tale sign of having just thrown up—and I've never seen her so pale. I want to hug her, but I don't know if that would be okay—if that would make it worse somehow, if it's better if I don't touch her. Besides, our relationship isn't exactly at the spontaneous hugging stage. Sometimes it felt like we were nearly there, but then this whole thing happened, and now I don't know.

"Does it hurt?" I ask, stupidly. I don't know what else to say.

"It's like really bad menstrual cramps," she says. "That's all."

But that's obviously not all, because her face crumples. I have to hug her now, don't I? I mean, that's what normal humans do for each other in these situations. I step into the bathroom and pull out a tissue from the box on top of the toilet. I hand it to her, and when our hands touch I kind of squeeze hers with mine. She half-smiles at me, like it's too painful to smile for real.

"I have my phone right here," I say. "Use that."

Ebba looks straight at me and says, "I'm sorry, Clara. We were going to tell you guys after the first sonogram. Tomorrow, as it happens."

Her eyes are leaking.

This is excruciating.

"It's okay," I say. "I figured it out weeks ago. I'm not stupid." I don't know why I felt compelled to add the last part. It's like my brain and mouth are pre-programmed to be mean to Ebba, and they run on automatic pilot, and I'm trying to shift them into manual, but I can't. The lever just won't budge. "I mean—" But what exactly *did* I mean? How do I make myself sound less callous in this situation? "I mean, there were signs."

"Yeah." She pulls the band out of her pony tail, shakes her hair out. Then she puts it up again with the same band. "This happened to me once before. A long time ago. I wanted to be sure before we turned all your lives upside down, you know?"

It's sweet of her to think of it that way. "I'll call Dad," I say. And then, idiotically, I add, "It's going to be okay," even though it's clearly not going to be.

"In the grand scheme of things," she says. "Yes. I've got you guys. And your dad. I'm happier than I ever thought I'd be."

Ebba winces, doubles up, clutches her belly. I dial Dad and pray he'll pick up quick. I don't know what I'm supposed to be doing here.

The phone goes to voicemail. "Dad," I say. "Call me. I'm going with Ebba to the hospital."

I realize as the words come out of my mouth that maybe the lever has budged, maybe I'm on my way to becoming a decent human after all.

"I mean," I say to her after I hang up. "I don't have to go with you. I don't know why I said that. But if you want—"

"I do," she says. "I would really like that. You don't have anywhere you're supposed to be, right? Orchestra or whatever?"

In this moment, I can overlook the fact that she's forgotten I'm not doing orchestra anymore this semester. The rehearsals are longer than I'm allowed to play for.

"No," I say. "That's fine."

I've never been in an ambulance before, and it doesn't quite feel real. There's a bed for her and a folding seat for me and more equipment than I ever thought you could fit in such a small space. It feels like the set of a TV show, like the ones Dad used to let me go to sometimes. Ebba seems okay. She doesn't seem like she really needs to be in an ambulance. She walked into it pretty much unaided. But still, I'm scared.

I take her hand. "I'm sorry," I say. And I realize my cheeks are wet and I'm sniffing. I think about how I hated the fact she was pregnant. How I hated this baby when I figured out it was going to arrive and disrupt all our lives. How I basically wished it was dead. And now it is. I know it's not logical to wonder if it might be my fault, but I wonder anyway.

Ebba opens her eyes, and squeezes my hand. "I know," she says. "I know." And I wonder how much she does know. If she understands me better than I think she does.

Fifty

They see us so quickly at the ER that by the time Dad arrives it's almost all taken care of, whatever it is they do in there.

"I was on set," he says, out of breath, when he sees me in the waiting room. My legs are sticking to the plastic orange chair. "I just got your message."

"It's okay, Dad." I don't know why I keep saying that when clearly nothing is okay. "I mean, she's going be okay."

"But the baby," he says. I shake my head. His shoulders slump. "The baby," he says again.

"I know," I say. I stand up to hug him. I'm almost as tall as him these days.

It's weird, me being the one comforting him.

I know the divorce wasn't easy on him. He put on weight and kept making these self-deprecating jokes like he's always made but with an ugly undercurrent of bitterness in his tone of voice. He never bad-mouthed Mom to us, just like Mom never bad-mouthed him, was always telling us how great he was. Like, Mom, we *know*, overcompensating much?

I wonder if it was a therapy thing. Like, *every time you're tempted to rag on your ex-husband to your kids, find something nice to say instead.* It was never, *remember that weekend he spent learning the piano accompaniment to the Hummel Kleine Suite, so he could play it with you?* Or, *remember that time he made you laugh so hard at breakfast that yogurt came out of your nose?* The nice things were always very general, but still, at least she tried. I guess at the time I didn't really think about how hard it was for them. Mostly I was thinking about me and how I didn't want to move and how crappy it would be to live with just one of them and even crappier to have to alternate houses every week. I'm used to that now. Mom is stricter on bedtimes and helpful with homework; Dad is more fun and a better cook but we have to share him with Ebba. There are trade-offs.

Anyway, the divorce was rough, but we're all starting to find our feet. Dad lost the extra weight quite a while ago now, started shaving every day again. That happened the summer Libby came to stay with us. I guess on some level, he was trying to impress her. Not that he really had to try.

The reason I'm telling you this is so that you'll realize how weird it is for me to be hugging Dad while he cries. It's always been the other way round, though these days when I'm upset I go to Katie or Netflix, not really to him anymore.

His shoulders are shaking now. He's a mess.

"We weren't trying, you know," he says. I wince. Wayyyyy too much information. I would prefer to believe this baby was the result of artificial insemination than the accidental by-product of—ugh—a night of passion. "But I was so happy. Which is crazy, because babies are a pain in the butt." He kind of snort-laughs and pulls away, so we can both sit down. I've blocked out the noise around us: squeaky wheelchairs, heels on the linoleum, a whining toddler, an intermittently ringing phone. But they come rushing back into my consciousness in the pause before Dad speaks again.

"I mean," he says. "They never let you sleep, and I'm too old for that crap. And they cry and cry and you can't stop them, no matter what you do."

"Kind of like you right now?" I say. He wipes his eyes with the back of his hand and smiles. Yay: points to me.

"But that soft skin and those round cheeks and that baby smell ... you can't beat those. That's why your mom and I had so many of you."

"I always assumed you just kept going till you got a boy."

Dad looks surprised that I've worked this out, like it's some great conundrum. Three girls, one boy. Not rocket science.

"Well," he says. "That, too."

He blows his nose with a tissue from his pocket and for a while we sit there in silence—well, not exactly silence, but not saying anything amid the din of people talking, machines beeping, kids limping out of rooms with a part of their body in a cast. Been there, bud. Good luck with that.

"When Ebba and me dated the first time," he says, softly, almost like he's talking to himself and I just happen to be there, "I used to daydream about having babies with her. Babies who'd have my freckles and her blue eyes. A perfect little amalgam of the two of us." Maybe he *is* talking to himself. He has to know this is making me queasy.

"Yeah." I pat his leg, in what could be interpreted as a reassuring gesture, but really it's a *stop talking, Dad* kind of pat. And then out of nowhere, and surely against my better judgement, I say, "You can always try again."

"Yeah," he says. "None of us are getting any younger, though."

"People much older than you both have babies."

"They do. But it's complicated. And it's complicated for our family, too. But this one was just kind of given to us without us having to think it through. If we thought about it too hard, maybe we wouldn't do it, you know? But we didn't think about it. It just happened."

"I would be an excellent big sister to it," I say. Not that I'm that great of a big sister now, except maybe to Harry. Harry loves to curl up on my lap and watch Disney movies with me. I haven't had a ton of time for that these last few years. But the point is: if I wanted to, I could be the best big sister ever.

"I'm sure you would," Dad says. But it's the kind of *I'm sure* that really means, *I'm almost sure, but not quite*. And then suddenly I'm not quite sure, either. In the last half hour while I've been sitting here waiting for Ebba, I've been imagining the baby would have lived with me all the time. I've been imagining carrying her (him?) from Dad's to Mom's and laying her out on a mat in Mom's living room. But the baby would be with Dad and Ebba all the time. And I bet she would do all her new stuff on the weeks when I'm not there—the stuff babies do. I remember Mom and Dad getting ridiculously excited when Harry rolled over or laughed for the first time, or started talking or crawling then walking. They would talk in these silly voices and clap really close to his face so he'd do whatever it was all over again. Meanwhile, I'd be, like, *I got an A in that math test!* Or, *I was asked to play the solo at the Pasadena Junior Orchestra holiday concert!* And they'd be, like, *great, honey, that's great*, and barely notice when I stormed off upstairs.

But maybe I'd appreciate the baby stuff more this time around. And if I missed big moments they could send me video. But it's not the same, you know? And then I think about how much Ebba would love this baby. She's nice to us because she has to be, you know? But with her own? It might be kind of gross, how much she dotes on it. I know I haven't exactly made things easy for her, so really why should she bother trying with me anymore if she has this adorable little baby that will coo and smile at her because she's the actual mom? Meanwhile, Dad will be all, like, *look at this amazing child I made with my amazing new wife.* Barf. Okay, I take it all back. No trying again. Let's keep things as they are.

Ebba saves me from having to say any of this, though, because that's when she comes out of the exam room and is walking slowly down the hallway and toward us. I watch Dad go to her. There's more hugging, more tears. I get out my phone and scroll through Instagram to distract myself and wait for the emotions to be done with or at least to cool down.

"Okay?" I ask Ebba when she walks over to me.

She nods. "Okay." Not *okay* as in *yay! Everything's great!*, obviously. But okay as in life is not over. They're hand in hand, Ebba and Dad, and I feel like a third wheel as I walk behind them to the car. I'm still scrolling, but really I've seen all there is to see and now I'm just doing this so I don't feel awkward. Dad and Ebba slow to a stop. They wait for me to catch up. Dad links arms with me.

"Thanks for your help today, kiddo," he says.

"I didn't really do anything."

"You were there," Ebba says. "I really appreciated that."

"No problem," I say. It's an automatic reflex, but I turn my head and lock eyes with Ebba and realize that I mean it. That I'm glad I was there.

Fifty-One

You should have seen Tim's face when I walked into the Scrabble tournament today at Pasadena Convention Center. He looked exactly as surprised as I hoped he would. It could be that he was surprised because I'm a girl: the room is full to bursting with boys, and not in a good way. The smell of Axe body spray almost knocks me over, and I've never seen so many pairs of glasses or black t-shirts or unkempt haircuts in one place before. Not swoopy and beautiful haircuts like Tim's, just neglected, because these boys were too busy playing video games and learning anagrams to make it out to the hair salon, to get their noses out of whatever nerd activity long enough to even think about a hair stylist.

But it could also be that he's looking at me that way because I'm me, and because, like everyone else in my life, he did not see this coming.

"You know," my dad said when he dropped me off at the convention center, "I really thought a nice side benefit of you not playing the viola anymore would be that I could stop driving you places all the time."

"I don't not play the viola anymore."

"You know what I mean."

I do. He means what some people call *obsession*. What I call *focus*. Did he really think I could live my life without one?

♫ ♫ ♫ ♫ ♫ ♫

There's a break at lunchtime, and I'm sitting on the floor with my back against the wall, eating my peanut butter sandwich and staring into space, when Tim comes up to me. I have, of course, planned for this—for what I'll say when he asks what I'm doing there, so the truth doesn't accidentally fall out of my mouth: *ummm, I miss you, and I want to get to know you, and I thought this might be a good way? Also, I'm a scarily competitive monster and I thought this would be a good place to channel that energy.*

"I didn't know you were into Scrabble," he says.

"I'm not."

Except, I admit it: there's something satisfying about laying out those words, linking them up with others, watching your opponent's face freeze in anticipation as they mentally tally your points. And it's all so objective: something is a word or it's not a word. It's worth this many points because the rules say so. Math.

"You're not into Scrabble," Tim says, slowly, incredulously.

"I'm into it the regular amount."

He slides down the wall to sit next to me. "A regular amount would be not at all."

"I'm actually into nerdy boys," I say, giving myself a mental gold star for remembering the line I'd planned and placing it perfectly, like an S hook on a Scrabble board. "Really into them. Can't get enough of them. And I figured this was a good place to meet a boatload of them."

"A conference center load, yes." He laughs at his own not-very-funny joke. "The best place, some people might say."

"Those people would be right."

There's really nowhere to go from here, so I start chewing my sandwich again. Peanut butter with extra crunch, just the way I like my sandwiches. My dad definitely has his uses.

"Well," Tim says, after we both just sit there for a while, with me chewing, him staring off into the middle distance. "May the best nerd win."

"Are you calling me a nerd?" I ask, turning toward him. I should have waited to finish my mouthful but I couldn't leave this unaddressed for more than one second.

"Gross," he says, flicking crumbs off his sleeve. "You're at a Scrabble competition on a Saturday afternoon. Are you really going to try and make the case that you're not a nerd?"

"I just like nerds, is all."

"Yeah?"

He looks at me long and hard till I have to turn my face away. Damn it.

I never lose at this game.

This doesn't bode well for me if he and I ever play together. Scrabble, I mean. The flutter of butterflies in my stomach start to stir, to awake from a long sleep. I curse my choice of lunch. Peanut butter breath is the worst. Still, there's an argument to be made that it's not quite as bad as Axe body spray over a layer of sweat. Maybe that smell is overpowering this one. Let's hope so.

Tim slides his foot along the ground till it bumps into mine, almost by accident. It's no accident, and I'm no fool, but I leave mine there.

"You like all nerds?" he asks. "Or one in particular?"

"Pretty sure it's all of them." I'm going to make him work for this. Besides, though I wouldn't say I'm attracted to nerds, or even that I want to spend much time around them, I do like them. I like that they're driven. Focused. If you ask me, when the apocalypse comes, it's the nerds who'll save us, with their obscure knowledge and their determination. They won't be distracted by gossip or by friendships or social connections. They'll get the job done. See also: Mark Zuckerberg. Steve Jobs. No people skills, if the movies are to be believed. And yet, where would we be without them? Probably in this exact same hallway having this exact same conversation, but you know what I mean.

"I don't blame you for liking nerds," Tim says, running his hand through his swoopy hair. "We are pretty great."

Then he stands back up and leaves. "Good luck out there," he says over his shoulder when he's a few feet away. Luck has nothing to do with it, but still, it's sweet of him. And I'm kind of disappointed that he didn't stay and talk some more. I wanted him to stay and fight a little harder.

Maybe I've exhausted him.

I hope not.

It would be so disappointing if he just gave up on me.

Fifty-Two

I'm sitting on my bed reading over allowable two-letter words in the Scrabble section of my bullet journal when someone knocks on my door.

"Just a minute," I say, because I want to get to the end of the list. I get there and call out, "Come in."

It's my dad. My dad almost never comes to my room. I think he's a little bit afraid of it. He stands in the doorway tugging at the bottom of his t-shirt and I have to tell him again to come in.

"Hey, kiddo," he says. He sits on the edge of my bed and traces the outline of the patterns of my comforter with his finger. He clearly has a message of great importance to deliver. "I have something to ask you. I was doing some digging on the LACHSA faculty."

"Why?"

"I'll tell you why. Let me get there."

I hate when people do this, make you wait for the punchline. Like, give me the actual information first and then fill in the background. Don't keep me in suspense.

"I wanted to see if maybe I knew someone there who could help us."

The pillows behind my back have started to slip down, and I rearrange them. "With what?"

"With getting you another audition. For when your wrist is healed. Or for next year."

"They don't take rising juniors," I say. Surely he knows this. Surely I have drummed this hard enough into people's heads over the last year.

"They don't usually, no. But it turns out that an old friend was just promoted to head of the music department. We went to Juilliard together. He was a huge fan of *The Classroom*, and back in the day I got him a tour of the set and he got to meet some of the guys. It was years ago, but he still tells me sometimes how grateful he is, that it was one of the best days of his life. I could put in a call. Mention that my super-talented, super-hard-working daughter deserves a second chance."

It would actually be a third chance, since this was my second chance after not making it to the in-person stage the first time. Arguably, I've had my second chance already.

"Thanks, Dad." I realize I am holding my left wrist with my good hand, as if trying to protect it from being overworked and damaged again.

"No promises, okay? But I can try."

It seems unthinkable to turn this down. Unthinkable to do anything other than yelp in delight and smother my dad in hugs till he can't breathe. But for some reason, I don't feel like yelping. I feel less than thrilled. What is *wrong* with me? It sounds a little pathetic that a tour of the *Classroom* set could indebt someone to my dad for life, but then again, I know fans of that show are kind of … rabid. But something about this seems off. Dad hates trading on his fame like this. He usually compares this kind of thing to emotional blackmail.

Desperate times, desperate measures, but still.

"Lemme think about it, okay?"

Dad looks surprised. I don't blame him. I'm surprised too.

"Sure," he says. "Just let me know."

I feel a little bad, because he thought he was coming into my room like the clichéd white knight on a stallion and I've basically told him I'm not sure that I need rescuing. The thing is, six months ago not getting into LACHSA then Juilliard then the Symphony felt like the worst thing that could possibly ever happen to me. Now, all of a sudden, I've got another chance, and … I don't know.

My dad looks at me, maybe trying to read my thoughts—but good luck with that, because even I, for once, am not sure what they are. He gives up, stands, and kisses me on the forehead instead.

"Love you, kiddo," he says, before he leaves and closes the door.

I reach for my phone and text Katie.

Dad says he's going to try to get me another audition.

I watch dots appear immediately, then disappear again. Maybe she's looking for the right GIF to send?

OMG! How?

He knows someone.

Oh.

What does that mean? What does *oh* mean? I feel like she's packed so much into that tiny word. And the period is interesting. Am I overthinking? Maybe. But I also know my best friend pretty well.

I wait for her to say more, and when she doesn't, I ask outright:

What does oh *mean?*

Just, you know. It's nice that you have a dad who knows people. But what about people who don't?

It's not fair, I know it isn't. But what happened with my wrist was a dumb accident. That wasn't fair, either. It wasn't that I didn't work hard enough. It wasn't that I wasn't good enough. I was unlucky, and now I'm lucky. Right? The circle of life … or something?

I worked really hard to get in.

I know.

More dots appear on her side, and I'm writing, too, so she must be seeing my dots appear and disappear as I think this through. Why do I feel so weird about all of this? This is my dream, being handed back to me. I should take it, right?

I think about what Libby said in Cambridge—about how she was lucky to get in, because usually people from her kind of school don't. I think about how I told her that getting in should be based on talent and hard work. It's so easy to say that in theory, when you're discussing other people. It's so easy to get annoyed at other people's unfair advantages. But here I am, with one of my own. Maybe that's why I feel weird about all this. But still: a few months ago, I would have stuffed those feelings down and grabbed the chance while I had it. Getting into LACHSA mattered more to me than anything else in the world.

Now, I don't know.

And it unsettles me that I don't know.

Fifty-Three

"I have something for you," Ebba says, the morning of the Scrabble tournament. It's not my birthday till next week, June 12, and maybe I'm scrunching up my face in surprise and confusion because she laughs, not unkindly.

"I know it's not your birthday till next week," she says, and it's freaky, like she's read my thoughts in their exact wording. "I just thought that maybe this could help today."

She's holding a small, square box and I'm completely mystified as to what it could be, what could possibly have any relevance to today. It's not like we're allowed to have anything with us—it's just us and a brain full of words. Our phones and all our belongings have to be securely locked away.

I can feel my forehead scrunching further. Mom always says to be careful about that scrunch, or I'll regret it when I'm forty, which, like, okay, but then I'll be forty, which will be a way bigger worry than my wrinkles.

Ebba holds out the box. "You'll like it," she says, "I promise."

I don't know what to make of how sure she is. Maybe I really am that predictable. Or maybe she's confident in how well she knows me now.

I take the box from her and unwrap it, the paper crunching under my fingers. It's a jewelry box. I snap it open, and nestled inside is a necklace, the pendant shaped like an alto clef. It's a delicate rose gold, really beautiful.

Alto clef themed things like this are hard to find, not like treble clef items which you trip over as soon as you open up Google. Ebba didn't happen to see this in a store, say, in

Old Town San Diego, and think, *Clara would like this*. She went digging for this, on purpose, maybe on Etsy. And I love it. Maybe I am that predicable, and maybe she's right to be comfortable in how well she knows me. Well enough to know that despite the disappointment of the last year, not getting into LACHSA, not being able to play as much as I'd like to, not having the firm, steady bowing hand that I used to, despite, not to be dramatic, the death of my dream, the viola still makes me happier than anything else.

"I love it," I say, totally, one hundred percent meaning it. "Thank you."

And before I even have time to think about it, I'm hugging her. She smells of her usual perfume: rose, vanilla, jasmine, almond. Ebba is a really good hugger. Some people hardly apply any pressure when they hug you, and you wonder if they'd prefer not to be touching you at all. Others hug you a little too hard and it gets suffocating. Ebba does it just right. It's a Goldilocks hug.

"But what's an alto clef necklace got to do with Scrabble?" I ask, when I've pulled away.

"Nothing, in a way," she says. "But also everything."

I wait for further explanation. This is where the ability to raise an eyebrow would come in super-handy.

"I just find," Ebba says, threading her finger through the loop of her own necklace, and when I see her do that I know what she's going to say. "Playing with a necklace helps me to think. And maybe it'll do the same for you."

I grab a fistful of my hair and hold it up. Ebba passes the pendant around my neck and fiddles with the clasp. And as she does that, her skin on mine, I remember the time I saw her down in the ballet basement with Juliette. Of the word, *tender,* that I thought of then. I want to prolong this moment, this feeling of closeness, and so maybe that's why I voice what's been on my mind since Dad came into my room the other day with his offer to cash in a favor with an old friend.

"Did Dad tell you he might be able to get me another audition?"

She steps back from behind me, and I turn to face her.

"Yes. But he said you weren't sure."

"Yeah." I don't know how to phrase all the complicated things going on in my mind. "Isn't it a little weird that someone Dad knew a long time ago would do him this huge of a favor?"

"Well, first of all, I don't know that he'd actually do it. It's borderline unethical, you know?" I hadn't thought of it that way. I wonder if she and Dad have argued about this. "But also, people *really* loved *The Classroom.*"

Obsessed, is how I'd describe some of its fans. It's a little crazy. But part of me gets it, too. If someone introduced me to, say, Gustavo Dudamel, I'd do pretty much anything for them, maybe even ten years later. And I get Dad wanting to do his best for me, wanting to open every door than he can, and I'm grateful.

"Maybe I just don't want it that badly anymore," I say. I touch my necklace as I say it, as if I'm wanting to reassure the alto clef, and by proxy the viola, that this doesn't mean I don't love them anymore. "LACHSA," I clarify for Ebba. "I love the viola, still. But maybe there's a way for it to be part of my life in a different way, you know?"

I'm playing my viola for an hour a day instead of three, and I'm enjoying it. It's frustrating that my fingers are slower to respond than they were, but I'm getting there, almost back to normal, pre-skiing abilities.

I tell Ebba how playing with Dan, with an audience of one,

who was determined to be impressed no matter what we did, with no expectation that I would practice and practice until my fingers bled and I achieved perfection … well, that was fun—a really satisfying kind of fun. And what if that's the whole point? Not competition, not being the best, maybe not even being admired, but being swept up in it, enjoying the moment, enjoying the enjoyment of those watching?

"You're exhausted, right?" she says. "From all the other stuff, the effort of it."

And I realize that yes, that's exactly it. I've worked so hard for so many years, and then, after the injury, when I should have been resting, I worked even harder.

I nod.

"I remember," Ebba says. "From my ballet days. I loved dance. I never felt more like myself than when I was dancing. But there was some ugly stuff that went with it. After I fell, and we were waiting for the ambulance, I heard some of the girls whispering about my *Swan Lake* part, about who was going to get it since I wasn't going to be able to dance anymore. I was in the worst pain of my life, and these were my friends, and that was their reaction right then. I was really hurt by that, but I also had a long time to sit around thinking about things, and I realized that I wasn't so very different from them. That the same thought would've gone through my mind, too. And that wasn't me, you know? I loved dance but I hated what that world had done to me."

"You think that's what's going on with me?"

I'm not asking this angrily. There's a pang in the pit of my stomach that tells me that if she does think that, she might not be wrong.

"Only you know the answer to that," she says kindly, brushing my arm. "It took me a long time and a lot of therapy to figure it out. But taking something you love and making it your whole life— it's not necessarily uncomplicated, you know?"

"Yeah. I do."

Maybe I don't want to be at LACHSA, grinding away, playing mind games with other violists, pretending to be their friends while secretly plotting their downfall so I can get ahead. That does not sound like a fun way to spend the last two years of high school. Maybe what I want instead is to be at a normal school (as normal as things get in Pasadena, ha) and be one of the best, a big fish in a small pond, without having to trample on people. Trampling is no fun for anyone, actually. I don't want to be that person anymore. There's got to be a way to compete, to be the best without being horrible to everyone around me. There's got to be a way to get to be a damn good viola player, good enough to enjoy it, without maiming myself in the process.

I'm not gonna lie, it's going to be scary seeing the front page of my bullet journal covered in question marks. If I'm stepping off the LACHSA-Juilliard-Symphony train, then I'm not sure where that leaves me, or what to structure my life around. (Let's face it, it's probably not going to be Scrabble.) And maybe it will still be the viola, in a different way. Or maybe I don't even need LACHSA to get into Juilliard and I can step back on the train later.

Who knows.

Uncertainty terrifies me.

"Whatever you decide," Ebba says, "we're with you, okay? You're so talented, and we love you so much."

"Thank you for the necklace," I say, running my fingers over it, my way of saying *I love you too*. "It's perfect."

Fifty-Four

It's ridiculous that Tim and I have both ended up in this Scrabble final at the swirly-carpeted ballroom of the Marriott Hotel in downtown LA, but there you have it. If there's one thing I've learned in my almost-fifteen-years of existence, it's that life *is* ridiculous sometimes.

The rules of competitive Scrabble are, as you'd expect for a competition, but as you maybe wouldn't expect from Scrabble, pretty strict. You have twenty-five minutes total each to make all of your plays, usually about twelve to fifteen of them. You can't just make a word up, or you can but it's dangerous because the other person can challenge you and if they're right, if the word doesn't exist or you've misspelled it, then you get the score that word would have given you deducted from your total, and that matters a whole lot at this level because games are usually close. You can be within sight of victory and then, bam, like a skiing accident before your LACHSA audition, it can be taken away from you.

I've played seven games so far, moving from square table to square table to face nerd boy after nerd boy and the occasional actually pretty normal girl, and according to the screen showing everyone's points, Tim and I are neck and neck, right at the top of the scoreboard. Well, okay, not quite: he's three points ahead. But I'm playing him next, and we're far enough above everyone else that whoever wins our game wins this tournament. Needless to say, I'm ready for this showdown. I'm waiting for any tricks Tim might pull, any words he might invent. He'll never get past me.

Rumor has it, and I've done my research and verified this, that Tim's been into Scrabble for years. Apparently, his dad taught him. He got obsessed with it and learned all the two-letter words and all the other tricks like I have. Only, he did it over a period of years. I've crammed it all in the last couple of months. There's acrostics you can learn, tricks to remembering combinations of letters, kind of like when you're starting out with reading music and the first thing you learn is the treble clef and Every Good Boy Deserves Football as a way of remembering that the note that goes on the first line of the staff is an E, the second one a G, and so on.

I'm fingering my alto clef necklace now, and it's definitely been a lucky charm so far today. It was a risky strategy of Ebba's, though, giving the necklace to me, because the viola makes me sad, too. It reminds me of everything I feel I've lost, everything I've worked for that's come to nothing, the dreams that won't come true and the fact that the first page of my bullet journal looks like this now:

~~LACHSA~~

~~JUILLIARD~~

~~SYMPHONY~~

???

But for now, I'm looking at my seven wooden Scrabble tiles, poised to play a great game, poised to defeat Tim. He looks so serious and thoughtful under that swoopy hair. He looks so determined. I'm pretty sure that's what my face looks like a lot of the time, too. I hope so, because I don't think there's anything more attractive in a person than determination.

And, damn it, he's good. Because of course he is. He's the person playing opposite me in this Scrabble final. That's not something you just fall into. He clearly knows the entire list of two-letter words, all the useful one-letter prefixes. I wonder if there are Post-It notes with word lists on his bathroom mirror too. He probably spends more time in the bathroom than the average boy does, getting that hair to swoop just right.

He's good, but I'm better. Or, at least, I'm doing better in this particular game. I'm leading him by twenty-two points, and there are only four letters left in the bag, which by my calculations of the tiles we have already used and depending on exactly what he still has on his rack, might be As and Is and a P or an R or an L, and there's not a ton you can do with that, points-wise. But then he plays his turn, and it's a good one. A very good one. The word is *spurious*, and the P is on a double letter, and the second S is on a double word, and it links with *piece* to make *pieces*, so that's a lot of points, and it's a master stroke. It's really hard to pull that off at the end of a game, when there's hardly any space left on the board and just in general not much room for maneuver.

The thing is, though, is that how you spell *spurious*? I'm not sure that it is. I think that's the British spelling, and we're using the American Collins dictionary in this competition. I know the pain of almost getting a great word but being one letter short or of having a bingo, which is where you use all your letters in one go and get a fifty-point bonus, but just not having anywhere to put it. And what if that's what this is? What if he very nearly had it and has decided to take a risk? He definitely doesn't deserve the points if he's cheating on purpose and hoping I won't notice.

Nobody underestimates me and gets away with it.

I always prove them wrong.

Almost always.

I maybe should have listened to the PT and not forced

myself with the viola after my accident. But how did I know my story wouldn't be the kind of against-all-odds story that we cheer and make into movies? I was almost certain that it would be. Madison Harper could have been cast as me. Maybe for the viola parts they could even have used my real hands, made it look like it was her, playing me, playing the viola.

And now I'm here instead, in this room that's smelling increasingly of BO despite the Axe body spray, potentially becoming Southern California's Junior Scrabble Champion. A redemption story, of sorts. It's not LACHSA. It's not Juilliard. It's not the Symphony. But it's something. And it all hinges on Tim being wrong in his spelling of *spurious*.

I open my mouth to challenge him, but just as I'm about to, I see something in his eyes—something that looks like pleading. I think about the Zyzzyva app on his phone, his years of preparation, the triumph for him of getting to this final. I think about how for me this is a chance to prove myself and a lot of fun but ultimately just a hobby. It isn't everything, the way that playing the viola was. Is. Or the way that winning this competition is for Tim. And I think about Ebba, about that time she said she'd still love me if I didn't get into LACHSA. Achievement isn't the path to love. I know that now. Maybe Tim doesn't yet. Maybe he needs this win for reasons I know nothing about.

I close my mouth. I look at him as if to say, *you're welcome*. We finish the letters and he wins. He's the Junior Scrabble Champion of Southern California, and I've never seen him smile so wide, with all his teeth showing, his name flashing in bright white letters at the top of the score screen. I'd like to be that person. Because I like to win, because I'm used to winning, when I set my mind to something.

But you know what?

It turns out that being gracious feels a little bit good, too.

Fifty-Five

"Congratulations," I say to Tim after the medal ceremony, where he gets gold and I get silver and we're clapped like Olympic athletes which seems, you know, a bit much. What I actually want to say is, *You're welcome.*

"Thanks," he says, playing with the red, white, and blue ribbon around his neck. People are milling around us, starting to disperse. Our parents are hanging back, waiting for us to exchange gracious platitudes or praying that we don't rip each other's hair out. "I was really hoping you didn't know how to spell *spurious.*"

"I do know. It doesn't have a U."

"Yes, it does," he says. He pulls his phone from his jeans pocket—damn it, those dark jeans, they look so good on him, show his butt off just right—and taps on the dictionary app and shows me how wrong I am. I lean in to look. I can feel his breath in my hair, skimming my cheek. I realize that the plea I thought I saw in his eyes wasn't *please don't challenge me, I really want to win.* It was *please do challenge me, I want to win by a lot when you get this wrong.*

"Oh," I say, because I'm not sure how to process this, and also because I'm distracted by how very close our faces are. One more inch … "Well, then. Double congratulations. For knowing how to spell *spurious. And* for being Junior Scrabble Champion."

"Southern California only," he says. "Nationals are next."

"Good luck," I say. "Not that you'll need it."

"Thanks," he says. Man alive, I wish he wasn't so good-looking.

I wish that winners weren't so attractive.

I turn to go before my face burns so hard it starts to smoke.

"Wait," he says, before I make it all the way back to Mom, who's waiting for me at the back of the hall, biting her lip like she's anticipating a meltdown. I spin round and take some steps back to him till we're close enough to speak without shouting. "How come you didn't challenge me? You would have won if you'd been right."

That is an excellent question. It all made sense in the moment, but I can't remember right now. Right now all I know is I want to punch him in the mouth. With my mouth. And maybe a little less force than a traditional punch. And more tongue.

I grab hold of what's left of my senses and swallow hard. "It seemed like it really meant something to you, winning this."

"It does." He pauses and looks at me and my palms are sweaty. How does he do that? With those long eyelashes under that swoopy hair, obviously, but like, *how*? "But you let me win?"

I can see how that's disappointing. When I was a little kid, I used to have tantrums when I didn't win at board games, so sometimes Mom and Dad just let me win, because it was easier for everyone. But then sometimes I'd realize they were letting me win, and I'd be even madder. I like to play by the rules and I like to win by the rules. Fair and square. Even if I'm realizing now that life is more complicated than that.

"You, Clara Cassidy? You let me win? After, you know … everything?"

"It's not like winning a Scrabble competition was going to get me into LACHSA," I say. His face falls. My stomach lurches, because I didn't mean in the way it sounded. I was just explaining why logically it didn't make all that much sense for me to cling onto this victory.

"I really am sorry," Tim says. "I don't know how else to say it. I know flowers are kind of a pathetic attempt, but—"

"They were nice flowers." Objective fact.

He kicks one foot against another. "But not enough."

"No," I say. "Not enough. But I'm not sure that there's any way you can make it up to me, really. You can't undo what's done. The flowers were a good effort. Plus, I have time for this Scrabble thing now that I can't play my viola as much."

He's confused. I can tell. "You don't sound mad," he says.

"I'm so tired of being mad. Mad at you, mad at my parents for not staying together, mad at Ebba, mad at my sister for being boring and my other sister for being too cute and talented. I thought maybe I'd try not being mad for a while."

"Wow," he says, which is kind of what I'm also thinking. This was not what I'd planned to say to him. I didn't even know that was how I felt, not really, not, like, in *words*.

"I know. I'm as surprised as you are."

"Think maybe you can try not being mad for long enough to hang out with me sometime?"

My face flushes. I don't want to ask this, but I have to. It's important for certain things to be clear. "Like a date?"

"Like that, yeah."

I think about the Tres Jolie lingerie languishing in my closet. About the fact that I'm almost fifteen and, damn it, I want to be kissed.

"I guess we could go get celebratory ice cream or something sometime. Seeing as how we're Junior Scrabble Champion and Runner Up."

"Southern California only."

Somehow we've both ended up way closer than we were—so close that I can feel Tim's breath on my face. We were both taking steps toward each other without realizing it—in our friendship, I guess, or whatever this is, as well as physically. But now I'm very much realizing it, and so are my butterflies. But I just about get the words out. "So we'll get two scoops. Save the three-scoop celebration for after nationals."

"You're gonna do nationals with me?"

With me. I thought I was done with the Scrabble thing. But that could be fun. And nationals involves traveling. Hotel rooms. Beds.

"That depends," I say.

"On what?"

I lower my voice conspiratorially. "On whether you're ever going to kiss me."

A little desperate, maybe. And maybe not the most logical reason to want to compete at Scrabble. But like I said, it's important that everyone is clear on what the situation is. I spin around and walk to my mom, leave him standing there, the challenge and the promise hanging in the air. I'd like to say that was all planned for maximum effectiveness, but mainly it's because I can't believe I said that and I think I might have scrunched up my face weirdly as I got the words out and now I'm a little embarrassed. That was forward, even for me.

"You look very pleased with yourself," Mom says, hugging me.

"Oh," I say. "I am."

"But you lost."

"I came second, Mom. I didn't *lose*."

"Wow," she says, pulling away and looking into my eyes, like she's trying to read my thoughts in them. "Okay. I'm not sure what is happening here, but okay."

"I'll tell you someday," I say. What I mean is, after I've had the chance to use that teal lingerie. Long, long after that.

Fifty-Six

What is happening is that I'm realizing there are things in life that are better than winning. There are feelings better, even, than the feeling of being clapped after a viola solo.

There is, for example, the feeling you get from putting on the lingerie with the gentle scratchiness of lace—not that I expect Tim to see it, not yet, but just for me, to give me confidence, to make me feel good, and yes, okay, maybe to be prepared, just in case. It has never in my almost fifteen years hurt to be prepared. And putting it on under my normal clothes feels like a secret superpower.

There is the feeling of anticipation: I am going on a date. With a swoopy-haired boy who doesn't know or care who Madison Harper is. He texted me last night to say that he couldn't wait for the ice cream, that he was sitting in his room listening to a Brahms viola solo, thinking about how I want him to kiss me. It took me forever today to choose just the right outfit, my jean shorts and my off-the-shoulder red shirt, and then to do and redo my hair half-up and my makeup until it looked like I hadn't spent much time on it, just woke up naturally looking amazing.

I stand by the bay window in the living room, waiting for him to pull up, because he can drive himself now. When I see his Toyota RAV4, I walk away from the window so that he won't know I was waiting. I give it a second or two after he rings the bell to open the door so I don't seem too eager. In that second or two, I catch Ebba's eye and smile, and I remember what she said at the kitchen table in the middle of the night that time, *you are a wonderful young woman*, and I think maybe she meant it. I take a deep breath and open the door.

"Hi," I say. "No flowers today?"

I don't know why I make this joke. In all my planning of this moment—and trust me, there has been a *lot* of planning—I have never anticipated making a joke like this. But now he's standing there, looking nervous, like he was six months ago, with the flowers, and here we are.

"I'll bring flowers next time," he says. I can't tell if he's joking back, or if this is his way of apologizing, if maybe he didn't get that I was kidding. I don't know him well enough. I don't know him at all, really. This is harder than I thought, this dating thing. At least when I was too busy for boys because the viola was taking all my time, that was predictable. You start off terrible, you practice, you get better. Guaranteed results. This thing, it feels slippery. Like nothing is guaranteed. It unnerves me. But it's also exciting.

"I'm kidding," I say, just in case.

"I know," he says. He stands there, still, in the doorway, kicking his feet together, smiling at me. His eyes keep flicking down to my chest. *One thing at a time*, I want to say, but I also don't. The teal lingerie must be working its magic already. See: superpower!

"Bye, Clara," Dad shouts, down the stairs. "Have fun!"

"I think that's our cue to leave," I say to Tim.

"Let's do it," he says. Then he blushes. I've never seen him blush before. I think I didn't realize that boys could blush. "I mean, not like that. That's not what I—"

"I know," I say. "It's fine." He's so different, standing here, than he was at school that first week. He seemed so self-assured then, so confident. I shut the door and take his hand. I was trying to do it casually, like, no big deal, but no-one warned me what happens to your arm when you take the hand of a boy you like. How sparks run up and down it. How the butterflies in your stomach start performing *Swan Lake*. We start to walk down the driveway to his car, and I realize I'm going to have to let go of his hand if he drives and suddenly that seems impossible.

"Want to walk?" I say. We're less than fifteen minutes from Bengee's and it's not so hot today. Walking feels more romantic somehow.

"Sure," he says. There are all these long silences between our sentences. This is so unlike him, unlike both of us.

"Are you nervous?" I ask him, because I'm worried that if one of us doesn't say something this could get way too awkward way too fast.

"Is it that obvious?"

"I mean, yeah. You're usually way more talkative than this."

Tim interlaces our fingers, and that sets off a fresh chain reaction of sparks. What's the science behind that? And why do I care about science right now?

"I'm not usually on a date with you," he says.

"But when you see me by my locker—"

"I take a deep breath. I make myself seem more confident. The first time I saw you, I *was* confident. I had no idea how terrifying you were. I had no idea I'd wind up liking you so much. So much that even when you made it clear you weren't interested anymore I wouldn't be able to stop thinking about you."

That's his favorite word for me, *terrifying*. But I focus on the next part, the part where he likes me so much, present tense, even after everything. Now I'm the one who can't think what to say next. So instead of anything intelligent, I ask him what ice cream flavors he likes best. He likes the combination of lemon and mango. I like mint chocolate chip, but only if the mint is white and the chocolate isn't too sweet. I explain the hierarchy: the very best is Three Twins mint confetti (extra points for the cute name), but you can only get that in Santa Monica. It has a perfect ratio of mint to chocolate. Häagen Dazs is not far behind, though, and the newest addition to the list is Graeter's, which you can finally get in Pasadena. The creamy texture is amazing and the big shavings of dark chocolate are A+. And then it's Ben and Jerry's, always reliable, but a bit too cakey on the chocolate chip front. We're on safe ground now, conversation-wise, or really Clara-monologue-wise, and we both desperately want to stay there.

But at Bengee's I take the chocolate-covered strawberry, because how can you not? Tim lets me try his mango-lemon combination after he buys it, right there by the counter, and I have to admit that it's a good one, that the flavors complement each other perfectly, one smooth and sweetish, the other a little sharper. Not unlike us. It turns out that how it feels to try your boyfriend's ice cream is also better than how it feels to be clapped after a viola recital, especially when he looks at you the way Tim is looking at me.

"What?" I say, stupidly, ruining the mood.

"Nothing."

He's smiling, though. Grinning, almost. So I ask him again. "What?"

"I was wondering when I get to kiss you, is all."

The butterflies in my stomach are doing the part in *Swan Lake* where Odile spins round and round thirty-two times doing *fouettés*. They're all doing that. Every single one of the twenty million butterflies is doing it.

"Not right here." And not outside right in front, either. Del Mar is a busy street. It doesn't seem like the right place.

"Think that maybe that's what the courtyard behind Lemonade is for?"

"I do," I say. "I think that's exactly what that courtyard is for. That's the purpose for them building it there."

It's not like this in the movies. In the movies, no-one discusses kissing before they do it. There's a moment, romantic music plays, they lean in, and bingo. But I am nothing if not a planner. I guess Tim must be too. How else do you become Southern California's Junior Scrabble Champion, if not by planning? We walk out and turn right onto South Lake. I have a block to finish my ice cream. I sneak glances at Tim, and he eats fast, fast, fast. I linger with mine. I want this moment to last, this anticipation. And also, now that this moment is here, now that I'm finally going to kiss a boy, I'm nervous. What if I do it wrong? Is there a way to do it wrong? They never do it wrong in the movies.

"You almost done with that?" he asks me after we turn into the courtyard with its two red British phone boxes. (I've never understood why they're there, but now isn't the time for such questions.) Tim's done waiting, and I don't blame him. I nod. He takes the little tub from me and reaches to throw it into the trash can. Clean and tidy. I like that about him. He takes me by the hand and leads me to the pebbly gap between the phone boxes.

All those months chewing gum just in case, and in the end we'll both taste of ice cream.

"I don't know how to do this," I say. I'm leaning against

one of the glass doors, which is lucky, because I'm not sure I'd still be standing otherwise. My legs are jello.

"Like this," he says. He leans in and so do I, and I can smell the tangy lemon of his ice cream, the softness of the mango, smell it so close it's almost like tasting, and his lips are on mine, and there it is, the taste, the *kiss*. I don't want to rush past this, like scales before the more fun part of viola practice. I want to remember this moment—the tiny sparks in my lips, the way they radiate out down my neck, down my arms, down my entire body.

But then, there's the tip of his tongue on my lips, and more sparks, and I open my mouth, and his tongue finds mine, connects with it, chases it.

Somehow, I'm still breathing.

"Wow," I say, pulling away a little before the sparks actually catch fire and burn me alive. So that's how."

"Pretty good, huh?"

"It's only going to get better from here, too."

"Practice makes perfect," he says, leaning in again.

I can't argue with that.

Clara's glossary of musical terms

Alto clef: At the beginning of each line of music, there's a symbol that shows you how to read the music. The only instruments that use the alto clef are the viola and the alto trombone. It looks like a three, or even, if you squint, like the side of a viola. So if you ever see someone with an alto clef necklace, you can be reasonably sure they're a viola player. You should tell them I said hi, and maybe lend them my book.

Arpeggio: When you break down a chord and play the different notes that make it up, it makes for a nice pattern that you can use at the beginning of practice to help your fingers and your ear warm up.

Bow: The bow is what you drag across viola strings to make notes. It's made of wood or carbon graphite and horsehair, which I know is weird. I don't really think about it anymore, but then I'll mention it to someone new and their eyes will go really wide and I'll remember, oh yeah, most people don't have daily contact with horsehair. At the beginning of each practice, you twizzle the end to tighten the hair, and at the end, you loosen it, to prevent it getting too tense and breaking. Even viola bows need a break.

Cello: The only instrument that comes close to being as good as the viola. Imagine singing *somewhere over the* *rainbow*: the difference in notes between *some* and *where* is the difference between the cello and the viola.

Double stopping: If you angle your bow just right, you can play two strings at the same time, which makes a chord. It's an advanced skill that takes a while to get right.

Étude: Some pieces are meant for playing in front of other people, but *études* are pieces that help you practice certain skills. It means *study* in French.

Fingerboard: The way you make different musical notes on the viola is with your fingers landing on different parts of the strings. That's called a fingering. The thin, neck-like part of the viola where you put your fingers down, is the fingerboard.

Legato: Playing notes really smoothly. It's more complicated than that, but that's all you really need to know.

Pizzicato: The other, less frequent way to make a note on the viola is by plucking the strings with your fingers. It's playful and fun, and it sounds like the *plink* of a raindrop.

Position: I know—almost as funny as *fingering*. There are eight places you can grip the fingerboard to reach the different notes, and positions are what we call those places. When you're just starting out and you learn how to do this, it makes you feel like a superhero.

Pitch: This is how you describe how high or low a note sounds. Some people have *perfect pitch*, which means that if they hear a note they can tell you right away if it's a D or an F sharp or whatever. Obviously, I am one of those people.

Practice: The never-ending thing that is sometimes enjoyable, sometimes tedious, but always necessary, because it leads to progress.

Rosin: A sticky substance you get from trees. You use it so that the horsehair on your bow can grip the strings on your viola better.

Scales: You're supposed to play these at the beginning of viola practice. They're a pattern of eight notes (or multiple of eights) that goes up in pitch slowly. There are *major* scales, which sound happier, and *minor* scales, which sound sadder.

Staccato: The opposite of *legato*. It's when you want to play notes that feel kind of jumpy.

Staff: A staff is a line of music. You've probably seen music written out, with five lines across the page, right? Five lines make up a staff.

String: The viola has four strings, and that's how you make music. When none of your fingers are down on any of them, they play a C, a G, a D, and an A. You can make all kind of notes, depending on where you put the fingers of your left hand. Strings are made of metal now, and you don't want to know what they used to be made of.

Tune: To make viola strings sound like C, G, D, or A, you turn the black pegs at the top of the viola's fingerboard to tune them. And you also need to adjust the tuning every time you play, with the fine tuners, which are at the opposite end of the strings.

Tone: It's really difficult to explain this in words, but the tone is basically the quality of the sound. How the sound *sounds*.

Transpose: When you play a piece that's meant for a different instrument, you have to change the notes in your head to fit your own instrument. That's transposing.

Velour: the soft fabric inside my viola case that keeps it protected.

Viola: the best instrument in the world.

Viola case: a long rectangular box-like thing that keeps your viola nestled in and safe from being bashed around when you're carrying it around to school and lessons and orchestra.

Warmups: when you start your viola practice, you don't go straight for the sheet music. First you play scales, arpeggios, and other exercises your teacher gives you. It helps get you (and your viola) in the mood.

Acknowledgements

This book started out as a first draft during NaNoWriMo in 2016, as a sort-of sequel to *Unscripted* after I couldn't get those characters out of my head. It's been a labor of love to bring it to eventual publication and I'm grateful for everyone who's been part of the process.

Massive thank you to everyone who helped with my endless questions about the viola and the American high school experience, especially Daniel Sumner, Jenn Whitmer, and Kathleen Swayze. Thank you to my early readers, especially the Spun Yarn, and the Romantic Novelist Association's New Writers' Scheme, whose expert help and encouragement helped me believe in this book from the start.

A million thank yous to Blake Dennis for your enduring and steadfast friendship and all your help with formatting, layouts, edits, covers, and so much more … including calming my anxiety!

Thank you to everyone who's been so supportive of my writing career, especially Jaime Amrhein, Selene Tucker, and my first superfan, Rebecca Kabat.

Thank you to Liz Dawson for insights into the hierarchy of mint chocolate chip ice cream brands and for making home a place where I was settled and emotionally safe enough to allow my best creative self to thrive during the crucial first draft of this novel.

Thank you to Mary Chesshyre for your thoughtful, kind, empathetic, and expert editing.

And thank you to Rocío Martín Osuna for my fabulous cover.

Thank you to the viola community for your excitement about this book and for welcoming me as one of your own!

Thank you to everyone who's ever shared my books online, bought or read anything I've written, said a kind word about it, or answered a question I had. I am so grateful for all of you. Sometimes, it feels like it takes not so much a village as the whole world.

And thank you to everyone who took a risk on an unknown writer and read this novel. There are millions of books in the world, and I'm so thankful you chose to spend a few hours with mine. I hope you enjoyed your time with it.

Note to the reader

Thank you for reading *Girl, Unstrung*!

If you liked this book, please tell your friends about it.

Social media posts are always great to see, too! I'd love to see you share your thoughts about this on TikTok and elsewhere. You can use #GirlUnstrung and tag me at @bookishclaire on Twitter and @claireandherbooks on Instagram.

I'd love a review on Goodreads, StoryGraph, and your preferred online bookstore.

If you want to read more about Clara's family, and especially about the summer when Libby came to stay, pick up my novel *Unscripted* wherever you get your books!

For bonus content, like a playlist to go with this novel, more information on learning the viola, or a link to sign up to my mailing list, use the QR code below!

Note to the reader

Thank you for reading *Girl, Unframed*!

If you liked this book, please tell your friends about it.

Social media posts are always great to see, and I'd love to see you share your thoughts about this on TikTok and elsewhere. You can tag @HildaHarmony and her team @bookshelfcafe on Twitter and @clairesellsbooks on Instagram.

I'd love a review on Goodreads, StoryGraph, and your preferred online bookstore.

If you want to read more about Clara's family and especially about the summer when Libby came to stay, pick up my novel *Beartribe*, wherever you get your books.

For bonus content, like a playlist to go with this novel, more information on the meaning the violet, or rather to sign up to my mailing list, use the QR code below.

Lightning Source UK Ltd.
Milton Keynes UK
UKHW040120251121
394548UK00001B/262